# The Chester Chasuble

# The Chester Chasuble

The umpteenth

Chronicles of Brother Hermitage

by

Howard of Warwick

From the Scriptorium of
The Funny Book Company

The Funny Book Company

Published by The Funny Book Company
Crown House 27 Old Gloucester Street
London WC1N 3AX
www.funnybookcompany.com



Cover design by Double Dagger.

ISBN 978-1-913383-39-8

Also by Howard of Warwick.

The First Chronicles of Brother Hermitage

*The Heretics of De'Ath*

*The Garderobe of Death*

*The Tapestry of Death*

Continuing Chronicles of Brother Hermitage

*Hermitage, Wat and Some Murder or Other*

*Hermitage, Wat and Some Druids*

*Hermitage, Wat and Some Nuns*

Yet More Chronicles of Brother Hermitage

*The Case of the Clerical Cadaver*

*The Case of the Curious Corpse*

*The Case of the Cantankerous Carcass*

Interminable Chronicles of Brother Hermitage

*A Murder for Mistress Cwen*

*A Murder for Master Wat*

*A Murder for Brother Hermitage*

The Umpteenth Chronicles of Brother Hermitage

*The Bayeux Embroidery*

*The Chester Chasuble*

*The Hermes Parchment*

The Superfluous Chronicles of Brother Hermitage

*The 1066 from Normandy*

*The 1066 to Hastings*

*The 1066 via Derby*

The Unnecessary Chronicles of Brother Hermitage

*The King's Investigator*

*The King's Investigator Part II*

The Meandering Chronicles of Brother Hermitage

*A Mayhem of Murderous Monks*

*A Murder of Convenience*

*Murder Most Murderous*

**Brother Hermitage Diversions**
*Brother Hermitage in Shorts* (Free!)
*Brother Hermitage's Christmas Gift*

**Audio**
*Hermitage and the Hostelry*

**Howard of Warwick's Middle Ages crisis: History-ish.**
*The Domesday Book (No, Not That One.)*
*The Domesday Book (Still Not That One.)*
*The Magna Carta (Or Is It?)*

Explore the whole sorry business and join the mailing list at
*Howardofwarwick.com*

Another funny book from The Funny Book Company
*Greedy by Ainsworth Pennington*

# The Chester Chasuble

## Caput I: Monks Will Be Monks

'I just don't want to go.'

The other three monks stopped their forward progress, again, and turned to face their young companion.

'Brother Hengard,' the leader implored with a weight of despair and some barely contained impatience. 'We have been over this. We did agree.'

'I know we did, Brother Paul, I know we did. But now we're here, I find second thoughts disturb me.'

'The time for that was before you volunteered.' Another monk spoke. This was Brother Brede, who never had any problem hiding his impatience with others; nor his irritation, anger or frustration. He frequently let them out, usually through slapping the palm of his hand against the other's head. And he was a big monk with a big palm. 'It's too late now. What's the matter with you, for goodness sake? We've not traipsed halfway across the known world for you to change your mind.'

'It all sounded reasonable when we were discussing it, but that was miles away. And days ago. Now the prospect is close at hand, I have worries that we are taking a dangerous step.'

'Dangerous?' Brother Brede retorted. 'You know perfectly well what's dangerous.' He gave a good hard glare. 'Pah. If your courage fails you, so be it. Wait here while we go ahead.'

'We support one another,' Brother Paul said gently. 'It must be all of us. You know the reasons.'

Brother Hengard remained hesitant. 'It's just, well, him.'

'We knew he would be here,' Brede explained, with a rubbing of his palms to get them warmed up. 'We went over it, and people were asked if they wanted to come or not. Some said they didn't. Some said they would rather do penance in the animal yard and clean the privy with their bare hands. You were not one of them.'

'I know, I know.' Hengard wrung his hands and rocked backwards and forwards under the force of his dilemma.

'It is our duty, Brother.' The final monk, Brother Girunde, spoke. A pious and devout fellow, his words were few but were thoughtful, and were always taken seriously by his brothers.

Brother Hengard sagged further.

'Come, Brother,' Paul encouraged. 'We have travelled far on our mission. Farther than many have ever been. To fall at this late stage would be to let down those who have put their trust in us.'

'The sin may be too great. Our eternal souls are in peril.'

Brede was ready for action. He stepped over and delivered his slap. 'Pull yourself together.'

'Brother!' Paul complained.

'Well. He needs more than a slap. Useless whelp. How do you get to determine where your duty lies?' He turned on his brother and was now pointing a finger. 'You have the instruction of your abbot and you decide to disobey. Is that it? You know better than the abbot? A man appointed by the bishop, who was himself appointed by the Pope, who is God's own representative on earth. There we are then. You know better than God.'

'No, no.' Hengard now buried his face in his hands.

'Come on.' Brede took his companion by the elbow and dragged him along the road. 'We are seeing this through whether you like it or not.'

Brother Paul looked as if he wanted to do something about

this, but as they were all moving again, he held off. He was pretty confident that there would be at least one more crisis before they reached their destination, but bridges could only be crossed once you stepped on them; or something like that.

The approach to the town brought even more fretful noises from Hengard. He started slowing his pace until Brede had to walk behind him and push.

The crossing of the boundary into the town proper was a struggle. The stroll up the main street was a challenge, and by the time Brother Paul had got directions for their final destination, and they were moving on, Hengard had come to a complete stop.

'If you don't move, I shall pick you up and carry you,' his herder warned.

Unsurprisingly, perhaps, the people of the town started to notice that there were four monks walking along their street, one of whom looked like he wanted to go in the other direction.

The sight of four monks together was unusual enough; to see them squabbling and pushing was quite entertaining.

'I should carry him, if I were you,' one fellow at the tavern called out.

'Brother, you are making a scene and a fool of yourself.' Paul now instructed obedience.

'I don't want to go,' Hengard now wailed. 'You can't make me. Help. Help.' He called to the townsfolk to rescue him from his awful plight.

The townsfolk looked on with folded arms, all of them genuinely intrigued about what was going to happen next. No one rushed forward to the rescue. There hadn't been this much entertainment in town since that old mummer came by and dropped dead in the middle of his play.

As the narrative had called for the death of the character he was playing at the time, it was several minutes before anyone realised the man wasn't getting up again.

That had provided weeks of lively conversation.

Brother Brede now took matters, and Brother Hengard, into his own hands. He simply grabbed his fellow around the waist and hoisted him up onto his high and strong shoulder, carrying him like a sack of bones.

Hengard's head hung over Brede's back and his feet swung out in front.

'Help me,' he called pleadingly to the now significant gathering of folk.

The significant gathering gave Brede a round of applause. They even started to wager whether the tall monk could pick one of the others up as well. He could even juggle them, perhaps? That would be good, juggling monks. One of their number claimed to have met a monk who could juggle once, but never one who could be juggled.

'Quickly now,' Brother Paul called. This was all getting completely out of hand and the sooner they got away from the public gaze, the better. There was no way their mission was going to have any privacy about it now.

Just when he thought they might escape the edge of the village without interruption, Brother Paul was brought up short by a large fellow standing in the middle of the road.

'What's going on here then?' the large one asked. It sounded as if he asked with a fair degree of authority.

'Oh, nothing, nothing,' Brother Paul tried.

'Nothing?' The man was clearly not persuaded that the scene before him was nothing. 'I am the head man of this town, and we don't have monks carrying one another through the streets.'

Both men considered one another and the sense that this statement made. At least the head man had the decency to frown at his own words, it being clear that monks carrying one another through town was not actually quite such a regular nuisance.

'I assure you that it is nothing to be concerned about. We are simply on a long journey and the brother here has reached the end of his strength.'

'Get me down,' Hengard called, quite strongly.

'His moral strength,' Paul specified.

'Where you taking him, then?' The head man clearly thought that the destination was the most important question whenever you came across a monk carrying another one.

'Where are we taking him?'

"That's right, where you taking him?'

Brother Paul looked up and down the lane and beckoned the head man to draw close so that a great confidence could be imparted.

'I cannot say,' he whispered in a low voice. He also nodded significantly, making it clear that this was not the sort of information that would be handed out to anyone. Not even someone as important as a headman would be privy to secrets like this.

The head man frowned some more. 'You'd better make your mind up soon; can't go on just carrying him all day.'

'No, no.' Paul let his impatience sharpen his words. 'I know where we're going, I just can't tell everyone. Or anyone.'

'Oh, right.' The head man nodded that he understood the words but shook his head that they made no sense.

'I don't want to go,' Hengard added.

'He doesn't want to go,' the head man let Paul know.

'Moral courage.' Paul shook his head sadly. 'There are many trials in life that we would rather not face, but our duty and our courage must make us do so.'

The head man sombrely agreed with this. 'And you have to carry him to this trial then?'

'It's not a real trial for heaven's sake. It is just something that we have all sworn to do, and this brother's courage is failing him as the end draws near.'

'I see.' The headman gave this some consideration. 'And this end is in these parts, then?'

'I cannot..,'

'I know, you cannot say.'

They were at an impasse.

'Perhaps you could whisper?'

'Whisper?'

'Yes. If you can't say, you could whisper. Whispering's not the same as saying at all.'

Paul wasn't ready to split that particular hair.

'And I am the head man,' the head man pointed out. 'I can be trusted. You wouldn't believe the sorts of things I could tell you about some of the folk around here. But would I? No, of course, I wouldn't. It's like your duty. It goes with the role of headman, keeping confidences.' He leaned in closer so that Paul would find whispering a bit easier.

Paul reluctantly shook his head. 'I would tell you if I could, but it really is the most awful secret; one that even I am sworn to keep.'

The headman looked disappointed and resigned. 'The lock-up it is, then.'

'The lock-up?'

'That's right. It's not what I would choose to do at all. Not me personally. But me as head man, I have to protect the community.'

'From four monks?'

'One of whom wants to go home,' Hengard threw in.

'I don't know what you're up to, that's the problem.' The head man folded his arms. 'I don't even know you're real monks.'

Paul was feeling quite out of his depth. 'What else would we be?' He held his arms up to point out that they were all dressed as monks.

'I don't know, do I. That's the point. You could be Normans.'

'Normans?' This really was getting ridiculous.

'That's right. Normans disguised as monks, the better to take us unaware.'

'When has anyone ever heard of a Norman wanting to take people unaware? We've heard that they ride in at full speed with swords swinging, that's how you tell that they're Normans.'

'You could be an advance party.'

'An advance party of Normans dressed as monks? What are we going to do, trick you all into prayer?'

'Not going to do anything now, are you? You'll all be in the lock-up. We'll take stinking Gerald out first. It's not nice with him in there.'

'And then what?' Paul was getting a little worried now.

'We'll have to call the town moot to decide what to do with you.'

'How long will that take?'

'Oh, not long. Next moot is in a month. It's a pity you didn't come yesterday, we only just had one.'

'A month? We can't wait a month.'

'Might be longer than a month. Moot might decide to keep

you longer if you don't tell them what you're up to.'

Paul's shoulders dropped. He took a deep breath. 'And you can keep a confidence?'

'That I can.' The head man sensed his victory.

'You're not the sort of head man who goes blabbing everything he knows in the tavern of an evening then?'

'Absolutely not.' The head man was mightily offended that such a thing could even be suggested. He also looked a bit worried that this monk might have been spying on him in the tavern.

'And you're the sort of head man who can carry this confidence to his grave.'

Talk of graves seemed to prompt some wariness on the part of the head man.

'Because it is the sort of confidence that kings would tremble to reveal.'

Now Paul beckoned the head man to draw near, which he suddenly seemed a bit reluctant to do. Taking the man firmly by the shoulder, the monk whispered their destination into his ear.

The head man stepped back sharply. 'Oh, right,' he said, looking a touch pale. 'Off you go then, on your way. Let's have no loitering. Move along please.' The head man shooed the monks along his road, very keen on getting them out of town as quickly as possible. He strode off quickly in the opposite direction.

All of this delay had done nothing to calm Brother Hengard. As expected, his complaints and struggles only got stronger the closer they drew to their goal. Even Brede, big and strong as he was, was having trouble controlling the wriggling load on his shoulder.

Finally, with a cunning combination of a roll to the right, a push with a hand and a kick, Hengard fell to the floor, Brother Brede staggering in the other direction.

'Stop him,' Brede called from the floor.

Brothers Paul and Girunde, who were far less used to this sort of thing, managed to grab handfuls of Hengard's habit before the younger monk could get to his feet and start the process of running away.

Unfortunately, their grips were not strong, only really being used to turning the pages of books, even if some of them were quite heavy pages.

Hengard pulled away from the restraining hands and looked around to see where was best to go. There was a large building to his left and the path went on past this and off into the countryside. He obviously decided that the countryside was for him and hitched the skirt of his habit to free his legs for a nice long run.

He'd only taken a few steps before the arms of Brother Brede wrapped themselves around his calves and brought him crashing to the floor.

His shout of complaint was only drowned out by Brede's holler of attack. He had obviously disposed of the last of his patience and was now ready to deal with Brother Hengard the way he really needed dealing with.

Spotting that this was getting out of hand, Paul stepped forward and beckoned to Girunde that he was going to need some assistance. Girunde gave a sigh at the frailties of the human spirit and followed.

Paul took hold of Hengard's shoulders while Girunde did Brede. They both heaved but had little success separating the two monks.

Brede was now growling in a very worrying manner, while Hengard's screams were reaching a higher and higher pitch.

They were soon accompanied by cries of "get him off me" and "murder, murder".

The two senior brothers had a firm grip, which was no help at all when the two fighters rolled over in the dirt. They took Paul and Girunde down with them and all four monks created a much bigger mound of monks on the floor.

Each had their own task. Paul and Girunde simply wanted to stand up again, Hengard wanted to get away, and Brede's aims appeared to be very unchristian, judging from the threats he was issuing.

'Stop it, stop it,' Paul cried, to absolutely no effect at all. 'In the name of our abbot and God almighty, stop this outrageous behaviour.' He managed to get himself back to his feet and considered the tangle of monks below him as he thought what to do next.

He didn't have to think long as a flailing leg caught him right on the back of the knee, and down he went once more.

Girunde was on his knees and crawled over to try and assist Paul. He only got halfway before the tumbling figures of Hengard and Brede rolled into him and knocked him onto his back.

By this time, the tangle of monks had managed to roll itself off the path and was trampling the tops of the turnips that were planted in neat rows nearby.

Paul managed to right himself now and offered a hand to Girunde, pulling him back to his feet. They both went over to Hengard and Brede, who were effectively one monk in two habits just at the moment, such was their confusion.

Brede appeared to be trying to strangle Hengard, while the young monk was just lashing out at random, perhaps hoping that he could manage to hit something vital and so stop the assault.

Paul and Girunde now stood on either side of the conflict and simply slapped their hands, completely ineffectively on the backs of the combatants insisting that they should stop this minute and behave themselves.

From an upper window in the building by the side of the road, the very slight figure of a young woman looked out at the display before her. For reasons best known to herself, her reaction was mild interest, rather than shock or horror or outrage.

As there was no sign of this conflict coming to a halt at any moment soon, she thought that perhaps she'd better do something about it. Her voice was part puzzlement, part curiosity but mostly resignation that this sort of thing was happening quite regularly now.

'Brother Hermitage,' Mistress Cwen shouted down from the upper room of Wat the Weaver's workshop, using the word "brother" as a mother would use her child's full name when she wanted to make it clear that such child was now in serious trouble. 'Why are there are some monks fighting in the vegetable patch?'

## Caput II The Usual News

This was not the sort of question Brother Hermitage took easily. His young and enquiring mind favoured well-structured, thoughtful enquiries into fine points of theology or biblical interpretation; preferably concerning the post-Exodus prophets. He did not cope well with random collections of words with a question mark at the end.

When people asked things that made no sense, it sent him into a sort of irritated daze. He knew that the words on their own worked quite adequately, but that they should not be put together in such ridiculous order. Monks and vegetables combined nicely, but fighting? Where had that come from?

As the duly-appointed King's Investigator, he had to focus on much darker problems most of the time, but then most of the time he tried to forget that ghastly title; often waking in the morning to think that it had all been some horrible dream.

At least he was waking in Wat the Weaver's workshop and not the truly revolting monastery of De'Ath's Dingle, which he still thought of as his official residence. He had become so settled here that he relied less often on Wat and Cwen to give him good reasons why he should not go back.

The latest, and it seemed, the conclusive reason for Hermitage to stay with Wat and Cwen was that this was where the King's Investigator lived now. It would be irresponsible of him, and probably against the wishes of King William, to be anywhere else at all. If he was wanted, who would think of going to De'Ath's Dingle?

This contradictory argument balanced the comfort of being with Wat and Cwen against the inconvenience of being the King's Investigator. No, inconvenience was the wrong word for this role. What would be best? Terror, perhaps?

But he understood the tone in Cwen's voice. She thought that monks fighting in the vegetables would be his fault. They were monks, he was a monk; what more was there to say?

And he had to admit that her conclusion was very likely correct. He certainly hadn't invited any monks to come and have a dispute in the middle of their vegetables, but he had little doubt that they were here for him. The coincidence would be too much to think about. Monks fighting just outside the workshop of the famous Wat the Weaver?

Monks even being just outside the workshop of the famous Wat the Weaver was going too far. Unless they were the pious type with missionary zeal who had come to throw things.

Not everyone knew that Wat had moved on from those old tapestries of his; the ones that did more for the understanding of human anatomy than most learned texts. The ones that caused offence to most decent people and did it in vivid colour.

As he put aside the rather worn sheet of parchment he was making his latest list of prophets on, he had an awful thought about where the fighting monks may have come from.

There was only one monastery he knew of where fighting amongst the brothers was common. Not only common but positively encouraged by the awful Abbot Athan as a fast and effective way of resolving disputes: De'Ath's Dingle.

Could it be that all his hiding from and avoidance of that dire place was now being visited upon him as some sort of punishment? Had some dread instruction gone out that Hermitage was to be recovered to De'Ath's Dingle by all means possible?

He could well believe that any two brothers of that place, sent out alone, would end up fighting in very short order. And if they weren't fighting one another, they'd have found some poor innocent on the road to do it with.

But then he reasoned that those brothers weren't usually allowed out at all. The monks of De'Ath's Dingle were there for a reason: to be kept in De'Ath's Dingle. High walls, thick gates and a ruthless abbot made sure of it. Unless there had been some complete breakdown, the brothers of De'Ath's Dingle would still be there, safely locked up.

And if the fighting monks were of De'Ath's Dingle, they wouldn't be restricting their activities to the vegetable patch; they'd be through the door by now.

There was nothing for it but to go out and see. Or perhaps pop up to the window with Cwen and look at what was going on. After all, it might be nothing to do with him. It could just be regular fighting monks on their way somewhere else completely.

'Well, come on then,' Cwen urged, as Hermitage's feet trod the wobbly steps up to the first floor.

He joined her at the window and looked out. He had to admit that there really were monks fighting in the vegetable patch. He'd thought it unlikely that this was the sort of thing Cwen would get wrong, but you never knew.

'Who are they?' Cwen demanded, pointing out at the increasing mess of monks and mud.

'I don't know,' Hermitage said, with quite some relief. 'They're not monks I recognise.'

Cwen gave him one of her looks. The one that said he needed to do something about a situation and not just consider it carefully. 'Either you're going to go out there and stop them or I am.' She folded her arms.

He knew that the monks in the vegetables would be best served by him going out to them and not Cwen. Her small stature frequently lulled people into making the most regrettable mistakes where she was concerned. The pain and the shock of her responses often arrived together; the recipient not knowing which one to be most impressed by.

'I'll, erm, go and see.'

'You do that. They probably want you, anyway.'

'Maybe not. Perhaps they are travelling on their way and are in some dispute about their route. It could be they only need directions.'

'Funny way of asking for directions. Go. Now. They're heading towards the peas.'

Hermitage skipped away from the window and back down the stairs. At the bottom, he met Wat coming the other way.

'What's she shouting about now?' Wat asked, brushing his unkempt dark hair from his eyes. He had a rag in his hands and had obviously been carrying out some maintenance on one of the looms.

'Monks,' Hermitage said.

'Shouting about monks. No point shouting about them, they won't go away. Too many of them.'

'More specifically the monks fighting in our vegetables.'

'Fighting over our vegetables?' Wat looked as if either he had gone mad, or Hermitage had. 'If they're hungry, I suppose.'

'No, not fighting over the vegetables, fighting in them. I'm just going out there to see what I can do.'

'I see. Join in, perhaps? Is it a thing monks do?'

'I think the idea is that I stop them.'

'Cwen's idea.'

'That's the one.'

'And how many monks are there? In the vegetables.'

'Four, as far as I can see. Two of them look quite old though.' Hermitage tried to make it clear that he might be able to deal with two old monks. Wat might like to come along to assist with any young ones.

'Come on then.' Wat beckoned to the door. 'I don't want monks in my soup.'

Hermitage stepped through the door with more confidence now.

'Although that's something I never thought I'd say.' Wat added.

By the time they arrived at the battle of the monks, the level of activity had fallen somewhat. The two main combatants seemed to have reached some sort of impasse. Brede was unable to deal the winning blow, and Hengard was unable to deal the winning getting up and running away.

Paul and Girunde stood nearby, having given up trying to achieve anything of use. They just wanted to wait until the two on the ground had exhausted themselves.

'Morning,' Wat said as he strolled up. He considered the monks on the floor as if he'd just found a dead fox surrounded by gloating chickens.

'Ah,' Paul said, looking up from his prostrate brothers.

'Brother,' Girunde said, addressing Hermitage.

'Brother,' Hermitage replied. He was grateful for confirmation that he had never seen any of these monks in his life. They were too well dressed to be from De'Ath's Dingle, and the two elder brothers had the look of senior members of an order about them. They were pale from lack of sunlight and were thin enough to see that they treated hearty nourishment with disdain.

'You must forgive this disgraceful display,' Paul urged them both.

'If you want a turnip, I'm sure you can have one,' Wat offered.

The head of Brother Hengard emerged from under Brede's arm and considered Wat. He screamed.

Wat turned to Paul with a shrug. 'I have that effect on some people.'

'Brother Hengard's resolve has failed him.' Paul shook his head in disappointment. 'I take it you are Wat the Weaver?'

'I am. Does he always scream at weavers, or is it just me?'

'Just you, I'm afraid.'

Wat nodded that this was quite understandable.

Hengard resumed his wriggling to try and get away, now trying to make the sign of the cross as often as he could, presumably to ward off Wat's evil.

'Brother, Brother,' Hermitage soothed. 'There is no need for such distress.'

'It's him, it's him,' was all Hengard could wail. 'Don't make me look.'

'Look at what?' Hermitage asked.

'The images. The images of evil. I will be cursed.'

'Oh, really.' Hermitage dismissed this nonsense. 'There are no images of evil. Wat has forsaken that work. He now makes appropriate and pious tapestries.'

'And he makes a lot less money,' Wat complained.

Hermitage gave him a warning glance. 'Come Brother. I am here, and I have not been cursed, have I?'

Hengard considered Hermitage as if he wasn't quite so sure about that. 'But, the sin?'

'It is for us to move him away from that sin, surely. Not cower in its face?'

'Well put, Brother.' Paul nodded his approval.

Wat leaned over to Paul and gave him some additional information. 'And the Normans don't go in for that sort of thing. They'd probably have my fingers off if they found out.' He grinned.

Paul did not.

'So,' Hermitage continued to soothe Hengard. 'Come inside. Tell us of your journey and your business. What brings you to the workshop?' Hermitage really didn't want to know what had brought them to the workshop.

It was clear that Paul knew perfectly well who Wat was, and people didn't tend to find that out unless they came looking. And these monks would not have come to commission a nice tapestry for their nave. Four brothers travelling together were clearly on a mission. He knew in his heart that the mission would be for him.

Hengard appeared to have recovered some level of control, so much so that Brede was prepared to loosen his grip and allow the young brother to stand. He was still on his guard though, as if expecting a break for escape at any moment.

Hengard looked at Wat as if the devils of hell were about to spring from his jerkin and devour them all, but at least he didn't actually run away.

'Do we have to go in?' he asked, trembling his head towards the workshop.

'It's where the food and drink is,' Wat replied. 'And the seats to sit on while you tell us why you've come all this way to destroy my vegetables.'

Hengard looked to Hermitage. 'You live here?' He asked part in admiration, part in awe.

'I do. And you will meet Mistress Cwen as well. She and Wat are good friends.' He doubted that Hengard was going to be one of Cwen's friends quite so easily. She was fond of turnips.

With Paul, Girunde and Brede forming a line to prevent Hengard's retreat, they edged towards the workshop, where Cwen was now standing at the door.

As the troop passed over the threshold, she stood silently to one side and simply considered them all one by one. Her most silent consideration was reserved for Brede and Hengard.

'Look,' Wat said brightly. 'We've got some more monks.'

Cwen sniffed.

'Let's go upstairs.' Wat indicated the steps. 'I'll get one of the apprentices to bring us some food and wine.' He beckoned to a small face that was peering around a wall towards the back of the entrance hall; a face doubtless nominated by its companions to find out what on earth was going on now.

Paul bowed his gratitude for this offer, which, it seemed, was very welcome.

Cwen led the way to the upper floor, the one usually reserved for Wat's favoured clients. Since the Norman invasion, those favoured clients, who had all been Saxons with a very particular taste in tapestry, were now either dead or pretending to be.

'We usually use the upstairs room for murder,' Wat announced happily.

A squeak clearly came from Hengard and not the loose step.

'I assume that's why you're here,' Wat went on amicably. 'We don't get many monks visiting the workshop. Not in packs, anyway.'

Paul gave a light cough.

'It must be Brother Hermitage you're looking for. And I'm afraid there's only one reason anyone comes looking for him.'

They were all upstairs now and most of them took the seats that were gathered around the fireplace at the far end.

The four new arrivals considered the luxury of the place with barely concealed worry. If there wasn't any sin actually going on anymore, the wages of it were on open display.

Hengard went over and sat on the bench by the window, perhaps thinking that he could jump out if things got very bad.

'So,' Cwen deigned to speak. 'Who's been murdered then?'

Hermitage had been hoping that it would take a bit longer to get to this point. A nice discussion of monastic matters would lead gently to conversations about well-being in general. Then there would be something about their journey and the order they represented before someone raised the regrettable topic of the demise of a specific individual; who might even have died of natural causes.

'A monk, I expect.' Cwen nodded at her own conclusion. 'What with you being monks and all.'

Hermitage was grateful that Paul also seemed a little reluctant to dive straight into the ghastly details of murder. 'We have come from the abbey at Chester,' he said.

'A fair step,' Wat observed.

'Just so. We heard of the achievements of Brother Hermitage from a Norman.

'We think this Norman sought to reassure us that King William is a just and rightful king. After all, he has appointed a Saxon monk as his investigator.'

'How much more just and rightful can you get?' Wat agreed with a broad smile at Hermitage.

'Did this Norman have a name?' Hermitage shivered as he

thought it could be King William's man, the awful Le Pedvin. That fellow had been involved in far too many of Hermitage's investigations, and not in a good way. The thought of seeing his disappointed and critical face again filled him with dread. He could appreciate that Le Pedvin didn't see the need for an investigator, but did he always have to be quite so personal about it?

'It was Adversane.' Paul replied.

'Adversane? Odd name for a Norman.' Hermitage was relieved that he'd never heard of the man.

'He has been in Chester for some time; long before William's arrival. He reported that the investigator, Brother Hermitage,' he nodded at Hermitage, 'has solved mysteries and identified murderers.'

Hermitage tried to look as if this was the last thing he wanted to do. Which it was.

'How did he know that?' Hermitage asked, hoping that word of his role wasn't spreading.

'From the Norman court, we gather,' Paul replied.

Well, that wasn't too bad. William and Le Pedvin knew of Hermitage, he just wished that they'd kept it to themselves.

'And so,' Cwen interrupted, 'when you had a murder of your own, who else to come looking for?'

'How did you know we were here?' Hermitage asked some slight, and wildly optimistic hope lingering in his mind that they'd come to the wrong place: the wrong weaver's workshop and the wrong Brother Hermitage.

'The Norman said you resided with the disgusting weaver.'

'Oh, now,' Wat complained.

'So, who else could it be?' Cwen could see that their reasoning was sound.

'Come on then,' Wat instructed. 'Out with it. Who's dead?'

Paul took a deep breath. 'Brother Abel.'

'Murdered, I assume?'

'Either that, or he managed to smother himself with his own chasuble.'

'And you think I'm disgusting?'

'It's a piece of ecclesiastical clothing,' Hermitage explained. 'A simple over-garment. From the Latin, casula, or little house. You know, casa, house?'

'Of course, we do,' Cwen said, with a roll of her eyes.

'Perhaps this Brother Abel was just careless putting it on?' Wat suggested.

'Careless putting it on,' Paul suggested. 'And then doubly so in wrapping it tightly around his head until he turned blue and died.'

'Hm,' Wat pondered. 'That would take some doing.'

'And so, the abbot sent us to find Brother Hermitage and implore him to come back with us and look into this awful business.'

There wasn't really anything Hermitage could say to this. He had to go, he knew he did. He didn't want to, but what did that matter?

'Of course, I shall come,' he said quietly. 'We have looked into such matters before, not chasubles, exactly, but murders. And we will see what we can do in this case.'

'We?' Brother Girunde asked.

'Oh, yes; Wat and Cwen always accompany me.'

They were distracted as Brother Hengard started screaming again and was climbing towards the window.

## Caput III Off to The Murder, Then

As ever, Wat the Weaver's pack sat ready to be taken up at a moment's notice. He could be out of the workshop and on the road in the blink of a fly's eye. His reasoning for this was that "you never could tell," whatever that meant.

Hermitage suspected that he needed his valuables close to hand in case he needed to run away from people who were chasing him; probably with very good reason. Perhaps, now that his more dubious activities were behind him, this was less of a risk. Still, old habits died hard.

Cwen was equally fast. Her belongings remained safe in the workshop, and she only ever took what she absolutely needed. She also argued that as Wat's pack was so well supplied there was no point in them both taking the same things; like money.

Hermitage, of course, had nothing at all. His slim volume of prayers was always in the small pocket inside his habit, so he had nothing at all to prepare.

And the monks from Chester had brought nothing and so were ready to turn around immediately. The suggestion that they might like to stay the night and set off first thing in the morning was politely declined by Brother Paul.

It was declined with another screaming fit by Brother Hengard, who was told he would be sleeping in the woodshed with this behaviour.

Unsurprisingly, it was Hengard who was hopping up and down at Wat's front door, urging everyone to hurry up. He didn't want to stay here a moment longer than was necessary as he said he could feel the drain on his soul.

Brother Brede promised that he would feel a drain somewhere else pretty soon if he carried on like this.

'Have you ever actually seen one of these evil tapestries?' Brede asked as they waited for Wat to leave his instructions with old Hartle, the weaving master.

'I most certainly have not.' Hengard was outraged.

'So, how do you know they're evil.'

'It's a fact.'

Hermitage shivered at this complete lack of reasoning.

'And how are facts determined?'

Hengard sighed. 'I don't think this is the time for a philosophy lecture.'

'It's not philosophy,' Brede informed him. 'It's called not being stupid. How do you know it's a fact? Because someone told you?'

'Everyone knows.'

'Everyone? All the people in the world? Even the Moors and the Vikings and the Turks.'

'Well, not everyone, obviously.'

'So it might not be a fact at all; if there is one person in the world who believes that it is not a fact.'

'What?' Hengard was looking rather confused.

'You have never seen one of the tapestries, correct?'

'Of course not.'

'And you've never met anyone who's seen one?'

'I wouldn't dream of talking to people like that.'

'So, without seeing one, or talking to anyone who has seen one, you've concluded they're evil.'

'Are you suggesting they're not?' Hengard sounded rather suspicious of Brede now.

'Not at all.' Brede was happy to accept this. 'They could well be evil. The point is that I don't know one way or the other. I wouldn't take the gossip in the marketplace as a determinant of any fact whatsoever. I'd want to see one for myself and then judge.'

'Yeuch.' Hengard looked horrified. 'I met another weaver who said his brother had seen one and that it was evil.' He clearly considered that his argument was won.

'You spoke to someone, who had heard from someone else? And that's how you make your mind up about things is it?'

Hengard clearly thought that it was a very sound way of doing so.

'You're an idiot.' Brede's own conclusion was clear.

'Brother Hermitage has probably seen one himself,' Hengard said. 'I bet he thinks they're evil.'

Hermitage smiled and shook his head. 'I haven't, actually.'

'But,' Hengard was thrown from his horse of reason. 'You live here, they must be all over the place.'

'Not at all. Wat doesn't make them anymore.'

'There you are,' Brede was happy. 'You've heard it from someone who actually lives in the workshop. And have you seen one while you've been here? Were there any hanging on the wall? No. As I said. You're an idiot.'

'You would let this evil fester?' Hengard accused.

Brede sighed. 'I thought we'd agreed that we didn't actually know there was any evil. Why have you gone back to the beginning again?'

'I did once see some that were similar in nature,' Hermitage confessed.[1]

'There you are,' Hengard was triumphant.

'They were very rude.' Hermitage nodded at the recollection. A recollection he'd hoped not to have to recollect again. 'But not actually evil, I would say.'

'Rude,' Brede gave the word heavy finality. 'The tapestry was rude. There are lots of things that are rude. Brother

1 *The Tapestry of Death* goes into some detail, but not too much.

Blinny is rude, isn't he?'

Hengard blushed.

'But he's not evil.'

'I'm not so sure about that,' Hengard muttered.

'All I'm saying is that you need to find out about things yourself, and not just take the word of anyone who twitters on about a subject; one they probably don't even know about themselves.'

Hengard was obviously not convinced and was shaking his head sadly. 'Next, you'll be suggesting that we should read the bible ourselves and not rely on church interpretation.'

Brede's jaw dropped, and his arm reached out to point his finger at Hengard like death's own digit. 'Don't be blasphemous,' he said.

'We ready then?' Wat asked as he appeared at the door.

Hengard shied away.

'I promise I won't make a tapestry while we walk.'

Hengard squeaked.

'Tell you what, Brother,' Brede said. 'Why don't you go ahead? You can tell the abbey that we are on the way, and you won't have to travel the road with the evil purveyor of tapestry.'

'How long will it take us to get to Chester?' Hermitage asked, having no idea where it was.

'Three or four days,' Wat replied.

'That's about right,' Brede agreed. 'There you are, Hengard. Three or four days on your own on the road with no evil to bother you at all.'

Hengard didn't look very keen.

'Or, you can stay with us, avoid the robbers and the Normans and anyone else who might want to kill a passing monk. Only thing you have to do is shut up. Can you manage that?'

'Brother Brede,' Paul spoke gently. 'And Brother Hengard. Now that we have achieved our goal and are on our way back to the abbey, perhaps we can just put this matter to one side.'

'We are taking Wat the Weaver to our abbey,' Hengard pointed out. 'I don't think that was in our instructions.'

Even Paul seemed to have some worries over this.

'Don't worry,' Wat put in. 'I won't stay. I'll find a nice tavern nearby. I always find abbeys and monasteries uncomfortable places anyway.'

'Why do we have to take him at all?' Hengard complained.

'Brother,' Paul admonished him for his manners. 'Brother Hermitage is the King's Investigator. If he says we need Master Wat and Mistress Cwen then there is no more to be said.'

Hengard did not look convinced.

'There is evil afoot,' Hermitage said.

'There you are. Told you so.'

'Evil in your monastery,' Hermitage added.

'Well, really!' Hengard was mightily offended.

'This Brother Abel has been murdered, yes?'

'Oh,' Hengard saw the point. 'Yes, he has.'

'An event quite blatant in its evil, you would agree?'

'Of course.'

'So, who better to spot evil than someone as evil as Wat the Weaver?' Cwen concluded for them all.

'Don't you start helping,' Wat complained.

'It's not that at all,' Hermitage insisted. 'We are all brothers of the cloth, yes?'

'Well, yes, obviously,' Hengard sulked.

'Brother,' Paul spoke up. 'We are engaged in conversation and have a long journey ahead of us. I would ask you to keep a gentle tongue in your head or I will ask Brother Brede to do something about it.'

Brother Brede looked like he had several things he could do with a tongue.

Hengard said nothing.

Hermitage went on. 'Can I assume that we have all been in our orders for some time? From a young age, perhaps?'

The other monks nodded their agreement at this.

'And so, our understanding of the world and its ways is limited. Limited to those interactions a monastery has with its surroundings. We have no business with true wrong-doing. The most we have to manage is a monk who perhaps takes too much from the wine sack. Or two brothers in dispute over whose turn it is for fresh straw.'

Paul and Girunde were obviously familiar with such disputes.

'Monks do not murder one another. Well, not as a general rule. They do not engage in the common behaviours of the outside world.'

'Wat does,' Cwen said.

'Well, I wouldn't have put it like that, but in essence, yes. Both Wat and Cwen bring fresh thinking. They have never lived in a monastery.'

'I should think not,' Cwen said.

'So, they know what the outside world is like and how the people there behave. I can offer no conclusions at this early stage, of course, but I would say that it is unlikely Brother Abel was murdered by another monk.'

Cwen reminded Hermitage of previous investigations. 'We have done murderous monks before, you know.'

'Well, sort of. But they were largely mad. Are any of the brothers of Chester mad?'

Paul shook his head carefully. 'Like any house, we have had those who were more, what can we say, confused about the world than others. But none were truly dangerous.'

Girunde nodded his support for this. 'We are no De'Ath's Dingle,' he said.

The brothers of Chester all crossed themselves at this.

'Now that is a monastery I've lived in,' Wat said, with his mischief in full flight.

The monks stopped walking and looked at him.

'What?' he asked. 'You should try it.'

'It is a long story,' Hermitage explained without explaining. 'From my very first investigation of a murder.'[2]

'If it was at De'Ath's Dingle, I'm surprised there was only the one.' Paul said.

'I first met Wat as he was passing by, and he helped me with a very complex issue.'

No one looked very convinced.

'And Mistress Cwen?' Paul asked.

'Ah, yes, we met Cwen when we were dealing with the murder of Wat's weaving friend, Briston.'[3]

'A lot of murder,' Brede grumbled.

'And I wouldn't say Briston was a friend,' Wat added.

'It is for Brother Hermitage's expertise in this area that we have come,' Paul reminded his companions. 'I am sure that he does not seek out murder.'

'Absolutely not,' Hermitage confirmed. 'It seems to find me all on its own.'

'And we have brought another to your door,' Paul apologised.

'That's all right,' Cwen said. 'We haven't had one for

[2] *The Heretics of De'Ath;* where it all started to go wrong

[3] *The Tapestry of Death;* hence the name.

weeks.'

They strolled on along the road in silence for a few minutes, each deep in their own contemplations of the events before them. The Brothers of Chester were perhaps sobered by comparing their own single encounter with an unexplained death with Hermitage's much more regular experiences.

Hermitage was yet again wondering how he had got into all this, despite the fact that he knew perfectly well. Still, at least this time he was helping out his own brothers and was not looking into some ghastly murder at the behest of the even more ghastly Normans.

Wat and Cwen looked as if they were out for a nice afternoon stroll without a dead monk at the end of it at all.

Wat said that they should aim to get to Brailsford tonight, which was a reasonably sized place, and would have somewhere they could rest. Under old Earl Waltheof, it had been a fine place of nearly thirty households and rumoured to be worth almost three pounds; a staggering sum.

Of course, Earl Waltheof's support for King Harold at Hastings turned out to be a bit of a hiccough. Rumour was that Waltheof had since decided that it was William he meant to support all along and was hopeful of being Earl Waltheof again any time now. In the meantime, the number of people and the value of the place would plummet.

'This Brother Abel?' Hermitage asked as he resolved that he was going to have to deal with this murder whether he liked it or not. 'What can you tell us about him?'

'Well, he's dead.' Cwen shrugged off the look she got.

'Was he young, old; did he have any special role? What were the circumstances of his death?'

'A lot of questions, brother.' Paul gave a resigned smile. 'As I said, he appears to have been murdered with his own chasuble. He was found in the chapel. The cloth was wrapped tight around his head and he had been left before the altar.'

'Shocking.' Hermitage was solemn.

'And he had not been with us long. Only in the last year did he arrive from another house; would you say that's right, Brother?'

'Aye,' Girunde confirmed. 'About a year. He was a devout fellow of middling to late age, I would say, about fifty, perhaps?'

'Where had he come from?'

'The abbot would know,' Girunde replied with little interest in the question. 'We are a quiet and contemplative order. The brothers would seldom give time to the consideration of such questions.'

Hermitage cast a glance at Hengard, thinking that a young fellow like him might find such a community quite trying.

'But he was a priest?'

'For the chasuble?' Paul asked.

'Eh?' Wat interrupted.

'The chasuble is a clerical robe,' Hermitage explained. 'A normal brother would not have one.'

'He was,' Paul confirmed. 'Although he never presided at mass.'

'Never?' Hermitage thought that was a bit odd.

'We have a priest who visits, and the abbot, of course, is delegated by the bishop. And Abel was relatively new.'

'But it was his chasuble?'

'Most definitely, He brought it with him.'

'Well, he must have done,' Girunde added.

'Why do you say that?' Hermitage enquired.

'Because no one had ever seen it before.'

'That's very interesting.'

'Is it?'

'The first time you saw this chasuble it had been used as the murder weapon?'

'I suppose so.'

'Maybe the other one brought it,' Hengard spoke up. Now that he was a considerable distance from Wat's workshop, he seemed to have calmed down a bit. He still twitched whenever he looked at the weaver, which was not helped by Wat sticking his tongue out or making rude gestures in return.

'The other one? The other one what?'

'The other new arrival. The monk in the tower.'

Hermitage usually got lost quite early on in his investigations, but this time he hadn't even arrived. He looked to the other monks for some guidance.

'Brother Hengard, you disgrace us with your behaviour and with your gossip.' Brede reprimanded the younger monk, who didn't show much sign of humility.

'What monk in the tower?' Cwen asked. 'Why is there a monk in a tower?'

Paul was reassuring that this was nothing to be concerned about. 'There is simply another brother who joined our community recently, but who has been taken ill.'

'Not dead as well then?'

'Not at all. The abbot received him, and he is now being tended in the tower by the herbalist.'

'And no one else has seen this monk?' Wat asked. 'The one they keep in a tower.'

'He is being tended there to protect us all from disease.'

'But not the abbot or the herbalist.' Wat was thoughtful.

'I'm not sure I see the connection,' Girunde commented.

'Mysterious monks in towers and others killed with their own clothes?' Wat asked. 'You want to deal with some more murders, you do.'

## Caput IV Charming

There was very little for Hermitage to report about the journey to Chester for those fictitious Chronicles he occasionally considered. He thought that posterity might be interested in a record of all the goings-on he had to deal with. More frequently, he thought that posterity must have better things to do with its time.

He supposed that his little band of travellers actually constituted quite a large group, and so were safe from the dangers of the road. Five monks journeying together would be more than most robbers would want to take on. Primarily because the possessions of five monks would be five times nothing at all. Which, if his calculations were correct, would still equal nothing. How five of anything could still equal nothing was not something he wanted to try and get his head around.

Wat and Cwen obviously looked better off, and Wat's pack, in particular, would be an attractive prize. Wat looked like he could handle himself though. And if he couldn't, he would send Cwen in. Throughout the journey, she looked as if she was hoping to spot a robber or two just so she could deal with them.

They passed through various towns, large and small, most of which paid them very little attention at all. There were the usual enquiries about the Normans and what they were up to. The smaller places had yet to see any significant impact from the Norman invasion, they just carried on as they always had. If the lord was a Saxon or a Norman it made very little difference; they still wanted your tax.

Hermitage didn't like to hint that any impact from the Normans was likely to be very significant indeed, particularly if the town in question gave any indication that actually they weren't that keen on having the Normans in.

For most places, their departing Saxon noble had gone off to Hastings and become fully departed. The Normans hadn't arrived yet, and if no one asked you for your tax, why would you pay it?

The closer they got to Chester, the more it felt that the country was carrying on as if nothing had happened at all. Clearly, Chester was a long way from Hastings, and William had to consolidate his hold on the south first. Still, Hermitage could comfort himself that the life of a religious community would hardly be disturbed by the comings and goings of kings and nobles in any circumstances.

But, as Chester approached, his familiar trepidations returned to make themselves felt. It had been easy to talk about the death of Brother Abel when that death was miles away. Now it wasn't so many miles away anymore.

After one last overnight camp, it was soon after daybreak that they approached the outer walls of the town, the usual gathering of poor and beggarly folk huddled in their rude dwellings and called out rude things to passers-by. Monks were a favourite target for this sort of thing, and Hermitage resigned himself to making passage through a torrent of lewd and just plain disgusting suggestions.

'The gathering of people here does seem to be a large one,' he commented to Brother Paul, as the first word of some passing monks started to spread amongst the disreputable community. 'Most towns I have visited have similar people, but never in such numbers, I think.'

'Space inside the walls is limited,' Paul replied. 'And expensive, of course. Between the king, the Ealdorman, the bishop and the church most of the houses are taken up.'

'Really?' Of course, this was perfectly normal and reasonable, but Hermitage had doubts. It was most likely that the king referred to was Harold, and the Saxon Ealdorman was probably as dead as his king by now. The Normans would have a new earl for the area in no time, but until then surely the houses were empty? He was certain that the bishop didn't live in his house.

'Our own house, Saint Werburgh's. has several houses,' Paul said with some pride.

Hermitage was starting to see why most of the people had to live outside of the walls in hovels. 'Ah, the blessed Werburgh,' he said. 'Her remains brought here by nuns fleeing from the Danes if I am not mistaken.'

'You are not.' Paul seemed impressed by this knowledge. 'And she has protected the city ever since. The Welsh King Gruffudd was besieging the walls some years ago when Saint Werburgh intervened.'

'Wonderful,' Hermitage said, wishing he'd been there to see it. 'What did she do?'

Paul held Hermitage's eyes with a solemn gaze. 'She made him go away.'

'Go away?' That was a bit of a disappointment.

'I know. Isn't it a great miracle?'

'He just went away?'

'He did. Gave up and went home.'

'She didn't appear in a golden haze or turn his weapons to water? Nothing like that?'

'Nothing so mundane, Brother. She must have spoken to him in the night and told him to go home. When he got up in the morning, that's just what he did.' Paul smiled broadly at the very satisfactory outcome.

Hermitage could see that a siege just stopping was a

marvellous thing. He couldn't help but think that sometimes sieges just stopped; for no other reason than they'd gone on so long without a result that everyone got bored and gave up. Or, more likely, the Ealdorman of the town spoke to King Gruffudd in the night and gave him some money. That sort of thing usually stopped sieges quite effectively.

He quietly reprimanded himself for such faithless thinking. Of course, Saint Werburgh protected the town. There was no reason to think otherwise.

'And so we offer our lives and our devotions to the blessed saint for her continued support.'

Hermitage nodded that this was a very reasonable and pious approach.

'Lucky charm, Brother?' a voice called to Hermitage from the crowded dwellings pressed hard against the walls.

'We have no need of such things,' Hermitage replied with a bow of the head. These poor people must be pretty desperate if they were trying to sell charms to monks.

'Keeps off the Normans,' the seller pressed the advantages of his product.

'Keeps off the Normans?' Hermitage couldn't help but stop at this ridiculous suggestion.

'Oh, yes,' the charm merchant clearly sensed a sale. He didn't realise that Hermitage was a real monk, one with no money whatsoever.

As the man with all the charms drew closer, he appeared to be a well-presented fellow, for someone who lived in a hovel and sold charms. He was young enough to be out working in the fields somewhere, rather than hawking his wares on the road. His clothes all seemed in good order and he even had solid shoes on his feet.

'How can a charm keep off the Normans?'

'Wards them off with its powers.'

'Powers? What sort of powers?'

'Powers to ward off the Normans.'

'Don't bother with him, Brother,' Paul said. 'Such things are nonsense, as we know. If not blasphemous nonsense.' He gave the trader a glare.

'But it works,' the man insisted. 'Do you see any Normans round here?'

'Not yet,' Hermitage said with some feeling.

'And you won't. Because of the charms.'

'So,' Wat eyed the charm merchant now. 'If the charm is already keeping the Normans away, why would we need to buy one?'

The man seemed a bit confused by this and looked as if he was giving the problem some serious thought.

'The powers will expire if people don't keep buying the charms.'

'Is that right?'

'Oh, yes. Everyone knows that. You have to keep buying charms to keep the powers going. You stop buying the charms, the powers run out and lo and behold.'

'Lo and behold what?'

'Normans. Soon as the powers are gone, they'll be popping up all over the place.'

'I rather think they're going to do that anyway. They just haven't got round to popping up here yet. And the need for people to keep buying the charms is nothing to do with your need for new leggings or another pair of those fine shoes?'

The man ignored the suggestion. 'The charms are keeping them away. Everyone's got one.'

'Not everyone,' Paul pointed out.

'She's got one,' the charm seller said with deep significance.

'She?' Hermitage asked.

'Now then, enough of that nonsense.' Paul was brusque with the man.

'Who's she?' Cwen asked this question, ignoring Paul completely.

'Why would she have come here if it wasn't for the charms, eh? Tell me that, mister clever monk.'

'Who is she?' Cwen repeated herself, much too close to the charm-man for comfort.

The charm seller looked carefully up and down the road to make sure that no one was listening; no one other than the seven travellers. 'Lady Ealdgyth.' He tapped the side of his nose.

'You did say Lady Ealdgyth? Not Eadgyth?' Cwen checked.

Hermitage could understand. If Cwen was going to bump into her mother, Eadgyth, again, she'd need to be prepared.[4]

'Who's Eadgyth?' the charm man asked.

'You don't want to know,' Cwen said. 'It just sounds like Ealdgyth.'

The man thought about this. 'No, it doesn't,' he said, giving Cwen a very odd look.

'This Lady Ealdgyth has got a charm then?' Cwen asked, with little real interest.

'That she has. Earl Edwin bought it for her.' The man glowed with pride.

'Come, come,' Paul urged everyone to move on.

'Just a moment,' Wat stopped them. 'Earl Edwin, Lady Ealdgyth?'

'That's them,' the merchant confirmed.

'Would that be Lady Ealdgyth the wife of King Harold, by any chance?'

[4] A Murder for Mistress Cwen will explain Cwen's caution

'I couldn't say.' The man had the look of someone who knew perfectly well but was only prepared to confirm it for money.

'Erm?' Hermitage asked.

'Yes?'

'I thought Harold was married to Edith Swanneck or is that the same person?' He didn't really follow these matters. He just did what kings told him. He knew William had a wife, and everyone had heard of Harold's.

'Well, sort of.' Wat said.

'Sort of married?'

'Married in the old way.'

Hermitage didn't like the sound of that. He knew that the "old way" was a common excuse for all sorts of sinful goings-on.

'A hand-fast marriage. The way the Danes do it.'

Now there was serious concern. The way Danes did things was almost always bad; and consistently unchristian.

'But then he married Ealdgyth early in ten sixty-six. Properly, in church and everything.'

'What happened to Edith then?'

'Oh, she's still about. The Ealdgyth thing was really a marriage of convenience. She was Mercian, you see.'

No, Hermitage didn't see at all.

'Harold needed their allegiance. And she'd been married to King Gruffudd.'

'The one who besieged Chester?'

'Very likely. But then Harold killed him in battle.'

Hermitage's head was starting to go round. 'Let me get this straight. Harold, dead king Harold, the one killed at Hastings, was married to Edith and killed Gruffudd. He then married Gruffudd's widow, Ealdgyth, while he was still married, only in not quite the same way.'

'That's it.' Wat seemed to think this was a perfectly reasonable explanation of things.

'It's disgraceful,' Hermitage concluded.

'It's quite normal. Kings and earls and the like are doing this sort of thing all the time.'

'Well, they shouldn't.'

'You can tell them, then.' Wat turned to Paul. 'Were you going to mention that Harold's widow had taken up residence in Chester at any point?'

'I'm sure it would have come up,' Paul said, with little concern.

'You'd think she'd start to wonder what's going on,' Cwen said. 'Every time she marries a king, they die. Need more than a charm to fix that.'

'Is it important that she's here?' Hermitage asked.

Wat was still considering Paul with a thoughtful look.

The charm seller waved his charms in their faces as if this tale only confirmed their need for his wares.

'Perhaps we'd better discuss this in private,' Wat said, indicating that they could move on through the town gate.

'Aren't you going to buy one?' the man of the charms complained.

'Certainly not,' Wat said.

'Oh, bloody hell. All that for nothing?' He looked down the road and saw some more travellers arriving. He skipped quickly away from the monks. 'Luck charms,' he cried. 'Get your lucky charms. As worn by the Queen of England.'

'So,' Wat continued as they entered the town, past the disinterested eyes of a couple of town guards. 'The until-recently Queen of England is here?'

'She arrived soon after the battle,' Paul said, showing little concern. 'There have been no problems. She was sent for safety by her brother, Earl Edwin, and has been residing here ever since.'

'Hm.' Wat sounded very cautious.

'Are you thinking this could be connected to the death of Brother Abel?' Hermitage asked. 'Surely a queen wouldn't do it?'

'No, of course not. It's the coincidence I don't like. Kings and queens and earls and the rest always mean trouble.'

'Trouble for a monk?' Hermitage asked.

'King William is no trouble for you, then?'

'Ah, well, yes, but that's different.'

Paul tried to reassure. 'Ealdgyth and her people have been here for some considerable time now. Apart from attending mass, they have nothing to do with us. They keep to themselves. They wouldn't have even known who poor Brother Abel was. And he only died a few days ago. There's no connection.'

'We'll see. It's not necessarily the nobles themselves, it's the sort of people they attract. Lowers the tone of any town, having nobles about.'

'How do you know all this about them, then?' Hermitage asked.

'Well, Harold was a very good buyer of tapestry. Knew what he liked and paid well for it.'

'I dread to think what he liked,' Hermitage said.

'But if the king liked them.' Wat took the opportunity to nudge Hengard in the ribs. 'Him being the anointed of God and all, the tapestries can't be all bad, can they?'

Hengard shied away. 'At least you tell one truth, master weaver.'

'Oh, yes. And what's that?'

'That the sort of people nobles attract are the very worst.' With a pointed sniff at Wat, he walked off into the town.

## Caput V Monk vs. Monk

Within its walls, the city of Chester was a hive of activity. Hermitage supposed that people who had large walls around them would be able to relax a bit more and get on with their lives. Being outside the walls would be far less comfortable, particularly if any besiegers turned up and found you in their way.

The population also looked as if they were a reasonably wealthy group. Everyone was well dressed and many of them were carrying bread, or skins of wine that they must have bought from the merchants.

It had sounded as if most of the houses in here belonged to nobles or to the church. Neither of them was the sort of people to be scrabbling in the dirt, begging for their next meal.

It also seemed that Saint Werburgh's was a well-endowed institution. If they had houses, someone must have put a lot of money into the place at some point. Hermitage was thinking that their accommodations would be quite comfortable. No De'Ath's Dingle style of dwelling for this place. They probably even had doors on the rooms and straw on the beds.

Brother Paul led the way through the narrow and crowded streets, exchanging a word here and there and a simple nod of the head quite frequently.

As they turned one corner, Hermitage saw another group of monks heading in their direction. There were four of them, and they wore simple habits with their cowls raised. Perhaps this was a welcoming party that had heard word of Paul's return.

The street just here was cramped, both by the buildings on

either side and by the press of people who jostled their way hither and thither. The two parties of monks occupied the middle of the way and would meet in only a few paces. Hermitage smiled his welcome at these new brothers.

'Make way,' a voice from inside one of the cowls called. Called in quite a brusque manner, Hermitage thought.

'Make way there,' Paul replied.

Both parties of monks came to a halt in the middle of the road, neither showing any sign of letting the other pass. Doubtless, they would exchange hearty greetings at any moment now.

'Make way, I say,' the cowl repeated. 'Make way for the brothers of Saint John.'

Paul gave a heavy sigh and Brother Brede stepped to the fore.

'The brothers of Saint Werburgh do not make way. The brothers of Saint John must move aside.' Brede sounded very sure about this.

Hermitage thought he heard Girunde mutter "Oh, no. Not again", or something like that.

'The brothers of Saint John move for no one.'

Hermitage quickly worked out that these new monks were the brothers of Saint John.

'They'll move for a punch up the cowl,' Brother Brede suggested, rolling his sleeves up.

'Typical response of Werburgh.' The cowl was thrown back revealing a very young brother who had a very ugly look on his face, which was itself quite ugly, to begin with. It reminded Hermitage in many ways of the awful Le Pedvin. It was almost as if the young man's skull had been painted with skin, rather than be given a proper filling.

'You're in enough trouble already, Brede.' The young man

pointed now. 'I wouldn't get in anymore if I were you.'

The way this monk used Brede's name made it sound as if it was the sort of thing found at the bottom of a privy. Hermitage thought that this was no way to speak to your elders. It was no way to speak to anyone, really.

'Move out of the way, Skull Longor, and there won't be any trouble,' Brede responded. Longor was down there in the privy as well, then.

Hermitage could see why the name was appropriate, but it was a bit rude to single out this young man's appearance, instead of simply calling him brother.

Hermitage seldom picked up on the nuances of human behaviour, but even he could tell that monks insulting one another would soon lead to trouble if something wasn't done. He also wondered if the sight of the monks fighting in Wat's vegetable patch might not have been as unusual as he thought at the time.

'That's Brother Longor to you.' Longor instructed. 'And you move.' He reinforced his suggestion with a shove on Brede's chest.

Hermitage was rather alarmed to note that Brede didn't even wobble. In fact, he clenched his fist and looked ready to return the blow in a much more vigorous manner.

'Brothers, brothers,' he stepped forward.

Longor and Brede considered him and his interruption.

'We are nearly at the end of our long journey. Surely we are brothers in Christ and have no dispute?'

'Who the devil is this?' Longor looked and sounded pretty disgusted.

'I am Brother Hermitage.' Hermitage bowed.

'Stupid name for a monk,' Longor commented, turning up his nose at the same time.

'You mean stupid name for the King's Investigator,' Brede said with very un-monkly superiority.

'The what?'

'The King's Investigator. The king's own man come here to look into the death of Abel. If you want to obstruct the king's man as he goes about his business, that's up to you.'

Longor did have a look of concern about him now.

'I've never heard of a King's Investigator.'

'Probably because King William hasn't thought it necessary to inform you. Us, on the other hand? We know all about the King's Investigator and have brought him here.'

Hermitage was wishing they'd stop saying King's Investigator quite so often.

The passage of people up and down this lane had come to a halt now. Maybe because there were two groups of monks facing up to one another and there wasn't room to pass, or maybe because there were two groups of monks facing up to one another and they thought there might be a fight.

Hermitage noticed that Wat and Cwen had wandered over to join the onlookers, rather than stay with the monks. They both had looks of eager anticipation, which was rather disconcerting.

'Abel.' Longor almost spat the name. 'It doesn't surprise me that the monks of Saint Werburgh get their brothers killed and then have to go looking for help to sort it out.'

'The king might want the brothers of Saint John looked into as well,' Brede suggested. 'After all, they regularly make unchristian threats towards Saint Werburgh's. No one would be surprised to find them involved in this. And that's before we even consider the other goings-on that Saint John's is famous for. That could turn up all sorts of worries. Very devout, King William is; won't want his religious communities misbehaving themselves. I dread to think what he'd do.'

'You are quite right,' Longor agreed with a vicious looking smile. 'The sooner he rids us of Saint Werburgh's the better. Doubtless, this King's Investigator will uncover the truth and that will be the end of you.'

With the emphasis given to his title, Hermitage felt as if the bottom of that privy was getting quite crowded.

'We all know why Abel was killed.' Longor looked very smug. 'Saint Werburgh's is cursed. The whole city knows it.'

'Typical superstitious nonsense from a monk of Saint John's. If you're even proper monks,' Brede sneered. 'It was only last week you said our pious abbot deserved to go to hell. Who knows what you did to poor Abel.'

Longor ignored the allegation. 'Dead monks in the chapel? Sick monks in the tower? The king's whatnot has to come and sort you out? The whole place is falling apart by the sound of it.' He turned to his own brothers to encourage some laughter and contempt out of them. Two joined in, but the third seemed a bit more reticent.

'Actually,' Longor went on. 'I suppose we had better get out of the way. Wouldn't want the curse of Saint Werburgh rubbing off on us. Might be our priest who gets smothered in his own chasuble next.'

'You have a priest? Not a real one, surely? You do surprise me. From what the city knows about the goings-on at Saint John's, I wouldn't think a priest would go anywhere near you.'

'On your way, Werburghs.' Longor stepped aside with great show. 'Get back to your monastery before the rest of you are taken by the devil that's obviously moved in.'

The monks of Saint John followed the lead and moved to the edge of the street. Paul indicated that his group should move on, and pointedly did not look at the others as they passed.

The small crowd in the street also returned to their business, grumbling their disappointment that they hadn't been given the entertainment two groups of fighting monks should have offered.

Once they were safely out of sight of the other band, Hermitage risked a question for Paul. 'There is some dispute between the two houses, then?'

'Well spotted, Hermitage.' Wat had joined them again.

'They're irreligious, sinful, foul and degraded fiends,' Brede summed them up.

'Now then, Brother,' Paul cautioned. 'It is as Hermitage says. Despite our differences, we are all brothers under the habit.'

'I wouldn't let one of them under my habit. I know what they get up to.'

'Why is there disagreement at all?' Hermitage asked.

'It has all built up over the years. The sin of pride is at root,' Paul said. 'You can imagine that an endowment is treasured by any house. How do we survive if not through the generosity of others?'

'Those nobles again,' Wat pointed out.

'Just so. The house of Saint John was founded by King Aethelred of Mercia around the year of our Lord seven hundred. The body of the blessed Werburgh was brought here almost two hundred years later, and we were endowed by Queen Aethelflaed.

'Ever since then, Saint John's have considered themselves to be the senior community. They even suggest that Aethelflaed endowed the wrong place by mistake; that the blessed saint isn't a saint at all but just someone called

Werburgh who happened to die nearby, and that all the relics we have been granted are false.'

'Oh, dear,' was all Hermitage could think of. He knew that churches argued with one another and were subject to human failings, like everyone. Perhaps their being in such close proximity made things worse.

'So,' Cwen said, looking quite thoughtful. 'They really don't like you.'

'They do not. And they are only encouraged by their abbot, Kenwald. He is a most difficult fellow and seems to consider it his life's mission to have but one ruling house in the city.'

Hermitage had never come across anything quite as bad as this. De'Ath's Dingle had been a truly appalling place, but at least it wasn't in competition with anyone to see who could be even worse. It kept all its horrors within its own walls; they were especially thick and tall for just that purpose.

'Are there no other churches in the city?' he asked. 'It seems quite a large place to have only two houses? Can they not bring the two of you together?'

'There are others, of course,' Paul confirmed. Saint Oswald's, Saint Bridget's, but they are small and tend to avoid having any dealings with either of us.'

'Don't blame them,' Cwen said. 'What does your own abbot say?'

'He tells us to ignore them. They are an ignorant nuisance and do not know their place in the world. Recognition will come to them, but in the meantime, we must turn the other cheek.'

'A wise counsel,' Hermitage said.

'But we're running out of cheeks,' Brede put in, clearly unhappy with this approach.

Wat addressed Brede with a serious look on his face. 'You

suggested they may have had something to do with the death of Abel.'

'I certainly did.'

'Now then, Brother,' Paul cautioned. 'Evil conjecture is quite inappropriate.'

'It's the only kind they deserve.'

'Would they really be involved in a murder?' Cwen asked.

Brede seemed to back down a bit. 'Well, they might.' He turned his head away and just grumbled a bit.

Paul continued the tale. 'They even complain to the bishop that we are a house in disarray and that we must be dealt with.'

'And what's the bishop done?'

'Nothing.'

Hermitage thought that was quite normal for a bishop.

'So. If one of your number was murdered, that would not look good,' Cwen said.

'Of course not. But that's not why we sought out Brother Hermitage. We need to find a killer.'

'Naturally. But if he finds that someone in Saint Werburgh's did it, I imagine Saint John's would be quite pleased.'

'Pleased?' Paul sounded horrified. 'Who on earth could be pleased with such a death?'

'The killer? Probably be quite unhappy if the killing didn't result in at least one death. Couldn't call yourself a killer if no one's dead.'

Paul just gaped at Cwen.

'It's all right,' she said. 'We deal with this sort of thing all the time.'

Hermitage shrugged that it was regrettably true.

Paul gave Cwen a very worried look. 'Are you now

suggesting that someone from Saint John's killed Abel just to make us look bad?'

'More than look bad; to get you disbanded by the bishop, or whatever it is happens to places that kill their own brothers.'

'I don't think there's actually any precedent,' Hermitage said. He too, found the idea truly repulsive, but with his experiences behind him, he could see that it was a possibility. 'And in any case, I don't think it would be the whole community of Saint John, just one deluded individual. That's all it normally takes.'

Paul shook his head in sorrow. Girunde joined him, while Hengard was looking quite worried.

'I knew it,' Brede piped up. 'That's Saint John's for you. Just the sort of thing they'd do.'

'Now, now,' Hermitage tried to calm the situation. 'This is all pure speculation. All we have seen is one falling out in the street. We have heard that you have a dispute, but it is a very long way from that to murder.

'We need to look into the events surrounding Abel's death and see what we can find. I think it extremely unlikely that Saint John's has anything to do with this. Despite your differences, they are a religious house. Religious houses do not go around murdering people just to make others look bad.'

'You don't know Abbot Kenwald,' Brede muttered.

'Are you saying he has murdered someone before?'

'Well,' Brede mumbled, 'not that we know of.'

'There you are then.'

'But there's always a first time.'

'And does no one at Saint John's ever die?' Cwen asked.

Brede looked a bit lost. 'Well, yes, of course, they do.'

'There you are then.'

'There I am. what?'

'Next time someone in Saint John's dies, you go into town and spread the rumour that Abbot Kenwald has killed another one. You know, just mention it in taverns, that sort of thing.'

A troubling smile was starting to spread across Brede's face.

Hermitage stepped forward and blocked Cwen's line of sight to Brede. 'Come along Cwen,' he said. 'Let's get to Saint Werburgh's.'

'What?' Cwen complained. 'I'm only trying to help.'

'Yes, well, let's try helping with the monk who's already dead and not worry about the ones yet to come.'

'Oh,' Cwen said, with some lively enthusiasm. 'Are there going to be more?'

## Caput VI You Wait Ages for One Dead Monk...

'There's been another one,' the abbot of Saint Werburgh's announced, even before there had been any introductions. He sat behind the desk in his study and held his head in his hands.

'Another one?' Hermitage asked, wondering what the abbot was talking about. Another one of what? He tried to think what they'd already had one of. Ah, yes, murder. They'd had one murder, hadn't they? The abbot meant that there had been another murder. Oh, dear.

'Brother Pendle.'

'Brother Pendle, I see.'

Girunde, Brede and Hengard all gasped together and sat on stools that lined the study walls. Paul stepped over to his abbot, offering comfort.

'I don't understand.' The poor abbot looked to be in quite a state.

As soon as they had met, Hermitage could tell that this man's advice about turning the other cheek would be genuine and sincere. He was an abbot of the old ways: pious, dedicated, almost holy in his own right. He was quiet, humble and unassuming. Dealing with the difficult people of Saint John's would be a trial to him. Having his brothers murdered around him would be simply unimaginable.

'Father,' Hermitage tried consolation. 'Your brothers have brought us here now. We will start to look into things straight away. The death of Abel is known to us, but what can you tell us of this Pendle?'

The abbot seemed to notice that they were there now, and emerged from his slough of despond. He rose and walked around the desk to join them. 'Of course, of course.' He tried a smile, but it looked very painful and forced. 'Brother Hermitage, is it not?'

'It is, Father.'

'Abbot Fulmer,' the abbot introduced himself. 'And who are your companions? We were not expecting any others.'

'Aha, yes my companions.' Hermitage realised that poor Abbot Fulmer was having a bad enough day already. Telling him that Wat the Weaver had arrived could be the final indignity. 'Well,' he began, wondering how he could get around this problem. He cast a glance at Wat and Cwen who were looking on with interest to see how he was going to get around this problem.

'After I was appointed King's Investigator, I left my monastery, De'Ath's Dingle, you know.'

The abbot gasped and sat down again.

'I resolved a murder at that place.'

'That does not surprise me.'

'And with events that followed, I found myself taking up residence, with erm, that is to say, I have a room at the workshop. A weaving workshop.'

'A weaving workshop?' The abbot looked at Cwen and Wat now and seemed to peer hard through rheumy eyes. The rheumy eyes widened to such an extent that it looked as if they wanted to leave the face altogether. 'Good God, it's Wat the Weaver.' The abbot now clutched his chest for good measure. 'You've brought Wat the Weaver in here.'

'Ah,' Hermitage said, rather weakly. 'You've met?'

For once, Cwen seemed less keen to have her status as a weaver pointed out to the room.

Wat gave Hermitage a look that said if he had ever met the abbot, he didn't recall it.

'Wat the Weaver,' the abbot was now gasping for breath

and was indicating one of his brothers should bring him some wine. 'In Saint Werburgh's.' The abbot gulped his wine and it seemed to help a bit. 'If Saint John's ever get to hear of this, we shall be finished. Finished.' The head went back into the hands.

'Told you,' Hengard muttered.

'Two dead monks not being enough, then?' Cwen said so that only Hermitage could hear.

'What have you brought him back here for?' Abbot Fulmer asked Hermitage from between his hands.

'Brought him back?'

The abbot released his face and pointed it at Wat. He followed up with his finger. 'That man was expelled from the city only three years ago.'

'Oh.' Wat nodded with happy recollection. 'That was you, was it? I always wondered.'

'Not just us, if you recall correctly.'

Wat smiled at Hermitage, a smile that said he quite enjoyed being expelled from the city, particularly as several people were involved.

'Do you know what sort of thing he was selling?'

'I can imagine,' Hermitage acknowledged.

'Selling very widely,' Wat put in, unhelpfully. 'To the most surprising people.'

Abbot Fulmer tried to block his ears.

'Master Wat has moved on from such things.' Hermitage tried to offer some comfort. 'I am pleased to say that since my time with him began, he has produced not a single work that would cause offence to anyone.' He sounded quite happy about this.

'Not one,' Wat confirmed, not sounding happy at all.

'The offence has already been caused,' Abbot Fulmer said.

'And if word gets out that Wat the Weaver is back in town, I dread to think what the outcome may be.'

'Lots of commissions that I'm not allowed to complete, I expect,' Wat mumbled.

'Why have you brought him, brother?' Poor Abbot Fulmer was suffering once more, and if there were going to be any more dead monks, he could be next. At least this one would be natural causes.

'That's what I asked,' Brother Hengard said.

Everyone looked at him as if they'd forgotten he was there; which they had.

'Master Wat gives insight,' Hermitage said. 'He understands how the ordinary man thinks and behaves.'

'I'll say he does,' the abbot confirmed. 'Far too ordinary, if you ask me.'

'If the murder of poor Brother Abel was committed by someone from inside a religious community, it may be possible for us to find them. But if, as seems likely, it was someone from outside, well, we need Master Wat's knowledge.'

'It won't be much help if he's thrown out of the city gates again.' The abbot was shaking his head but seemed resigned to just one more feature of a truly awful situation.

'You said there had been another one,' Hermitage prompted, thinking that moving off the topic of Wat the Weaver might be helpful. 'Brother Pendle?'

'Ah,' the abbot almost wailed. 'Yes. First Abel, now Pendle.' His eyes were still drawn to Wat, almost as if they were trying to make the connection from Wat to the deaths.

'What happened to Pendle?' Paul asked this.

'Dead,' the abbot said.

'Erm, yes. But how?'

'Strangled.'

'Strangled?' Paul sounded completely stunned by this.

'With an amice.'

'Nasty,' Wat whispered close to Hermitage's ear.

Hermitage sighed and explained to Wat and Cwen. 'The amice is a rectangular piece of cloth, sometimes placed over and around the head, like a hood, but more usually folded down and worn around the neck.'

'Not so tightly that it stops you breathing, I imagine.' Wat looked surprised at the glares of offence he got from everyone.

'Murder, then,' Brother Paul sagged down onto one of the stools. 'There can be no doubt.'

'Did you doubt Abel's murder?' Hermitage asked.

'I suppose I held out some vestige of hope that it might be an accident.'

'Smothered by a chasuble? Accidentally?'

Paul shrugged. 'Your expertise is greater than ours. You might have found that he tripped, or got tangled up, or, oh, I don't know.'

'If Abel had some sort of fit while he was putting on his chasuble I suppose it might be possible. But being strangled with an amice would be a pretty remarkable accident.' Hermitage said.

'Chasubles and amices, eh?' Cwen asked.

'What about them?'

'Both things that religious people wear.'

'Priests, you mean.'

'If you like. Bit suspicious, isn't it? Both of them being killed with clothing? Quite a clever thing to do, when you think about it, murder someone with cloth.' She noticed that the brothers of Saint Werburgh were all looking at her quite intensely. 'It's usually a knife, or a sword,' she explained staring back.

'Where would a knife or a sword come from?' Paul asked.

'Killers tend to have them to hand.' Cwen gave a sigh of exasperation. 'Tools of the trade?'

'It's probably that they were just the things nearby,' Hermitage said. 'Abel was wearing his chasuble, presumably, and Pendle his amice.'

'And the abbey's supply of swords is quite limited,' the abbot put in, with another glare at Wat.

'Killers do bring their own,' Wat pointed out.

'Anyway,' the abbot went on, 'Pendle didn't have an amice.'

'Ah.'

'He wasn't a priest or a canon. He was a simple brother. A man who did harm to no one.'

'So, someone brought along this amice especially for the job,' Cwen said, with some satisfaction. 'And if they went to that trouble, they could have brought a knife or a sword. Instead, they chose this amice. It's very significant.'

The room looked at her to find out why it was significant.

'For some reason,' she explained.

'Whose amice was it?' Wat asked.

The abbot gave a visible shudder as if he'd managed to forget for a moment that Wat was there. 'No idea,' he said, with a shake of the head.

'No idea because you didn't recognise it, or no idea because you haven't looked to see if any are missing?'

Abbot Fulmer didn't reply.

'So, perhaps it would be a good idea to look and see if any are missing?'

'Mine is over there.' The abbot indicated a shelf in the corner as if challenging Wat. There is only one other in Saint

Werburgh's who has one. Or rather there was only one, Brother Abel.'

'Aha,' Cwen said. Everyone looked at her and she shrugged.

Never one to turn down a challenge, Wat went over to the shelf. 'Just to see what one looks like,' he said, to Hermitage's look that said he was being very rude.

'This thing?' He held up the garment from the top of the pile.

'Of course not,' Hermitage said. 'That's an alb, isn't it?'

'Alb, of course. Silly me.' He put the alb down on the abbot's desk. 'This then?' He picked up the next.

'A stole.'

'Ah. This is a belt.'

'Cincture,' Hermitage corrected.

Wat put the stole and cincture on the desk and held up the next one for identification.

'Maniple.'

'Maniple,' Wat repeated, holding the strip of cloth away from him as if he was worried about something rubbing off.

'Sometimes called a sudarium,' Hermitage said. 'From the Latin for sweat-cloth.'

Wat held it even further away before dropping it in the growing pile. He picked up two more pieces. 'How many of these things are there?'

'Tunicle and Dalmatic,' Hermitage identified them. 'And that one on the shelf will be the chasuble.'

'Ah, the famous chasuble, eh?' Wat said.

'Infamous, you mean,' Paul said.

Wat considered the heap of garments. 'It's no wonder priests look hot most of the time.' He considered the clothing, a lot of which had fine embroidery on it and was of the very highest quality. 'Looks expensive,' he said. 'Who erm, who makes all this for you?' He sounded as if he was about to offer a better price.

'That's hardly the question of the moment,' Hermitage said, quite pointedly.

Cwen now stepped over and took the chasuble from the shelf. She held it up and considered it as if trying to work out how to use it as a murder weapon.

'That's it, is it?' she asked, looking at the now empty shelf.

'That's it,' Hermitage said.

Cwen sounded very nonchalant as she asked her next question. 'No amice, then?'

'I beg your pardon?' Abbot Fulmer said.

'Granted. No amice. On your shelf. There's no amice. It's not here.'

'I wonder where it could be?' Wat said, in a very odd voice.

'You know,' Cwen sounded very thoughtful. 'I think it could be in the proximity of Brother Pendle.'

'You could be right,' Wat agreed.

The abbot flustered over to the shelf and looked at it. He then looked under it. After that, he moved his hands about all over it as if the missing article had been rendered invisible. 'It must be there,' he insisted. 'I put all the vestments on the shelf after every mass. And that's where I get them from.'

'You're going to be one amice short of a mass next time, then,' Cwen said.

The abbot turned away from the shelf and worked his way through the clothes on his desk in a rapid manner. He then did it again more slowly. Then he took each one in turn and shook it and turned it inside out before placing it back on the shelf. 'The amice is not here,' he told the room.

'I think I said that,' Cwen snapped. 'Remember what I said

earlier? Perhaps Brother Pendle's got it.'

The brothers of Saint Werburgh all looked at one another, clearly trying to work out why Pendle would have the abbot's amice.

'Wrapped around his neck?' Cwen added clarity. 'That amice, that neck?' She shared a bewildered shake of the head with Wat as they considered the members of the religious community before them.

'Good Lord, you don't mean..?' Paul said.

'That the abbot's amice is the one that strangled Pendle?' Cwen asked. 'My goodness, there's a thought.' She waited for a moment. 'Of course, I mean the abbot's amice strangled Pendle. What do you think I've been talking about?'

'It's not possible.' Paul shook his head.

'Oh, well,' Cwen said. 'Brother Hermitage is our expert on what's possible and what's not.'

Hermitage was a bit surprised to hear that.

'What do you think, Hermitage? Is it impossible that the abbot's amice was used to strangle Pendle?'

'Impossible?' Hermitage knew that it was perfectly possible and that the brothers would come to realise that. He didn't know why Cwen had to be quite so rude about it. 'No, it is not impossible. The amice could have been taken from the abbot's shelf for the purpose.'

'Ah,' the brothers saw it now.

'There you are,' Cwen held her hands out. 'When a monk explains it, it's perfectly reasonable.' She dropped herself onto a stool now, shaking her head at the room while Wat gave her a consoling pat on the shoulder.

'It is a bit odd, isn't it?' Paul said.

'A bit odd?' Hermitage thought that the whole thing was more than a bit odd. Mind you, he'd only been here a while, so didn't really know what these people considered odd. Murder by vestment must count as odd to most people, surely.

'Abel killed with a chasuble and Pendle with an amice.'

'That was me again,' Cwen almost shouted. They all looked at her in surprise. 'Why are you repeating the things I already said, as if you'd just thought of them?'

The brothers looked quite confused and rather lost about why the shouty woman was picking on them.

'They are monks,' Wat explained. 'You have to make allowances.'

'They're idiots,' Cwen concluded. 'Look,' she said, so forcefully that the brothers leaned back in their chairs. 'I already told you that both murders were committed with priests' clothing, yes?'

The monks nodded.

'And Pendle was done with the abbot's amice.'

'We'd need to confirm that by seeing the amice in question, but it seems likely,' Hermitage added.

'Thank you, Hermitage.' Cwen seemed to be quite testy today.

'So, what do we conclude?' she asked the room, like some awfully demanding teacher.

A couple of the brothers looked at the ceiling, while the others considered their sandals. They had intensely thoughtful looks on their faces as if they were working very hard at this problem and would get the answer just after it was given to them.

Cwen sighed. 'Come on. This is easy.'

Brother Brede raised a finger, then he had some more thoughts and put it down again.

'It's obvious,' Cwen said. She surveyed the faces that were

turned away and then held out an arm to indicate the only possible conclusion. 'The abbot did it.'

## Caput VII The House of the Dead; and the Smell.

'What?' Abbot Fulmer shouted out.

'It's obvious,' Cwen said. 'Your amice, you did it.' She shrugged as if this was really not her fault.

'I most certainly did not.'

The rest of the room rose in uproar at the suggestion. All the brothers of Saint Werburgh were protesting at once. Hermitage said things like "ah well", "now then", and "I don't really think", none of which helped.

Only Wat was standing by the shelf of clothing, smiling to himself for some reason.

Brede managed to make his voice rise above the others. 'How dare you suggest that our abbot would have anything to do with this. It's outrageous.'

'Of course, it is,' Cwen said calmly.

'And I will see to it personally that you, erm, what?' Brede came to a halt.

'Of course, he didn't do it.'

Brede now just looked very lost indeed.

'Why would he send for Hermitage after the first murder if he'd done it? And then why would he go and do another one?'

'But, you said..,' Brede didn't know where he was going.

'I know I did. Woken you all up a bit, hasn't it? I told you it had to do with priests' clothing and hours later you decide it's something to do with priests' clothing. I said the abbot's amice was the murder weapon, and then Hermitage had to say it before you listened. Pay attention in future.' She glared at them all.

Every one of them looked as if paying attention was now their favourite thing.

'We need to have a look at Pendle,' Cwen told them, at which some of them gave her quite worried looks. 'To see if it really is the abbot's amice?' She gave them quite worried looks as well; worried that they were all so stupid they probably wouldn't spot a dead monk if he fell on them.

'Aha, yes, erm,' Brother Paul spoke up. 'Is that not the sort of thing the King's Investigator does? You know, look at dead bodies and the like?'

'You've seen a dead body before, surely?' Cwen asked. It was hard to imagine even the youngest child who had not seen a dead body at some time or another.

'Naturally.' Paul sounded offended at the suggestion that he might be reluctant to take a look at the corpse. 'But our brother has passed on. It is our custom that only the abbot and Brother Merle deal with our dead.'

Cwen cast a glance at Hermitage.

'It is quite normal.' He nodded. 'Brothers become skilled in different tasks and so they naturally fall to them. You know, physick, herbalist, provisioner, that sort of thing.'

'And this Brother Merle became skilled with the dead then?'

Paul shrugged. 'He seems to like it.' It looked as if this was the moment that the brothers all thought there might be something a bit peculiar about Brother Merle.

'Let's go and find Merle then,' Cwen said. 'Has he got Abel and Pendle?'

'If he hasn't, I think we have even more problems.' The abbot beckoned that they could leave the room and he went to the door to lead the way.

Paul, Girunde, Brede and Hengard noticeably stayed where they were as the others passed, but they were granted a derisory snort from Cwen as she left.

Abbot Fulmer led their way through the passages of the house of Saint Werburgh's as they headed for the deceased. Hermitage took great comfort from the familiarity of stone walls, stone floors and even from the smell of a monastic house, which seemed to have its own unique flavours, not found anywhere in the secular world; the secular world usually doing something about smells like that.

Wat and Cwen were sniffing quite loudly and Wat had placed his perfumed square of silk over his nose. Perhaps those flavours weren't as comforting for everyone.

As they walked, the abbot indicated where they were in the quite complex collection of buildings by giving a commentary. This way led to the chapel, that was the door to the refectory, the other passage went to the dormitory. Anyone would think that taking a party of visitors to see some dead brothers was just part of a normal day.

They were taken out of the main buildings and across a small open courtyard towards a lean-to building that rested on the outer wall of the whole establishment.

It was a dark-looking place, and Hermitage felt a small churn of worry move about inside as he considered the very solid door that barred the entrance.

The abbot knocked firmly on this and they waited a moment or two before there was a scraping noise from the inside. After a bit more waiting, the door creaked and moved and presented the very smallest opening to the outside world.

'Yes?' A voice asked the question, and Hermitage concluded that it really was the only sort of voice that could possibly answer a door where there were dead people inside. It was only a whisper but was a very worrying one; the sort of whisper that people used when they wanted to tell you something horrible and were taking some pleasure in doing it.

'Brother Merle,' the abbot said. 'This is Brother Hermitage, the King's Investigator. He has come to look at Abel and Pendle.'

'Oh, yes?' The worrying, whispering voice now became quite disturbing, as if it was grateful to have found a fellow with common interests. 'You'd better come in then.' The door opened wide and Merle presented himself to them all. He raised his eyebrows at the sight of Wat and Cwen.

'These are the investigator's companions,' the abbot explained. He said no more.

'Oh, yes?' Merle repeated, sounding both suspicious and quite interested at the same time.

While Hermitage had been pretty sure that he would rather not enter the building where the dead bodies were stored, now that he had seen Brother Merle, he was absolutely positive. He got the distinct impression that Brother Merle would rather all his visitors were dead, but not in a nasty way.

The Brother was a small man, short and thin, but was also as pale as those he cared for. It could well be that he only emerged from his room to attend upon the dead, after which he brought them home with him.

He was also fairly advanced in years and there was something in his eye that said he had spent most of those years talking to his charges. Conversing with them, probably, as he looked the type who claimed to hear the dead.

'They're all prepared.' Merle said this in a tone that indicated "preparation" was a pretty unpleasant, yet enjoyable task; for Merle, anyway.

'In we go then,' Cwen said, with remarkably good cheer.

Brother Merle stepped back to let them pass and they filed

into the small space of what Hermitage could only think of as some sort of mortuarium; a room for the dead.

The presence of the deceased was immediately clear, and Cwen snatched Wat's perfumed silk from his hand, planting it over her nose and breathing deeply.

'Bloody hell,' Wat said when he was forced to take a breath.

Hermitage had to admit that the odour of this place was the sort that didn't require a nose to make itself felt. An open patch of skin was all it needed to get you.

Merle was obviously used to it, unless it was coming from him, of course. Hermitage doubted that anyone still alive could generate this strength of pungency. If the smell was Merle, he wouldn't be surprised to see the corpses trying to leave.

The abbot was showing remarkable restraint, although one side of his face was twitching slightly.

Ignoring the truly appalling smell, which was impossible, the inside was quite a comfortable dwelling; apart from the two dead bodies lying on tables at one end; the ones whose fragrance dominated everything.

Brother Merle had settled himself very well and had perhaps selected his speciality to keep visitors to a minimum. At the far end of the room there was a fireplace, empty now, but the scorch marks on the wall said that it was in regular use. Drawn up in front of this was a single, comfortable-looking chair with a length of old cloth thrown over a stuffing of straw. Against the wall to the side was a bed. Merle obviously had no qualms about sleeping with his charges.

'There they are then. All comfortable and sleeping soundly,' Merle said.

'Good, good,' Hermitage managed to say. He sidled slowly over until he was close enough to make out the features of the two deceased brothers, and far enough away not to have to look too closely. He noticed that Wat and Cwen stayed by the door. They then opened the door and shoved one another to see who could get their nose out first.

The brothers were definitely dead. And Brother Abel was definitely deader than Brother Pendle. Both men had the look of those whose souls had left this world some time ago. Their bodies were now following, just more slowly.

'Tidied up nicely,' Merle said, looking at his work with pride.

Hermitage dreaded to think what "tidying up" involved. He had certainly seen worse dead bodies than these two though. They were clean, were dressed in neat habits and did have looks of peace upon their faces.

'Not like when I brought them in.' Merle nodded at the recollection.

There was no way Hermitage was going to ask what they had been like when Merle brought them in.

'Do you have the amice?' he asked instead, noticing that it wasn't still around the neck of Brother Pendle. 'The one that it is said killed the brother.'

'Oh, yes,' Merle leered as if this was a prize possession. 'Got it safe.' He smiled at them, which was not at all nice, and went to his sleeping area. He pulled a wooden box out and opened the lid before rummaging around inside. As he did this, he talked to himself, plainly reminiscing over the contents. The names of various monks were mentioned, and Hermitage dearly hoped that he wasn't going to have to look in the box.

'Here we are,' Merle emerged clutching a length of

embroidered cloth. He brought it over for examination.

Hermitage took it, not without some trepidation, and held it up so that they could all see.

'That's it,' Abbot Fulmer said with a heavy sigh. 'That is my amice. How did it get here?'

'Came with the body,' Merle explained, happy to help.

'I mean, how did it get on the body in the first place? Last I saw it, it was on my shelf.'

'We're not going to have to go over all that again, are we?' Cwen called from the door.

The abbot looked at her and recalled his lesson. 'Just so. Taken from me and used to kill poor Pendle.'

'Right,' Cwen congratulated the answer.

'Why would anyone do such a thing?' The abbot was in genuine distress as he considered the deceased. 'First Abel and now Pendle.'

Hermitage was grateful that his experiences of dealing with murder, revolting though they were, were going to be of some comfort to Abbot Fulmer. 'That is what we shall discover,' he said. 'We have seen that they are dead, and Brother Merle has shown us the amice in question.'

'I've got some more,' Merle said as if hawking something quite disgusting.

'More?' Hermitage was horrified at what this might mean. 'More what?'

'I've got the chasuble. The one what killed for Brother Abel.' He nodded towards the table to indicate which of the dead was which.

He scurried back to his box and brought it out. He then presented it to his audience, as if knowing that it was just what they'd been waiting for.

'This is Abel's own chasuble?' Hermitage asked.

'Yes,' the abbot confirmed. 'He brought that with him.'

'And I've got the bones.' Merle added, sounding as if he was getting a bit carried away now.

'The bones? What bones?' Hermitage trembled slightly.

'The bones that murdered Brother Hugo.' He grinned broadly and nodded quickly as if encouraging them to ask him to go and get the bones.

'Another murder?' Hermitage was horrified. What on earth was going on here?

'Now then, Brother,' the abbot calmed Merle. 'You know that Brother Hugo choked on a chicken bone in the refectory, and by the time we could deal it, he had passed on. He was not murdered.'

'Murdered by the chicken,' Merle concluded, happily.

'The chicken was already dead,' the abbot said. 'We have been over this.'

Merle turned up his nose and appeared to sulk. 'Still got the bones,' he said.

'You went to the brothers where they had died?' Hermitage asked, quite anxious to move Merle back to the dead in hand. He feared that spending too long in Merle's company could affect someone quite badly.

'Oh, yes,' Merle nodded with pride. 'I took them.'

'And Abel had the chasuble about his head, and Pendle the amice about his throat?'

'That's right,' Merle was happy to confirm the details. 'Both of them all blue.' He now held his breath, which only made him turn red, but he seemed to think demonstrated the process.

'Strangling with an amice, I can understand,' Hermitage said. 'But smothered with a chasuble? It's a large garment.'

'Wrapped round and round, it was,' Merle explained with

enthusiasm. 'Round and round his head. Over and over.'

'I see.'

'Again and again.'

'Yes, thank you.'

'All chasuble it was, his head.'

'Right.'

'Couldn't see him at all. Until I unwrapped him. Then you could see him. All blue.'

'Yes, we got the blue. So, you were the very first to go to them?'

'As soon as we have a death, Brother Merle is sent for,' Abbot Fulmer explained. 'It was clear that Abel was dead and had been for some time. The same with Pendle. There was no point trying to do anything, other than ask Merle to prepare them.'

'Prepare,' Merle repeated with a gleam in his eye; the sort of gleam that shines off a stagnant pool at midnight.

Wat now ventured away from the door slightly. It still looked as if he was trying to avoid breathing. 'And there was nothing else?' he asked. 'No one else about, no other signs, no clothes?'

'Oh, they had clothes.' Merle even cackled. 'Not like Brother Risely.'

'Brother Risely was a long time ago,' the abbot cautioned. 'We're not talking about Brother Risely anymore. Remember?'

Merle looked as if he'd just been reprimanded.

'Er, right,' Wat sounded confused. 'But there was nothing unusual about Abel or Pendle.'

'They was dead,' Merle confirmed. He seemed to think that was all you needed.

'You didn't see anything else? Notice anything? Nothing

out of the ordinary? Apart from them being dead.'

'Like what?' Merle asked.

'I don't know, I wasn't there, was I? Any people there who shouldn't be? Anyone skulking about. Something dropped on the floor. A message?'

'What?' Merle sounded interested. 'Like a parchment or something?'

'Exactly.' Wat was triumphant that he had got through and that there was something else. 'Exactly like a parchment.'

'No,' Merle said. 'No parchment.'

Wat hit himself on the forehead.

Merle did give it some more thought but shook his head. 'Just them. Nothing else.'

'Who actually found them?' Cwen asked. 'Who was the first to see they were dead?'

'As I said, Merle deals with all the bodies straight away,' Fulmer said.

'Yes, but who told Merle? Someone must have found the dead and then told Merle. Unless he was wandering the corridors looking for something to do; or someone to do it to.'

For a moment, Hermitage thought that was perfectly possible, if not actually likely. He even wondered if Brother Merle wouldn't go round strangling brothers when things got quiet. It was ridiculous, but even so, he would put the idea away, in case it came in handy.

'Oh, I see. Erm, let me think.' Abbot Fulmer rubbed his chin.

'The herbalist,' Merle said.

'It was the herbalist who told you?'

'That's right.'

'In both cases?' Hermitage asked, thinking that would be a

bit of a coincidence.

Merle nodded.

'Where was Pendle found?' Cwen asked.

'Dead,' Merle said.

'Not how. Where?'

'Yes, where. Here, with the dead.'

'He was here?' Hermitage couldn't help the squeak break out of his voice.

'Where were you?' Cwen asked.

'Out,' Merle said, without giving any explanation.

'And the herbalist found Pendle here? As well as finding Abel in the chapel?' Wat joined in.

'That's right.' Merle nodded, clearly not worried about this.

'What was the herbalist doing here?' Wat asked. He nodded towards Brother Abel and actually took a step closer. 'Bit late for herbs, I'd have thought. Unless he's got some really strong ones.'

'Humours,' Merle said, as a complete explanation, which it wasn't.

'Humours?' Hermitage couldn't see the connection.

'The herbalist says this place is full of bad humours.' Merle obviously couldn't see a problem.

'I think he's right,' Cwen said. She had snatched the cloth from Wat, who now seemed more interested in the body than its smell.

'He brings herbs to ward them off.'

'And you immediately throw them out,' Cwen concluded, gagging slightly.

'Oh no, I put them about. Don't notice that they do anything.'

'You must be dead as well then.'

'I think we need to talk to the herbalist.' Hermitage felt sure that a conversation in the herbalist's rooms would be far more comfortable than in Merle's. There was also a real interest. If this herbalist had found both bodies, he would surely have something of use to tell them.

'If you're going there.' Merle sounded very serious. 'You must beware.'

'Really?' Hermitage asked. Perhaps there was more to this herbalist than just herbs. Could he have something to do with the deaths?

'Yes.' Merle even pointed a bony finger at them as they moved to go. 'You must prepare yourselves if you go to his workshop. The smell is disgusting.'

## Caput VIII It's All in the Herbs

As they left Merle's very individual establishment, walking very gratefully and with regular gulping intakes of fresh air, Wat pulled Cwen and Hermitage to one side, out of the abbot's earshot.

'I know him,' he hissed.

'Know who?' Hermitage asked. He couldn't think that they'd met anyone new recently.

'Abel the dead.'

Hermitage couldn't follow that at all.

'Before he was dead,' Wat explained.

'Who is he?' Cwen was intrigued.

'I don't know.'

'You don't know who he is, but you know him?'

'I recognise him.' Wat's irritation at Cwen was clear.

'From where?' Hermitage wondered how Wat could know a monk at all. Then he recalled Wat's trade and realised how he could know a monk. Never mind murder, this had the potential to get very embarrassing.

'I can't bring it to mind, but I know the face. I'm sure I do.'

'From an abbey or a monastery?'

Wat was thinking hard. 'I don't think so.'

'But then how?'

'When I did business with the church or a monastery or the like, it was always with one person. You can imagine that the whole community wouldn't be involved.'

'I certainly can.' Hermitage knew that Wat's tapestries of old were just plain disgusting. He also knew that if monks or churchmen wanted to do something just plain disgusting, they tended to do it on their own.

'I just think I've seen him when I was doing business with

someone. It wasn't with him directly. I know the people I trade with. He must have been with someone while we were doing a deal.'

Hermitage and Cwen had nothing to offer but looks of encouragement.

'You've never seen him?' Wat asked Cwen.

She shook her head. 'No, not one of Briston's customers.'

Hermitage frequently forgot that Cwen had been in the same ghastly trade as Wat, only with Briston the Weaver. He liked to forget about it as often as he could.[5]

'A noble then? Or merchant?' Cwen offered.

'Most likely,' Wat agreed. 'He was probably a retainer or even a merchant himself who wasn't buying.'

'Very decent of him,' Hermitage said. He then realised this was all wrong. 'But Abel is a monk. A priest, no less.'

'He is now. Might not have been when I saw him. The monk's clothing is probably putting me off.'

'I don't think we want to undress him,' Cwen said. 'Although I think Merle would if we asked.'

Wat quickly waved that suggestion away.

'You didn't recognise Pendle?' Hermitage asked.

Wat shook his head. 'Never seen him before, dead or alive.'

'If he was a merchant, or some Noble's man, what's he doing as a dead priest?' Cwen held her hand out to demonstrate that this was a big question.

'Who knows? Hiding from the Normans? Becoming a priest would be a good way to disappear.'

'You can't just decide to become a priest,' Hermitage explained. 'It takes years of devotion.'

Cwen held his eyes with hers. 'Maybe he was lying when he said he was a priest?'

---

[5] The whole thing can be recalled by reading *The Tapestry of Death*

'Ah, yes, could be.' Hermitage could see this; not that he approved.

'It might come to me,' Wat said, as he indicated that the abbot was now saying his farewells to Merle. 'Let's keep this to ourselves for now. It might come in useful.'

Hermitage thought that sounded rather dishonest, but then so did pretending to be a priest, never mind suffocating pretend priests.

The abbot approached them now, coughing slightly as he escaped Merle's miasma, but trying to disguise the fact.

'How could this herbalist have found both the bodies?' Wat asked.

The abbot took a deep breath before answering. 'The herbalist moves around the monastery regularly, tending to the brothers who are sick or in need of his services. It would be no surprise.

'The chapel is open to all and so the herbalist could well be first upon Abel's body. And it is as Brother Merle says, his own particular function does tend to spread a bit of a pall over the place. Anything to counter that is most welcome.

'With Brother Abel freshly arrived, a distribution of fragrant herbs would be entirely in order.'

'So, he takes the herbs to deal with Abel and finds Pendle in the same state.' Cwen said. 'Question is, what was Pendle doing there?'

'And the question before that is why Abel was dead in the first place,' Wat added.

'There is that,' Cwen agreed.

'That reminds me.' The idea of the herbalist attending brothers around the monastery gave Hermitage an even earlier question. 'We're told there is a sickly monk in the tower?'

'Are you?' Abbot Fulmer didn't sound very happy about that. 'And who told you that?'

'I don't recall.' Hermitage really didn't want to get anyone into trouble. 'I think it might have been Brother Hengard.'

'Yes, it would be.' The abbot's frown said that he would be having words with Hengard.

'It's true then?' Wat pressed the point.

'There is a brother in the tower, yes. And yes, he is unwell. The herbalist is attending him.' The abbot seemed more concerned with Hengard's gossip than with the monk in the tower himself.

'We do know he's still alive, do we?' Cwen asked. 'I mean, a visit from the herbalist seems to be pretty fatal in these parts.'

'He is fine. Well, not fine, obviously, because he is unwell, but he is alive.'

'Seen him recently, then?'

'I have. Only yesterday.' Abbot Fulmer gave a smile.

'Plenty of time to die since yesterday. Perhaps we'd better go and have a look ourselves.'

'We can check with the herbalist.' Fulmer walked on.

'Not been here long, we hear.' Cwen wasn't giving up. 'A new arrival goes straight into the tower to be tended by the herbalist and has no visitors.'

'Quite right too.' The abbot was comfortable with this decision. 'The herbalist is still unclear what ails our brother and so we keep him away from others.'

'From everyone but the herbalist.'

'He is used to dealing with ague and pox and the like. He takes precautions.'

'And you?'

'I don't go too close. I do my duty to the brother to see that he is as well as can be expected. An abbot cannot neglect his community because of illness.'

'Where did he come from, this sickly brother?' Wat asked.

'I haven't had the chance to enquire. He is sick, and such details can wait until he recovers.'

Wat said nothing but moved his face around as if thoughts were squabbling inside.

'Is this brother of any relevance?' Fulmer asked.

'Everything can be,' Hermitage said. 'Anything at all might be helpful in identifying our killer.'

'The brother has not left his tower since he arrived. And I hardly think he's in any state to go wandering the corridors killing people.'

'We will gather many facts, and most of them will be of no help whatsoever.' Hermitage felt a wave of despair as he said this.

'What's his name, this sickly brother?' Wat asked.

'Brother Odwin.'

'Odwin, eh?' Wat repeated, slowly.

'Do you know him?'

'Never heard of him.'

Ah, thought Hermitage, another fact of no help whatsoever. It was so disheartening to know that he was going to have to go through a lot more before they discovered anything of use.

'Here we are.' Abbot Fulmer drew up at a simple door set into a wall of wattle and daub. Like Merle's home for dead people, the herbalist's workshop was a separate building from the rest of Saint Werburgh's. In this case, it was so that the herbalist could tend the garden that encircled the place: a garden full of the herbs and plants that were his calling.

It was a building on its own within the enclosure of Saint Werburgh's, and even from outside the sweet and pungent fragrances of herbs could be detected. The place even had an upper storey, which seemed a bit of an extravagance for a herbalist's workshop, unless some of the herbs were very tall.

Abbot Fulmer knocked on the door and waited.

Hermitage frowned at this. Surely an abbot was entitled to go wherever he wished in his own house, without hindrance.

'In case there is some delicate work underway,' the abbot responded to Hermitage's unasked question. 'A fermentation that might be disturbed by a sudden breeze from the door, that sort of thing.'

It sounded as if the abbot was reciting his instructions, rather than imparting his own knowledge.

After a moment or two, the sound of a bolt being drawn back was heard.

'Must be some pretty dangerous herbs,' Cwen said. 'If they need to be locked in.'

The door opened a crack and a face appeared, presumably the herbalist.

'Ah, Abbot Fulmer.' The herbalist smiled and opened the door fully. 'And some others.' The smile wavered a bit.

Hermitage had to admit that this monk did look like a herbalist. All the herbalists he knew appeared to be slowly turning into herbs themselves. Their fingers were grimy from working the soil and the plants, their habits were stained with all the colours of the rainbow and their general appearance was unkempt and uncared for. It was clear that their herbs were the most important things to them; far more important than the annual bath. Still, at least they tended to smell nice.

There were generally two types of herbalists, the old and the young. The old tended to be wizened fellows who looked as if they'd spent their long life doing things with herbs that really shouldn't be done.

The young were bubbling enthusiasts who considered that herbs presented the solutions to every modern ill if only other people could see it. Warts, pox, even the Weeping Dribble; everything could be cured by the right herb.

This brother was one of the young ones. It was obvious that his only topic of conversation would be herbs and their uses. That was why young herbalists tended to have very few friends.

'Brother Bodin, this is Brother Hermitage, he is the King's Investigator.' Abbot Fulmer did the introduction.

'Investigation eh?' Bodin sounded intrigued. 'A tracker, then. From the Latin, vestigare.'

'It is indeed.' Hermitage was delighted that Bodin appeared to be an educated fellow. This was not always the case with herbalists. Some came from the land and knew their herbs like the backs of their hands. Why their hands had backs in the first place just confused them. 'An appointment forced upon me, I fear.'

'And what are you tracking today?'

'We have come to look into the deaths of Brother Abel and Brother Pendle.'

'And you want to speak to me because I found the bodies. Fascinating.'

Hermitage smiled broadly. 'And this is Wat and Cwen,' Hermitage responded to a jab in his back from Cwen.

'Are they investigators as well?' Bodin's interest didn't wane. 'Is there a force of investigators across the land tracking the acts of ne'er-do-wells and rascals?'

'God forbid.' Hermitage couldn't stop the profanity escaping at such an appalling thought. 'And I pray to the Lord that this land will never need such a thing. They are my friends and companions who bring useful knowledge of the world outside the monastery to bear.'

'Common sense,' Cwen said. 'That sort of thing.'

Bodin nodded as if this was perfectly reasonable. 'Come in, come in.' He beckoned them all through the door. 'I shall tell you all that I can and see what light this throws upon matters.'

They stooped in through the door and entered a warm and comfortable room, so thick with the odour of herbs that Hermitage coughed.

A fire sat in the middle of the space, the roof open above to take the smoke, and over this hung three small cauldrons on an ingenious stand. Each one bubbled, popped and steamed with brews of one sort or another.

The roof was hung with so many stored and drying plants that it looked as if it had been planted and was starting to grow some sort of upside-down garden. Across one wall there was a long workbench with pestles and mortars and instruments of devious design and function.

The far wall had a simple bed and table and was obviously where Bodin slept. It was the least tidy and cared for area of the whole room. Besides this, a simple ladder led to the upper storey, doubtless full of even more herbs waiting for attention.

There was nowhere to sit, so Bodin indicated that they should gather around the fire to take its warmth, and so that he could tend his brews.

'Wat the Weaver, then,' Bodin said, sounding both impressed and surprised at the same time. 'I never thought Wat the Weaver would be in my workshop. Or in a religious house at all, come to that.'

Hermitage was amazed. 'The abbot told you?'

'I've not seen the abbot since your arrival.'

'Then, how?' Hermitage asked. Perhaps Bodin had been one of those taking an active part in throwing Wat out of town.

Bodin turned slightly to face Wat, who looked as intrigued as Hermitage.

'Master Wat is obviously a well-to-do fellow,' Bodin explained. 'His clothes are of the very highest quality as are his boots. Clearly, he is a merchant or trader or craftsman of some import and success.'

Wat bowed his head to acknowledge this.

'The fine belt he wears appears to be made in the style of a tapestry. The coloured wools are tightly threaded to create a charming image of deer and the other woodland creatures. No embroidery, that.'

Wat snorted at the very idea.

'His hands are clean and soft looking, so his work requires no use of great strength or tools that would harden the skin. A mason, for example, would have white skin from all the stone dust and would probably be missing a finger or two. Instead, Master Wat bears a couple of marks of old injury, seemingly from some fine instrument, like a needle.'

Hermitage was openly gaping now.

'Similarly, Mistress Cwen has the same signs.'

Cwen looked at her hands and nodded that Bodin was right.

'And finally, sticking from the top of Master Wat's left boot is a small fibre of coloured wool. Dyed with the madder plant, if I am not mistaken. The thread has clearly been cut as the edge is sharp, and it is too short for cloth or embroidery. Must be tapestry.'

'Remarkable,' Hermitage breathed.

'And how many successful tapestry makers called Wat are there?'

'One,' Wat confirmed.

Bodin shrugged that his conclusion was so obvious anyone could have reached it. 'Why Wat the Weaver and Mistress Cwen are accompanying a monk who is the King's Investigator is completely beyond me.'

'That is a very long tale.' Hermitage said. 'But your reasoning is remarkable. Such attention to detail.'

Bodin looked slightly embarrassed. 'I'm sure it is nothing to you who are the King's Investigator. Doubtless, you do this sort of thing all the time.'

'Oh, yes,' Cwen confirmed. 'It's nothing to Hermitage.' And she gave him a very peculiar look.

'My discovery of the bodies will soon be explained by your detailed scrutiny.' Bodin appeared to be looking forward to this.

Hermitage would be quite interested as well.

'Why don't you just tell us,' Wat said, with a rather hopeless glance towards Hermitage.

'Very well. There's little to tell, really. I went to the chapel with some herbs to be laid out.'

'Why lay out herbs in the chapel?' Cwen asked.

'A good question. I can see that the investigator's skills are shared by you all,' Bodin commented.

'We've all got them.' Cwen gave a heavy sigh and a look at Hermitage. 'Well, nearly all of us.'

'There is a very aged brother in our community, our gatekeeper, who suffers from the Stinking Leak. The other brothers asked if I could help as the chapel becomes unbearable whenever he is in there. I found a herb that was very effective at countering the worst effects. Every few days I lay a new supply. It was then that I discovered poor Brother Abel.'

'And how was he?' Hermitage asked.

'Well, dead.' Bodin looked a bit confused by the question.

'I mean how, exactly. Where was he? What was his position?'

'Ah, I see. Yes, very good. He was before the altar, on his back, with his chasuble wrapped tight around his head. At first, I thought he might be sleeping.'

'Sleeping?' It sounded like an odd way to go to sleep.

'Using the chasuble as a pillow, he had taken to the chapel for some quiet. But when I drew close, I saw that the thing was wrapped tight around his head. I called Brother Merle and we unbound him straight away, but it was clear that he was dead, and had been for a while.'

'What time was this?'

'It would have been between Prime and Terce.'

Hermitage nodded thoughtfully, even though he couldn't see how that piece of information was of any use at all. He just felt he had to ask something.

'I then informed the abbot, and Brother Merle took the deceased away.'

'On his own?' Hermitage asked.

'On his trolley,' Bodin replied. 'He has a special one for this sort of thing.'

'Trolley, I see.' Hermitage looked as if he was considering this trolley very carefully, while Cwen and Wat looked at him and shook their heads slightly.

'Yes. He frequently leaves the thing outside cells in the middle of the night. Some sort of joke, I think.' Bodin's face said that he didn't see the humour.

'Once Brother Merle has a body in his care, I go over and

spread more herbs about that place.'

'And that's when you found Pendle.'

'Just so. And he was also on the floor, but this time the amice was tight around his neck.'

'At least Merle wouldn't need his trolley.' Wat said, to scornful looks from everyone.

'Merle said he wasn't there.' Hermitage wanted to check that. Brother Merle seemed a very peculiar fellow. It could be that he had something to do with all this due to some disturbance in his head.

'That's right.' He came back later.

'Do you know where he'd been?'

'Not at all. Could have been the privy for all I know.'

'Was there anything to connect the brothers?' Hermitage asked. 'Abel and Pendle? Did they know each other?'

'No more than we all know one another.'

'Brother Abel was a recent arrival, I gather.'

'That's right. Been here for several months now though. There are brothers who came after him. In fact, Brother Pendle was one of them.'

'Really?' Hermitage thought that was interesting. He didn't know why it was interesting, but one thing at a time.

'Abbot Fulmer, you said Pendle was a harmless fellow.'

'Just so,' the abbot confirmed. 'He has not been here that long, but it is clear that his is a gentle soul.'

'Had a lot of newcomers recently?' Cwen asked.

Abbot Fulmer thought about this for a moment. 'I suppose we have seen more new arrivals in recent times than was common in the past. But then things have changed, have they not?'

'Have they?'

'The Normans?' the abbot prompted. 'We have little

knowledge of them here, but it is told that they are rough and impatient people.'

'Rough and impatient,' Wat said with a little grimace. 'Yes, that's them exactly; rough and impatient.'

'And so, brothers from other establishments may seek to move.'

'Run away from the Normans you mean,' Wat said. 'Probably very wise.'

'A bit odd that it's the new ones who are dead,' Cwen said.

'As Bodin says, they have been here for many months now, they are hardly newcomers anymore.'

'Hm,' Cwen was not convinced.

In the silence that descended as no one could think of anything else to ask, there was a thump from the ceiling above their heads.

'Heavy herbs?' Cwen asked.

Bodin looked embarrassed. 'Ah, no, that would be my erm, patient.'

'The monk in the tower?' Wat asked, obviously finding this unbelievable.

Bodin nodded.

'That's ridiculous.'

'Why so?'

Wat looked up. 'One upper floor does not make a tower.'

'With the roof on top, it is the tallest part of Saint Werburgh's.'

'Still not a tower. All you've got is a monk upstairs. That's not very mysterious, is it?' Everyone looked at him, clearly puzzled why he was worried about the nature of towers.

'Hardly the point, eh?' Cwen suggested. 'The monk in the tower is a new arrival as well, yes?'

'Well, I suppose so,' Bodin admitted.

'We'd better have a word with him then. As he's a new arrival who's still alive at the moment.'

'I'm sorry, that's out of the question.'

'Because of his ague?'

'Just so.'

'The abbot sees him.'

'Only from a distance,' Abbot Fulmer said. 'And just to exchange a wave to let me know he is content. Brother Bodin deals with him directly.'

'And that is the way it must stay,' Bodin said. 'I cannot risk anyone else being near him.'

'Could we shout at him?' Cwen asked.

'He is a sickly man. I don't think being shouted at will help.'

'I'm sure he won't mind being shouted at if it stops him being murdered,' Cwen retorted. 'And we've got to get some justice for the dead people. And help the living ones who aren't dead yet, but might be at any moment. Particularly if they're new, it seems.'

'I see your point,' Bodin said. 'But I must forbid it. Until there is some sign of recovery, he must stay isolated. And he will be safe here with no visitors. And he has most certainly not been out anywhere; murdering brothers or otherwise.'

Cwen was on the verge of arguing some more, only louder this time when Wat stepped in.

'That's very thoughtful of you,' he said. 'Of course, we must respect your wishes, you are the herbalist, after all. Perhaps we could return to the abbot's study and make a list of other monks who are new. Talk to them first?'

'That is a wise suggestion,' Bodin agreed.

'It's a short list,' the abbot mumbled, sounding rather saddened.

Not really knowing what was going on, Hermitage found himself leaving the workshop, promising to return as soon as the monk in the tower was ready to receive visitors.

'You go ahead father,' Wat said to Abbot Fulmer. 'I just want to check something with Hermitage and Cwen, we'll catch you up.'

The abbot looked rather confused but did as he was told.

Once he had gone, Hermitage turned to Wat. 'What is it you want to check?'

Wat was looking at the building. 'I want to check which one of us is best at climbing up the outside of a herbalist's workshop.'

## Caput IX Don't Do, Delegate

'Brother Hermitage, come quickly.' Abbot Fulmer called across the courtyard, putting paid to their tower climbing plans.

'Oh, Lord, what is it now?' Hermitage fretted. 'Surely not another death.'

'From the stock on the abbot's shelf there's still plenty of clothing to go,' Wat said. 'Murdered with a mani - whatnot,' he suggested with mock horror.

'Death by dalma thingy,' Cwen intoned.

'If you two could be some help, it would be much appreciated.' Hermitage shook his head and made towards the abbot, who was now beckoning rather frantically.

'What is it, father?' he asked when they got close enough.

'A delegation.' The abbot looked very worried and was wringing his hands as if he had not the first idea what to do.

'A delegation? Delegation from where? Of whom?'

'The town.'

'Angry townsfolk, eh?' Wat asked. 'They don't have burning torches, do they?'

'Wat, really.' Hermitage tried to look supportive for the abbot's sake.

'If they've got burning torches, it's not good.' Wat shook his head dolefully, which Cwen helpfully slapped and indicated that he should follow the abbot and shut up.

She hissed in his ear. 'Don't forget that you have a bit of history when it comes to the angry townsfolk of Chester. It won't be helpful if they recognise Wat the Weaver, will it? If they find that throwing you out of town didn't work, they might decide to set light to you this time.'

Wat's expression said that he got the message.

'Have they come about the murders?' Hermitage asked.

'I don't know.' Poor Abbot Fulmer really was in a dreadful state. As a pious and efficient abbot, he doubtless ran his community with care and devotion. Dealing with anything outside of the walls would be a trial. Delegations of people turning up was obviously too much. 'All I got was a message that there is a delegation from the town waiting for me in my study.'

'Then we shall accompany you.' Hermitage tried to sound much more positive and decisive than he actually was. The abbot would feel better for having Hermitage's company. And Hermitage needed Wat and Cwen there for the same purpose. 'Lead on.'

'I am most grateful.' The abbot touched Hermitage's elbow and gave him a very weak smile.

'Do you know exactly who this delegation is?' Wat at least sounded more serious now.

'I don't. I'm just told it's a delegation from the town.'

'No idea how many?'

'The Latin, delegare is not much help,' Hermitage said. 'It just means a sending or assignment. Could be just one person or could be several.'

'Well, that's very informative, thank you, Hermitage.' Wat gave Hermitage a very blank look as if he hadn't found the information helpful at all.

'The message was that they had been put in my study. Must be more than one.'

'Right,' Wat said with a tone and look that said he had a scheme in mind. Doubtless a very bad one. 'Abbot Fulmer, are there any more of those religious clothes about, you know, orbs and manticores and dalmations? Ones that aren't in your study?'

'Er, yes. There will be some items in the chapel.'

'Excellent,' Wat grinned, which worried Hermitage no end. 'Here's what we're going to do.'

. . .

The delegation from the town was growing impatient as it waited in the abbot's study. The duly-nominated representative of Saint John's, Brother Longor, who had organised this gathering, said that it was very small and poor for an abbot's study, but they would just have to put up with it. It was typical of Saint Werburgh's

Of course, Brother Longor had made sure they were all pretty impatient before they even got here. Tales of the horrific goings-on in Saint Werburgh's had got people nicely worried and annoyed. How long, he had argued, was it going to be before the ordinary townsfolk were being murdered in their beds?

It would have to be said that this delegation did not actually include any ordinary townsfolk. Ordinary townsfolk couldn't be trusted to shovel dung most of the time, let alone deal with complex issues. The problem would be that once all the ordinary townsfolk had been murdered in their beds, the killers might turn their attention to important townsfolk. And that would never do.

What was needed for a delegation like this were the significant citizens. The ones with all the money.

The Ealdorman himself had sent his second assistant, with instructions not to promise anything, or agree to anything, or preferably to say anything at all.

The bishop's office had despatched a junior clerk, who didn't really know where he was going or why but thought that it was nice to get out once in a while.

A senior servant from the house of Lady Ealdgyth had even been released, just to find out what was going on, and to provide a bit of gossip for what was otherwise proving to be a very boring existence for a king's widow.

More directly interested were a couple of merchants, who had come along in person. The wool and spice merchants had been delegated by their fellows, as they were generally acknowledged as being the most difficult and self-interested pair of heads in the town. No one would be putting anything over on them. The people of the town being murdered left, right and centre didn't bear thinking about; trade might suffer.

Finally, a representative of the town mint had come along. He attended as many meetings and gatherings as he could to protect the mint's interests. This was mainly because the town wasn't supposed to have a mint at all, and no one knew about it outside of the walls. If there was trouble, people in real authority might find out that Chester had been making its own money for years.

Those who ran the mint needed to know this sort of thing so that they could choose the right moment to run away. They'd already invested a lot of their profit in Ireland, and since the Norman invasion had kept a boat ready for a hasty departure.

This august gathering was crowded into the abbot's study and all the stools had been used up. The merchants and the man from the mint were seated, the rest had had to squabble over the remaining chairs.

'Where is the wretched man?' Brother Longor complained. 'Doubtless covering up more wrongdoing.'

The assembly grumbled that this was probably true.

'I shall summon someone,' Longor announced. 'The most important people of Chester cannot be kept waiting like this.'

The merchants and the mint man agreed.

As he reached the door, it was thrown open, nearly knocking him from his feet and narrowly missing his head.

Wat stood in the space as stiff and solemn as a church door. He moved his head to consider Longor, and his body said he was disappointed that the door had missed.

There was no chance of him being recognised as he had a cowl over his head which drooped down and shaded everything but his chin. Below the cowl, he wore a rather bizarre collection of religious vestments in entirely the wrong order. The abbot and Hermitage had pointed this out, but Wat said it looked the part.

'Be upstanding,' he bawled.

Cwen came in by his side and moved to hold the door open before bowing at the waist and keeping her eyes fixed to the ground. She too was covered from head to foot in variously the garb of a monk, a priest, a novice with, for some reason, a goose feather at her belt.

Abbot Fulmer had solemnly explained that Saint Werburgh once raised a goose from the dead. The goose had been called Grayking, apparently. Cwen had taken this information and managed to control the shaking of her body; and not laugh out loud.

Even in the presence of all this regalia, and a feather, those on the seats didn't move.

Wat drew his cowl back slightly, keeping his hands up to avoid the risk of recognition. He gave them a very dirty look. 'Be upstanding,' he ordered. 'For William, Duke of Normandy, King of England's most high representative.'

Now they stood up.

Wat stepped away and joined Cwen in the bow.

After a moment or two, when nothing happened, he turned his head to survey the room and looked utterly horrified that they were still upright. He gestured that they'd better bow as well, or King William's most high representative would have their heads.

They bowed. All except Brother Longor, who just nodded a bit and looked very suspicious.

After counting to ten, which was what Wat had told him to do, Hermitage walked into the room. He was wearing every bit of religious regalia that had been left over, and he felt very stupid and quite blasphemous. They had even taken a cowl threaded with gold from a statue of Saint Werburgh and put it on top of his head. He had really protested at this but the abbot had given special dispensation; after Wat and Cwen told him to give a special dispensation, which he wasn't sure he had the power to give anyway.

Wat had promised they would put it all back afterwards and Hermitage could complain about it as much as he liked on the way home.

Wat and Cwen now rose from their bows and stood straight.

Abbot Fulmer came humbly in behind Hermitage.

Wat turned to face the room and in a loud and pompous voice made his announcement. 'The King's Investigator attends upon you. Draw near and give heed. All with business before the most revered investigator may make their case. The King's own ear will hear you.'

The man from the mint was starting to look quite worried now.

Cwen stepped away from the door and walked across towards the abbot's desk. Anyone who stood in her path got the most horrible glare from under the cowl, which simply got more intense until they moved out of the way.

Once the route was clear, she bowed again to Hermitage, who crossed the room and took the seat behind the desk - the one the wool merchant had been sitting on.

He had to move the ridiculous amount of clothing he was wearing out of the way to avoid falling over, but he took his place and gave the room a condescending appraisal; having been shown how to do one by Cwen.

The room stood in quiet, waiting for something to happen. Hermitage said nothing. Wat had told him that this was the very best strategy for putting the fear of God up people. If someone from King William came to your house and just looked at you for long enough, you'd eventually go mad.

'He's just a monk,' Brother Longor eventually broke the silence. 'I saw him arrive with Brother Paul and the others.'

Wat looked at Longor as if he'd just spat on the king's shoes. He walked slowly over to Hermitage, keeping his eye on Longor all the while, and then whispered in the investigator's ear. What he whispered was, 'Take a quill and that bit of parchment from the desk and write his name down. And look serious about it.'

Hermitage, not having any idea what was going on, did as he was told.

'Brother Longor, isn't it?' Wat asked.

'Yes,' Longor replied indignantly.

'Brother Longor,' Wat repeated slowly for Hermitage's benefit.

Longor watched as the quill was taken up. 'What's he doing?' he asked, sounding a little less sure of himself now.

'The King's Investigator is writing your name down,' Wat said, sounding very worried about this step. 'It may be needed.

Later.' Wat made "Later" sound as if it might be the moment on Judgement Day just after all the dead had risen from their graves before the sinful ones were put back in again.

There was a bit of shuffling in the room.

'In fact,' Wat went on, turning his cowl to each face in turn. 'King William's Investigator will want all your names.'

The delegation started looking at one another now, some doubt on their faces.

'What is your business with the investigator?' Cwen asked in that way only Cwen could manage; invasive, highly personal and with the sort of undercurrent of threat only very high waterfalls can manage.

This generated a general conversation of suggestions, all of them along the lines of "nothing really", "just passing by" and "my goodness, is that the time?".

'Just a moment,' Longor protested as the man from the mint got up to leave. 'We want to know about these murders.'

'I'm sure there's nothing to worry about,' the wool merchant said. 'It sounds as if the king has got things under control.'

'Murders?' Cwen asked, very pointedly. 'What murders?'

'What murders?' Longor almost shouted. 'The murders here. At Saint Werburgh's, what murders do you think we're talking about?'

Cwen pinned Longor down with a very heavy gaze from under her cowl. 'I thought we were talking about the murder of Brother Abel. Murder, you see, not murders. Are you aware of another one?'

Longor paused for just a moment, a moment which told even Hermitage that he was uncomfortable.

'The other one.' The Brother of Saint John waved a

nonchalant hand as if everyone knew about the other one.

'We have only just discovered the death of Brother Pendle ourselves. How did you know about it?'

Longor shook his head as if Wat was being obtuse. 'You can't hide a dead monk in Chester. Word gets around, you know. The fact is that Saint Werburgh's is killing people.'

'And I'm sure the King's Investimataker will sort it all out,' the man from the mint said as he walked very quickly out of the door.

The two merchants were now engaged in a private discussion and managed to leave the room while ignoring everyone.

The bishop's clerk still looked vaguely interested in what was going on, but that could be that he just didn't want to go back to work.

'Where are you going?' Longor pleaded as the Ealdorman's assistant now left as well. 'Come back.'

The assistant turned at the door and gave a shrug, saying that Longor had lost this one.

The clerk now headed towards the door, trying to look as if he wasn't going at all, but was merely stretching his legs. He gave Wat and Cwen a vacant look before bowing to Hermitage and wandering out, examining the door with interest as he passed by.

Longor looked to the last person in the room for any vestige of support. This was the servant of Lady Ealdgyth, and he seemed to give Longor a warning glance, telling the brother not to dig himself an even deeper hole than the one he was standing in.

'We'll be off then,' the servant said as he stood. 'Good to see King William is taking our troubles seriously.' He took an only slightly protesting Longor by the arm and steered him towards the exit. As he did so he whispered in the monk's ear and they both gave glances back to Hermitage. Neither of them bowed.

Once they were out of sight, Wat went over to the door and stuck his head out, listening hard.

With everyone else out of the room, Hermitage was free to drop his head to the desk and start breathing again. 'That was awful.'

'That was wonderful,' Cwen said. 'Did you see them? Talk about scared rabbits.'

'There's obviously a lot going on here that people would rather the king didn't find out about.' Wat came back to the desk. 'I suspected there might be.'

'I'm still not sure that was strictly honest,' Abbot Fulmer took one of his own stools.

'And I'm pretty sure none of them is either,' Wat said.

'And Hermitage really is King William's investigator,' Cwen pointed out. 'That's honest.'

'Dressed up like this?' Hermitage complained.

'Who's to say? I'm sure the king would let you dress up if you wanted to.'

'At least it has got them out of the place,' the abbot breathed deeply. 'For now, anyway.'

'Oh, it's done a lot more than that,' Wat smiled at them.

'In a good way?' Hermitage asked hopefully.

'In a very good way. Did you see Longor and that servant of Ealdgyth's? Whispering away as if they have secrets to keep.'

'They did seem to know one another.'

'Which is a bit odd, isn't it? King Harold's widow and the monks of Saint John's. When it's Longor who rallies them all and comes marching in?'

'How do you know he was Lady Ealdgyth's servant?'

'I listened to them talking. He said he'd report back and that Longor had wasted all their time.'

'I'm not sure you should be listening to other peoples' conversations,' Hermitage chided.

'Except when there's a murder on,' Wat said, which did seem to be a reasonable excuse.

'Do you think they had anything to do with it then?' Cwen sounded as if she was answering her own question, and the answer was yes.

'Saint John's do seem to have a lot to gain from all this. Mainly Saint Werburgh's losing its power and authority.'

'We never seek such things,' Abbot Fulmer said.

'Which probably annoys Saint John's as well.'

'But the others?' Hermitage asked.

'They couldn't get out of the room fast enough.' Wat snorted at their antics. 'I'd be surprised if those merchants haven't gone home to pack for the journey to Wales. Get out of the king's way as fast as they can before he catches them, holds them and taxes them to death.'

'So, what do we do now?' Hermitage asked. 'We've still got two murdered brothers to worry about.'

'We investigate,' Wat said with some relish. 'And it's all working out nicely. We've got three paths to follow and there's three of us. How convenient is that?'

Hermitage had a sinking feeling that it wasn't going to be convenient at all. 'Go on.'

'Right. We've got Brother Longor and that lot at Saint John's to find out about. Hermitage, you're a monk, you can do that.'

'I can what?'

'Go to Saint John's, look around, ask about. See what's

going on.'

'But they know me. How will I discover anything? They'll throw me out. If that Brother Longor spots me, I'll be finished.'

'Just make sure Brother Longor doesn't spot you, then. You've got a cowl. Pull it down over your head. Most monks do that anyway.'

Despite this completely ridiculous suggestion, Wat seemed to think it was agreed.

'Cwen, you can go to Lady Ealdgyth's.'

'Why me?'

'Because Hermitage is a monk and would stick out like a monk. You'll slip into a great lady's court much easier than I would.' He leaned in close and whispered to Cwen. 'And if Abel was in some Saxon Noble's household, and then turned up here as a priest, a dead one at that, you might pick something up.'

'Such as?' Cwen looked rather worried about what she might pick up.

'Was Abel known to them? If he was some old enemy of Ealdgyth's, could be she got rid of him.'

'And Pendle?'

Wat shrugged. 'Not a clue.'

Cwen shook her head that she wasn't happy about this but seemed to have no choice 'And you?' she asked aloud.

'Me? Forgive me Abbot Fulmer, but I'm going to climb up your great tower and see what this sickly monk is all about.'

The abbot looked most alarmed at this.

'A herbalist who keeps his workshop locked? Who won't even let his abbot go near his patient but who attends him personally? A herbalist who finds all the dead bodies there are to be found? There's something going on there and I want to know what it is.'

## Caput X The Towering Tower

Each in their own personal way, they prepared for their oncoming trials.

Wat asked if the abbot had any old clothes he could borrow; he didn't want to get his nice jerkin and leggings dirty climbing up the outside of the so-called tower. The only thing the abbot had to offer was what the monks put on when they shovelled out the privy. It was either that or an old habit, which wouldn't be much good for climbing.

Wat said he'd try the habit. Hermitage seemed to like the things so there must be something in them.

Cwen accepted that she would need to look different if she was going to slip into the court of Lady Ealdgyth without being spotted. Her comfortable leggings and top looked fine for ordinary, hard-working folk, but Lady Ealdgyth would spot an ordinary, hard-working person a mile off and have them thrown out straight away.

Naturally, the abbot had nothing to offer, having no idea what women wore at all, or why. He didn't even like to talk about the topic, and so Cwen said she would have to go out into town and find something.

Wat grudgingly concluded that this would mean him giving her some money. With a glint in her eye that could only be described as evil, she said that wouldn't be necessary.

When Hermitage pressed her on what she was going to do she advised him not to ask, which was never a good sign. All she would say was that if she was going to look like someone from Lady Ealdgyth's court, it would be best to dress exactly the same, even to the extent of wearing exactly the same dress. If someone else was wearing it at the moment, that was a problem she would deal with.

In preparation for his own task, Hermitage simply sat and fretted quietly. Eventually, he garnered the courage to ask the abbot for directions to Saint John's.

Hearing that it was not far at all, he sat and fretted some more.

'When do we come back?' he asked the others, secretly thinking it quite likely that he might not make it back at all.

'When we've got something to report,' Wat said.

'That could be days.'

'Days? How slowly are you going to go? Work quickly. Get around as many people and places as you can. Listen to what's being said, watch who's doing what and going where, particularly that Longor. Then get back here. There should certainly be no need to stay overnight.'

'Overnight?' Hermitage's shock at this idea was obvious from the way he almost screamed the word. He put his hands on his knees to stop them knocking together. 'I don't know how I'm going to hear what Longor says and not get spotted by him.'

'Saint John's is a very large establishment.' The abbot comforted Hermitage. 'There are very many brothers there, and the place tries to appropriate any visiting monks or priests who pass by. I suspect this is to prevent them coming here and to build their own prestige.' He shook his head at such shameful pride. 'One more brother in his habit and cowl will not be detected.'

Hermitage raised his eyebrows. 'That's very interesting.' He was wondering how Abel and Pendle managed to avoid the ministrations of St John's. But something even more interesting bothered his mind.

'There you are, then,' Wat said. 'Not so dangerous after all.'

'No, no, I mean detected, what an interesting word. De tegere if I am not mistaken. De for reverse and teger for cover, to uncover, to detect.'

'How absolutely fascinating,' Wat said, looking at the ceiling for some reason.

'One might even say that the process of investigation could lead to detection.'

'Might one? Really? How exciting. And what's the Latin for get on with it?'

'Erm, proficitis cum eo?' Hermitage suggested. 'Oh, I see, you mean get on with it.'

'Well done.'

At least the diversion into etymology had taken Hermitage's mind off what "getting on with it" actually meant. He now resigned himself to his fate.

'It's getting late already,' Wat said thoughtfully. 'I wonder if we'd actually be better starting this in the morning.'

Hermitage thought that was a very good idea. Next, they could debate which morning in particular. Perhaps one several weeks away would be best, give them plenty of time for planning.

'No,' the weaver concluded, making Hermitage's heart fall. 'Get started this evening and we meet back here after sunset, even if there's nothing to report, we should be able to scout the lay of the land. Then we can start afresh in the morning.'

Hermitage knew that he'd feel anything but fresh if he'd scouted out the land. Wat and Cwen seemed almost keen for their expedition to begin and he felt guilty for thinking that if he walked slowly it might be sunset before he even got to Saint John's.

'Right.' Wat clapped his hands. 'Where's this dirty old habit I can put on?'

. . .

Abbot Fulmer seemed so bemused by the goings-on around him that he found the habit for Wat and followed him out into the courtyard in some sort of daze. He was clearly a man who liked to think about things carefully and give them due consideration. Due consideration requiring several days in normal circumstances.

Being rushed into this bizarre series of activities was more than he could cope with, and so he just went along with it all.

Wat was standing and appraising his approach to the climb up the tower, assessing what might be the easiest route to the summit. As that summit was a window only some fifteen feet or so off the floor, it was not a challenging task.

'I don't suppose you've got a ladder?' he asked, his voice a low whisper in case the herbalist could hear through his own walls.

'A ladder?' The abbot replied equally quietly. His bemusement was reaching paralysing levels.

'For climbing up things?' Wat explained the purpose of the device.

'I think we may have one somewhere. For repairs, you know.'

'I do.' Wat considered the building again. 'Second thoughts, perhaps Brother Bodin would notice someone putting a ladder against his building and climbing up.'

'Can't we just ask?' The abbot inquired, meekly.

'Ask for a ladder? From the herbalist? Do herbalists usually keep the ladders? And anyway, I think it would tip him off as to what we're up to.'

'No, no. I mean can't we just ask the brother about his

patient. He is an estimable fellow. If I ask directly, I am sure he would tell.'

'I'm not,' Wat said blankly. 'He seems to be going to a lot of trouble to keep people away from him.'

'Perhaps because his illness is a risk to us all?'

'It's possible, but I don't believe it. I have a sense for when people are hiding things, usually the amount of money they've got, but the principle is the same.'

Abbot Fulmer started wringing his hands again. 'I am really not sure that Wat the Weaver should be climbing up the walls of Saint Werburgh's chasing after the sick.' As the words came out, the worry on his face increased.

'Two of your brothers are dead,' Wat pointed out. 'Me climbing your walls is the least of your worries.'

'What if it's true though? What if Brother Odwin really is sick with some horrible pestilence and you get in there to see him? You could fall to his disease.'

'I'll be surprised if there's a Brother Odwin up there at all. I am sure that if there is, he's not really sick.'

'I've seen him,' the abbot protested.

'Close up? Seen his face? Would you recognise him in chapel?'

The look on the abbot's face said that he did not have a satisfactory answer to these questions.

'When did he arrive, this sickly brother?'

'Several weeks ago.'

'And he went straight to the loft of the herbalist's workshop?'

'It was Brother Bodin who received him at the gate.'

'Was it?' Wat sounded very interested. 'Is that normal? The herbalist happens to be standing at the gate when new arrivals turn up? Shouldn't he be tending his herbs?'

'When Brother Odwin arrived, he was already sick. It was quite natural that the herbalist should take care of him straight away.'

'And were you there to see this, or is it only what you've been told?'

'I welcomed Brother Odwin immediately afterwards. My brothers do not give me falsehood.'

'I'm not so sure about that either.' Wat gave the abbot a rather hopeless smile. 'You're not related to Hermitage, are you?'

'Not that I'm aware of.' Abbot Fulmer looked very puzzled by the question.

'You have the same approach to people. Think the best and get used to being disappointed. Very commendable in an abbot, I'm sure. Not so good for an investigator of murder.'

'Hence the investigator's companions,' the abbot said, without rancour.

'Exactly.' Wat congratulated the abbot on his reasoning. 'That's why I'm climbing up your herbalist's tower and why we're off to Ealdgyth and Saint John's. Think the worst and be pleasantly surprised now and again.'

Abbot Fulmer shook his head that this was a sad way to approach the world.

'And I don't get pleasantly surprised very often.'

'Then Brother Hermitage?' The abbot's question was clearly what Hermitage's role in all this was at all.

'Hermitage puts it all together. We go tramping about upsetting people mostly, Cwen and I, we're good at that. We find some things out, Hermitage finds out some others and then suddenly, Aha.'

'Aha?'

'Hermitage says "Aha". Or he looks like he's thinking it.

Soon after that, he explains everything and the killers get dealt with.'

'Simple,' the abbot said.

'Not usually, no.'

Wat paced around a bit now and decided that he would use a small bush that grew at the rear of the building as his first step. From there he thought he could reach one of the timbers of the place, and then haul himself higher.

'All right. Now I need you to do your bit.'

'My bit?'

'Exactly. Go and get Brother Bodin.'

'Go and get him?' The abbot looked from building to bush to Wat and back again. 'What, to come and help?'

'No, of course not to come and help.' Wat hissed with some irritation. 'We're hardly going to be able to sneak into his workshop without being spotted if we ask him to come and help, are we?'

'Well, I thought not, but then I'm not familiar with these sorts of goings-on.'

'Funnily enough, it's the first herbalist's workshop I've climbed up as well. I'm just using some common sense.' He looked hard at the abbot. 'Are you sure you're not related to Hermitage?'

The abbot's look was confused and largely vacant.

'What I want you to do is go and distract Brother Bodin.'

'Distract him?'

'From the fact that someone is climbing up his walls. He might notice, ladder or not, and I'd rather find out about this sickly Odwin without interference.'

'If I go and get him, I think he'll notice.'

Wat sighed very heavily. 'You don't go and get him and bring him here. You distract him. Take him somewhere else.'

'Where?'

'I don't know, do I? It's your Saint Werburgh's.' Wat gave it a moment's thought. 'Ask him about some herbs.'

'Herbs.'

'For heaven's sake. The things the herbalist looks after.'

'I know what they are.'

'Excellent. Some progress at last. Just knock on his door with some questions about herbs. Keep him there while I climb up the wall at the back.'

'But I don't have any questions about herbs.'

'Make some up,' Wat's instructions were getting increasingly short and pointed.

'Make some up? Dishonestly?'

'How can a question about a herb be dishonest?'

This was obviously too much for the abbot to cope with.

'What is wrong with you?' Wat asked.

'There's nothing wrong with me.' The abbot seemed pretty clear about which of them had something wrong with them.

'No, I mean what's wrong with you? What ailments do you have? We've all got something or other. I've got weaver's finger. Cramps up at the wrong moment. I'm told there's some root or other I should be taking but I've never bothered. A few more years and I might be living on the stuff. What's wrong with you?'

The abbot pulled at his ear as he thought. 'Well, I suppose I get a touch of Angry Foot now and again.'

'Angry Foot, there you are.' Wat was familiar with the aching of the feet. Standing at a loom all day was almost certain to bring it on. 'And what do you take for that? The leaf poultice?'

'Usually, yes.'

'There you are then. Tell Brother Bodin that your feet are

angry and you'd like some poultice.'

'But they aren't angry.'

'But you tell him that they are.'

Abbot Fulmer looked horrified at the suggestion he should lie.

Wat took a step towards him and laid his hands on the abbot's shoulder. 'Abbot Fulmer,' he said, looking the man in the eye.

'Yes?' The abbot looked suspicious and worried at the same time.

'Does Angry Foot bother one foot more than the other?'

'Erm, the left, mainly,' the abbot looked grateful for the concern.

'In which case, I am truly sorry,' Wat said as he stamped on the abbot's left foot.

'Ow,' the abbot cried out as Wat clamped a hand over his mouth. Some very un-abbot like expletives sounded as if they were trying to follow.

'Now your foot's angry you can go and ask for some poultice.'

Once the howls of the abbot into Wat's hand had diminished, he released his grip and nodded towards the door of the workshop with a smile.

The look he got in return was not one that belonged on the face of any abbot or a man of God at all, come to that.

Listening for the knock on the door, and the response from within, Wat timed his climb and got his feet onto the bush and his hands up onto the timber with ease.

A further timber, jutting from the wall of the workshop provided a foothold and Wat hauled himself further up. From here he could reach the edge of the window, from which access to the loft should be open.

The hold of his feet was tenuous as he got his arms over the window sill and rested for a moment.

The window itself was just a hole hung with a rough piece of cloth to keep the wind out, and Wat nosed this aside so that he could get his weight onto the frame.

With his head partly inside the building, he listened hard. There was a comfortable conversation going on below about angry feet and poultice, and which phase of the moon was best for application.

He hoisted himself the last couple of feet until he was more in the workshop than out. He leaned forward and found the floor beneath his hands. He pulled his legs in behind him as quietly as he could and squatted cautiously with his back to the wall.

Even if Brother Bodin had not spotted his arrival, it was unlikely that the man who occupied this room would be unaware that someone had just climbed in through his window. Assuming that there really was someone here and that he was not deep in some awful sickness.

The room was dark, and Wat's eyes slowly adjusted. Eventually, he could make out a cot at the far end, which had the shape of someone resting upon it. The rest of the space was piled with herbs stored in bundles and, like the room below, the ceiling was hung with drying and dried plants.

With no movement from the cot, Wat took a cautious step away from the wall. A board creaked under his foot and he stopped immediately.

He could feel his breath demanding to be let out but was aware that any noise might lead to discovery. Still, he was in now. Even if Brother Bodin came and found him at this moment, the secret of the sickly patient would be out. He stood to his full height and prepared to walk up to the bed.

That was before he almost jumped straight back out of the window as he was tapped on the shoulder.

'Ah,' he shouted out, unable to avoid the reaction. He spun on his feet and turned to face the figure that must have been waiting by the window from the moment he started to climb through. The shape on the bed was clearly a ruse.

The meagre light working its way through the cloth kept the face of this man in darkness. Wat's own face was still recovering from the surprise.

'Wat the Weaver.' The figure intoned the name as if it knew it well.

The man moved away from the window and drew close to Wat, examining him with care.

Wat recognised that face straight away. Recognised it and did not believe it. Something churned in his stomach and he could not control his reaction. He let out a scream and spun on his heels to get back out of the window as fast as he could. His terror mounted as strong hands gripped his shoulders and dragged him back.

## Caput XI Planning is the Better Part of Valour

Brother Hermitage's encounter with the monks of Saint John was meticulous in the planning. He was secretly hoping that if he made the planning meticulous enough, there wouldn't be any time left for actual doing. Then it would have to wait until morning, by which time Wat would be back with the answer from the herbalist's workshop.

With the abbot and Wat off climbing walls, there was only Cwen to see that Hermitage didn't spend the rest of the daylight hours in planning for his meticulous planning, followed by some reviews of the plans after which a good night's sleep was probably in order.

He had already decided that simply going to Saint John's was too obvious. A frontal assault would be the most likely route to discovery and that would be no good at all. He couldn't just march up to their door and knock on it asking if he could come in. The monk who answered the door might not recognise him, but someone would.

He needed to blend in with the place, and for the brothers there not to notice that he was among them, listening in.

He also found the words frontal and assault a bit of an issue. He wasn't at all comfortable with either of them.

He needed some guise under which his arrival there would be quite natural. There was still the risk of him being spotted by some of the brothers he had already met, but if he were to arrive with a group, for instance, there would be less chance of him being spotted. It was all terribly dishonest and underhanded, but perhaps better that than become the next murder victim himself.

Cwen pointed out that they didn't have a group of monks he could mingle in with and it was too late to find one.

He would go to the town gate he concluded. He could then mix in with the day's arrivals and get to Saint John's by happenstance.

'Proficitis cum eo,' Cwen said.

'Aha, yes, get on with it. Indeed.' He was starting to regret giving Wat and Cwen that particular translation. He had a feeling he was going to be hearing it quite frequently in the future.

'Well?'

'Ready to go,' Hermitage said. It was perfectly true that he was ready to go but that didn't mean he was going to.

'Down to the town gate,' Cwen prompted.

'Yes, quite. Down to the town gate. I will go down to the main gate and try to appear as an innocent brother arriving in town with no idea where to go.'

'And someone will direct you to Saint John's.'

'I hope so.'

'And if they don't?' Cwen appeared to be testing him.

'I say that I have heard great things and would be fascinated to see it.'

'Right, off we go then.' Cwen now took Hermitage's arm and lifted him from the seat upon which he was meticulously planning. 'The sooner you get down to the gate, the sooner I can go and find Ealdgyth's people and see what they're up to.'

'Why would Ealdgyth kill a monk?' Hermitage asked, genuinely bothered by the question but also interested in it as an alternative to going to the town gate.

Cwen was remorseless and dragged him from the room. 'We have our doubts that Abel even was a monk, don't we?' she said. 'If Wat's right, Abel could have been in a Saxon Noble's court before William arrived. If he ran off from the wrong people, they could well want him dead.'

Hermitage had to admit that this sounded perfectly reasonable behaviour for nobles.

'But Lady Ealdgyth is a noble anyway or was. Who knows why they do most of the things they do? It's just too suspicious, her court being in the same town Abel gets murdered. And her servant having quiet chats with Brother Longor. The Brother Longor you're about to go and find.'

'I'd better not let him see me.' Hermitage sought some assurance that this part of his plan had support.

'Oh, I don't know,' Cwen said, looking thoughtful.

'You don't know?' Despite Cwen's strong arm pulling him along, he stopped.

'Could liven things up a bit. If he thinks you're interested in him he could do something stupid.'

'To me?'

'No, not to you. He might give something away. I bet he's never seen the King's Investigator following him around before.'

Hermitage was quite keen that he didn't see it this time.

'I shall try to listen without being spotted,' he said, thoughtfully. 'Hopefully, he will have his guard down.'

Cwen gave a friendly smirk. 'Yes, Hermitage, you do that. Meanwhile, getting to the town gate seems to be the first of your challenges. One that you haven't managed to conquer yet.'

Hermitage started moving again.

They now reached the great main door of Saint Werburgh's, a large and impressive construction of wood and iron that rose at least ten feet from the floor. It was an arch split into two halves, secure and close-fitting, which looked as if it was well maintained. Great hinges held the doors in place and a large iron ring sat in the middle of each.

Cwen nodded to the brother who was sitting on a stool close by, as she reached to open their way out.

'What are you doing?' the brother asked, sounding quite shocked.

'Opening the door,' Cwen replied, nonchalantly. 'If you pull this thing here it opens, and you can get out.'

'I know that,' the brother was irritated now.

'Excellent. Well done.' Cwen shook her head and turned away.

'You can't.'

Cwen gave this a moment's thought. She looked at the door, looked at her hands and compared the two. 'I think I can, you know. My mother taught me door opening when I was quite small. One of the few useful things she did teach me. I knew it would come in handy.'

'What I mean,' the brother explained with a weary and patronising voice, 'is that you are not allowed to open the door.'

Anyone who knew Cwen would be aware that saying things like that only annoyed her, and people who knew her tried not to annoy her. 'I'm not allowed to open the door?'

'No one is allowed to open the door.'

'Must make coming and going a bit tricky.'

'It is the ceremonial door.'

'I'll open it ceremonially, then.'

'It is my job to make sure that no one opens the door.'

'You sit here all day, by a closed door and tell people they can't open it?'

'Not at all.'

'Glad to hear it.'

'I sleep here as well.'

'Which door should we use?' Hermitage interrupted this

engagement. He was happy to have his visit to the town gate delayed by any means possible, but he could see this situation descending into another of Cwen's "discussions" as she called them. He knew perfectly well that he was not capable of breaking up a discussion without help.

The brother nodded to the left of the main door. Set into the wall here was a small side-door, humble and overshadowed by its mighty neighbour.

'And may I open this one?' Cwen asked, overly politely.

The brother peered out of a small window set up in the wall above his head. 'You may.'

Cwen craned round to look out of the window as well. 'Sorry.' She nodded to the monk. 'I should have checked that I'm allowed to look out of the window.'

'I was merely checking that it is not yet sunset,' the monk informed her. 'Once the sun has set no one is allowed in or out.'

Hermitage understood that this was part of the rule; a very reasonable part as well. It did put a bit of an obstruction in the way of them coming back here after sunset to report their findings. They would just have to call for the abbot when they got back. Arguing their way in past this fellow was a task too much.

Cwen made a great display of going over to the door, opening it, and beckoning that Hermitage could step out. Just by the side of the door, someone had left a walking staff. It was a simple length of wood but had the sheen and polish that said it was well used. Perhaps some pilgrim had left it by the door as a reminder that he would be continuing his travels and was not at Saint Werburgh's for rest.

'Here,' Cwen said. 'Take this.' She took the staff and held it out for Hermitage.

'I can't take that.'

'Don't start this again.'

'It's not mine.'

'It'll make you look like a traveller.'

'It'll make me look like a staff thief.'

'Who does this belong to?' Cwen asked the door monk.

'That is Pilgrim Edgar's staff.'

'There you are,' Hermitage said. 'It belongs to a pilgrim called Edgar. I can't just take his staff.'

'He won't mind.'

'Cwen,' Hermitage did his serious and disappointed voice. It sometimes worked. 'This is the staff of a pilgrim. It would be the most awful thing to take it from him. What if he wants to leave and comes here to find his staff gone?'

'It's only a bit of wood.'

'A bit of wood that has travelled many miles, by the look of it.'

'Just the thing. People will look at the staff and not at you. They'll see you're a traveller and not ask questions.'

Hermitage said nothing.

'You are the King's Investigator. You're probably entitled to take it.'

'I cannot do it,' he tried to sound as final as he could.

Cwen called over to the brother of the door. 'Can you tell Pilgrim Edgar that the King's Investigator has borrowed his staff and will bring it back?'

'No, I can't do that,' the monk said.

Cwen's hands went to her hips, which was never a good sign.

'And why, exactly, is that?'

'Pilgrim Edgar's been dead for twenty years.'

Cwen looked at the monk, took the staff and bundled

Hermitage quickly out of the door. 'I don't even want to start on an explanation of that.'

Once beyond the walls, they looked up and down the street.

'You're for the town gate, which is that way, I think,' Cwen said. 'I'll just have to wander off and see how quickly I can find Ealdgyth's people.'

'Getting back in after sunset may be a challenge,' Hermitage noted.

'Why?'

'The monk at the gate will bar the entrance.'

'He'll just have to unbar it.' Cwen could see no problem getting a door open. 'Or we can prise it open with Edgar's staff.'

Hermitage shrugged. He had enough things to worry about without looking forward to that uncomfortable scene.

'How will you find Lady Ealdgyth?'

'I'll manage. Find the best-dressed person in town and follow them, or find the worst dressed and ask where the nobles are.'

'And the worst dressed person will know?'

'Of course. Where else do you go to get alms and a bit of food.'

'In my experience, those who have such things are reluctant to part with them.' Hermitage shook his head at this state of affairs.

'Ah, but if you're a horribly dressed and particularly smelly beggar, the nice people will pay you to go away.'

Hermitage nodded as he considered this.

'Town gate,' Cwen said. 'You. Go.' She even pointed, helpfully.

Hermitage raised his hand to acknowledge the instruction

and to wish Cwen good luck in her endeavour. He rather suspected that it was the court of Lady Ealdgyth that needed the luck.

With staff in hand, Hermitage now walked the short distance towards the main gate. He noticed that people did give their attention to the staff as if it was a sign of some sort. He thought that if he could pick up a scallop shell from somewhere, he could wear that as the badge of a pilgrim, and no one would disturb him at all. He quickly shook the awful idea of impersonating a pilgrim from his head. The whole situation of murdered monks was bad enough without him adding to the sum total of sin.

As he approached the gate, he saw that it was busy with comings and goings. This was hardly surprising, as sunset would see the closing of the town as well as Saint Werburgh's. Those who needed to get in or out before the end of day were hurrying to do so.

It occurred to him that he might even be too late for Saint John's. If they too closed their gates at sunset, he could be stuck outside. Then he really would have to go back and wait until morning; except he wouldn't be able to get into Saint Werburgh's either. At least, not without Cwen. He would be stranded in the streets of Chester after dark. He hurried towards the gate.

He had no idea what to do when he got there. There were some town guards on duty, but they were occupied with their preparations for closing up the town.

Everyone else was rushing about their business, and the last thing they would do was stop for a chat with a pilgrim.

He couldn't even see any other monks at all, let alone pilgrims, with whom he could mingle. And even if he did, there was no telling they would go to Saint John's.

As he leaned on his staff, watching the activity in and around the gate, he felt a presence at his right shoulder. Looking over, he saw a small boy watching him, as he was watching the gate. He nodded an acknowledgement.

The child could only be eight or nine years old and had a ragged but mischievous look about him. He looked the type who would beg for alms and then when he didn't get any, would steal them from you anyway.

'What you doing?' the boy asked, clearly suspicious that Hermitage was doing something he shouldn't.

Hermitage got the impression that if he said he was doing something disreputable, the boy would want to join in.

'I am a traveller.'

'You ain't travelling now; you're standing still.'

Hermitage was impressed by the argument. As he considered the boy, he realised that he was now going to have to make something up. Making things up had never been one of his strengths.

'That is true, but all travellers must rest, must they not?'

'Suppose. You going to rest here then?' The boy indicated the area around the gate.

'Not for the night,' Hermitage saw his chance. 'I shall seek lodgings from one of the religious houses here, although I don't know them. I have a pilgrim's staff, you see.' He held the staff out, grateful that he was able to tell the entire and honest truth. The fact that the pilgrim in question had been dead for twenty years was not something that need worry this boy.

'You want to go to Saint John's, you do.'

'Do I?'

'Oh, yes. It's the only place.'

'The only place? Surely there must be others in the town.'

'Well,' the boy seemed reluctant. 'There's Werburgh's, but they're all devils there.'

'Devils?' Hermitage was shocked that this boy believed such nonsense

'Everyone knows that.'

'I have heard that Saint Werburgh's is a peaceful house run by a pious abbot.'

'I thought you didn't know the places.'

'One hears things.'

'One what?'

'I mean I have heard of Saint Werburgh's.'

'Oh, right. Still, you don't want to go there.'

'No?'

'Definitely not. The monks of Saint John are best for you. I could take you if you like.'

'That is very kind,' Hermitage said. He knew that in all of his investigations he singularly failed to be suspicious about the right individuals. Wat and Cwen were continually chiding him not to think the best of people all the time, but he couldn't help it. It was just the way he was.

However, this small boy's invitation to take him to Saint John's made his knees wobble. He thought it unlikely that he would be murdered in the street by a nine-year-old, but he wouldn't put it past this one.

'I have nothing to offer you,' Hermitage said, holding Edgar's staff close in case the child took a shine to it. He thought it important to make it clear that he had nothing worth stealing before they set off.

'That's all right,' the boy shrugged. 'You're a holy man and they're holy men.'

'Well..,' Hermitage was too modest to accept that appellation.

'You have to do right by holy men.' The boy was sombre and serious.

Hermitage was grateful to hear this and relaxed slightly. He indicated that the boy could lead the way.

'What is your name, child?'

'Peter.'

'Peter, eh. A good biblical name.'

'Probably,' the boy shrugged.

He wasted no time leading Hermitage through streets that he already knew led towards Saint John's. When they walked up the street by Saint Werburgh's, the boy cast a warning glance and bade Hermitage beware of the devils.

'I don't see any devils,' Hermitage said.

'That's 'cos they're devils, isn't it?'

There was no argument for that.

A few more streets on, and the house of Saint John presented itself. This was a much grander edifice than Saint Werburgh's, as Hermitage had suspected it probably would be. Fine stone and glass in the windows told of money spent and hinted at luxury within. The abbot of this place would not be humble and pious.

He just prayed that he would be able to discover whatever it was he had come to discover quickly. Then he could get out; he hoped.

This place probably had its own ceremonial entrance somewhere, but Peter knocked on a small door set into the stone and waited for a response, smiling at Hermitage as he did so.

After a few moments, the door was opened, and the face of a monk appeared.

Hermitage started breathing again as he saw that this was not a brother he had met before. So far, so good.

'Ah, Peter,' the monk said, looking at the boy before turning his attention to Hermitage.

'I brought you another one,' Peter reported.

Hermitage felt quite uncomfortable as the brother of Saint John appraised him as if he was a freshly slaughtered lamb.

Peter held his hand out. 'Can I have my penny?'

The monk smiled and pressed a small coin into Peter's hand before reaching out and taking Hermitage by the elbow, pulling him towards the door with surprising strength.

He suddenly felt as if the lamb wasn't slaughtered at all, not yet, anyway.

## Caput XII Small Packages

Mistress Cwen roaming the streets and alleys of Chester for some means of entry into the court of Lady Ealdgyth was a bit like the fox that had been mistakenly invited for a look round chicken-town. Even the chickens who had never seen a fox before could tell that something wasn't quite right. The look in the eyes, the naked appraisal as their worth was weighed, it was all very discomforting. They couldn't say how they knew, but for one of them, the day was going to end very badly.

Great men of the town, women of import and significance, even guards and officials were given the sort of examination that made them cross the road. Even a physick dealing with ague of the nether parts wouldn't be quite so rude.

When one guard, who must be some sort of troop leader, started frowning at Cwen and looked as if he wanted to ask her what the devil she thought she was doing, she concluded she needed to be a bit more subtle. How to do subtle was more of a challenge.

Hermitage could do subtle so well that people didn't actually notice anything at all; even that he was in the room. And Wat's version of subtle usually had people clasping their purses tighter.

Nonchalant, that's what she needed to be. Hermitage said it came from the Latin, naturally. Non calere, not warm. She had to be cool and calm, and that was not at all comfortable. She might be able to keep it up for a few minutes, but if she didn't find a target soon, someone was going to suffer.

Nakedly asking where Lady Ealdgyth was seemed a bit too blunt, even for her. It would tip people off that she was on the lookout. She needed to get close and listen in, find out what she could and then get away again. Knocking on the door and saying, "excuse me, have you killed any monks recently?" seemed a poor approach.

She scanned the street once more while trying to look as if she wasn't scanning the street. Most people were coming and going about their business, using the street as a simple means of getting from where they had been to where they needed to be. The beggars were having a poor time getting anyone's attention.

Churchmen and monks flitted hither and thither, but they were no good at all. Unless one turned out to be Lady Ealdgyth's personal priest, of course. But then how would she spot that? They all looked alike.

Ah, there was one. A well-dressed young man who was not going anywhere. It looked as if he was simply out for a stroll and was enjoying the activity of the town as it buzzed around him. Who but a noble would have time for anything like that? People had jobs to do, normally centred on putting food in their mouths. Even in a rich town like Chester, where the people inside the gates were so wealthy they had houses to live in, there would be daily tasks.

This was a fellow who looked like he didn't do daily tasks, or he had someone to do them for him. He would go back to his house this evening for some feast, no doubt. No simple noon-day meal to see him through from one day to the next.

And no one was paying him any particular attention. This meant that he was not known to the townsfolk. He was not the Ealdorman or one of his high officials. Such a fellow would be bothered by everyone passing as they pursued their own interests. This one would want dispensation on their rent. That one sought permission to set up a new stall in the market. The other one confirmed that they were going to court to recover the debt that some old woman owed them, even though she had nothing; and even though she was their mother.

The next question was how to approach. Or even whether to approach at all. Perhaps a simple following through the streets would suffice.

Before she could make up her mind, the man was approached by a servant who was obviously bringing some sort of message. It was clear the second one was a servant. He was more poorly dressed, kept his distance and bowed when he spoke.

The idle fellow looked rather annoyed by the message and threw his hands in the air, at which the servant shrugged that it wasn't his fault.

Shoulders sagging, the man indicated that the servant could lead the way and set off up the street. Cwen followed, much to the relief of all the other folk around, who could now relax again.

The route led them away from the main thoroughfare, into small streets where the traffic was less but the houses grander. They were still huddled together, as if for warmth, but the windows were well set with clear glass, doors were solid and well-polished and the filth on the street outside was notable by being in neat piles rather than just spread about all over the place.

Without hesitation, the servant went to one door and pushed it open, standing back to allow his master to go first.

Cwen was close enough to hear as the man entered the house

'What is it now?' he wailed like some child told that they had to wash the horse before they could go out to play.

There was a reply from inside, but it was indistinct.

Whatever was said, it was enough to have the man stomping in as if he wanted to break the floorboards.

The servant followed and closed the door behind him.

Cwen weighed up the situation. She still had her normal clothes on, so would not be able to pass for a noble. From seeing the way they behaved, she wasn't sure she could carry it off, even if she did have the right outfit.

She could simply walk into the house, the door was obviously left open, but then what would happen? There could be people inside who might hesitate for just a moment before throwing her onto the street.

She might try approaching the servant, striking up a conversation and finding out what was going on.

Before she could reach a conclusion, the door opened again and the man emerged once more, this time in the company of two other men and a woman. These others were also well-dressed and were busy in conversation. If they did notice Cwen loitering outside, they didn't pay her any attention. They wandered off, chatting amongst themselves and Cwen caught snatches of their words. She followed along to make sure she could hear the rest.

'I don't know where we're going to find one,' the first man said.

'It's ridiculous,' the woman replied. 'How are we expected to know anyway?'

'God, I hate this town,' another man moaned.

'I want to go back to London,' the fourth chimed in.

'What? And get eaten by that awful William Normandy?'

'Let's go and ask the Ealdorman, he should know.'

'Oh, he's awful. Ghastly man. What would he know?'

'Who else do you suggest? It's not as if we're experts in looking after babies either, is it? They're horrible, smelly things. Why she had to ask us, I do not know.'

'She hates us,' the woman concluded. 'She's doing this on purpose. I'm a lady in waiting, not a wet nurse.'

'What is a wet nurse, anyway?' one of the men enquired.

'We don't need a wet nurse,' another man explained. 'The children are far too old for a wet nurse.'

'Ohh,' the others all sang in mock surprise. 'You seem to know a lot about it.'

'I had a younger brother,' the first explained. 'We just need someone who can look after them. Clean them, feed them, that sort of thing. Bring them when they're wanted, take them away when they aren't.'

'Which is most of the time, I hope. And she thought I was going to do it?' The woman sounded truly horrified.

'She should have brought someone with her.' One man raised this as if it was an old refrain.

'We did have to leave in a hurry,' the woman replied. 'We were lucky to have got away ourselves.'

'What happened to the old woman who was doing it?'

The others all shrugged. 'No idea.'

'Probably died,' one man said. ''They're always dying, old women.'

The others nodded at this profound wisdom.

'Hello,' Cwen said, managing to appear out of a side alley, having ducked in just before.

'Er,' the woman looked at her with disgust. 'Who are you?'

'The Ealdorman sent me,' Cwen tried a smile at them all. She always found it hard to smile at people who didn't deserve it.

'Why?' One of the men looked at her as if she was just the sort of person they didn't need.

'He heard that your old woman died. The one looking

after the babies?' Cwen couldn't actually believe that she was going to try this. Babies? Horrible, smelly things, she agreed. Mind you, most adults she knew were awful and children were appalling, so babies were just the start of the chain; or the end, depending on how you looked at it. People; that was the problem at root. Well, other people, obviously.

'And you're here to look after the babies?' One of the men beamed at the others, clearly unable to believe their luck.

'That's it.'

'You're a bit young, aren't you? Shouldn't you be an old woman?'

'I will be,' Cwen said. 'I'm working up to it. All old women start young.'

This was too much for the four minds to contemplate. All they knew was that there was someone in front of them who was going to take their problem away.

'She will be pleased,' the woman said. 'Us finding someone so quickly. What's your name?'

'My name?'

'Do you have one?' This appeared to be a genuine question as if the woman didn't know whether people who looked after babies had names or not.

'What was the name of your old woman?'

The four all considered one another. 'No idea,' one of the men eventually concluded.

'We can't just call you old woman,' another man went over the details of the problem. 'Because you're not old yet, are you?'

'I suppose not. Why don't you call me, erm, Weaver?'

'Weaver? What? Like a weaver?'

'That's it.'

'Funny name for an old woman.'

'She can call herself whatever she wants.' The woman was anxious to get on. 'Let's get back and tell Her Majesty.'

Cwen thought that the way this woman said "Her Majesty" did not show great respect. It was as if the majesty in question was behaving like a queen when she wasn't one.

They all turned and headed back up the street, Cwen trailing along behind the other four, who were now behaving as if she wasn't there at all. She had to tell herself that this was a good thing, and not that these people needed a good slap.

Back at the house, they pushed the door open and entered. The entrance hall was busy with people. Some were coming and going on errands or the like, others seemed to be just standing about chatting or were sitting quietly in corners.

The hall itself was not large and was not even that comfortable. A simple floor of stone slabs made it cold and unwelcoming, and even the seats that there were looked hard and uncomfortable.

'That was quick,' one of the figures in the hall commented as the troop of old woman hunters returned.

'When we're given a task, we get to it straight away. That's why we're trusted.'

Cwen gave a wry smile that these idiots were taking credit for something they hadn't done. She could only imagine what explanations they would come up with when she vanished.

'There's a first time for everything, I suppose,' another voice sneered. 'Still, it's best to give the simple tasks to the simple people.'

'Come, Weaver,' the woman of the group said, turning her nose up at the others. 'Let us take you to Lady Ealdgyth's children.'

From the sniffing, turning of backs and muttering that

went on, Cwen could see that these people had too much time on their hands. Their main occupation seemed to be showing that they were better than the person standing next to them. As none of these people appeared to be better than a dung sweeper, she thought their efforts were wasted.

She was also disappointed that she was going to be taken to these children and not to Lady Ealdgyth herself. Yes, she had got into the house, but it was unlikely a couple of babies were going to have anything informative to say about the murder of monks.

From the goings-on in the hall though, she could well believe that this lot might not stop at simply insulting one another. A quiet stab in the dark to remove some irritation or other was easily imagined. Obviously, they'd be doing it to one another, which would be no great loss to the world, but if this was how the court of Lady Ealdgyth behaved, it might be the sort of place that would have people removed if they were trouble. And if Abel had been trouble to one of this lot in his past? She had no idea about Pendle, but he could well be a dead noble as well.

Led up the narrow and rickety stairs, Cwen left a growing hubbub of conversation behind. Most of it included quite a few rude words. She couldn't tell if the mission to get a nurse for the babies had been a justified punishment or an unwarranted privilege.

At the top of the stairs, a single door stood barring the way, and the woman of the party knocked on it. There was so little room that Cwen was still halfway down the stairs.

There was no reply, but after some audible footsteps, the door opened.

Through the legs of the others, Cwen saw that this was a very well-presented man who looked more like an official than anyone she'd ever seen. He even held a staff in one hand, and it was hard to tell if the staff was the stiffer of the two. It was a much more official staff than Pilgrim Edgar's, even having what looked like silver on the top.

The holder of the staff looked down a very long nose at them all. Upon recognising the arrivals, he sagged visibly and suddenly became human. 'Oh, thank God you're here.' He stepped back and beckoned that they should all enter.

The party did so, and Cwen saw that they all bowed as soon as they entered the room.

'Is this her?' the man with the staff asked as Cwen reached the threshold.

'It is. We found someone straight away.' The woman spoke as if only she was able to achieve such a remarkable feat.

The man and his staff considered Cwen and nodded that she should enter.

Inside the room, which took up the entire top floor of the house, Cwen saw some very comfortable furnishings, including a cot. Before she could move another inch, or consider anything else at all, someone rose up in front of her and thrust two babies in her direction.

'Take them, take, them,' the woman who had been holding the children almost begged. 'They are driving me to distraction.'

'Erm.' Cwen couldn't help but put her arms out to take the infants, who seemed to be at risk of being dropped on the floor if she didn't.

Holding babies was not something she had ever done, nor had any desire to do. She'd seen other people do it, and it didn't look too complicated. But then, she'd seen other people fall down holes and that didn't mean she was going to give it a go.

A room full of people, all of whom expected her to hold the babies, didn't give her much choice. Somehow, she ended up with a baby in each arm. They were very heavy and smelled horrible.

As the woman handed them over, they started to complain about their treatment as well. Cwen had no idea how old they were. Babies were babies, then they were children. When the change occurred, she had not the first idea. The things in her arms cried, which was what babies did.

'Take them away and deal with them,' the previous owner instructed.

'Do as Lady Ealdgyth tells you,' the woman of the party repeated the instruction.

At least Cwen now knew that this was Lady Ealdgyth, and that these were her babies. She also knew what dealing with smelly babies involved. Her mother's tales of childbirth and the aftermath were what had put Cwen off babies in the first place.

She briefly considered Lady Ealdgyth's slim frame and small stature and wondered at how the two monsters in her arms had come out. Not without great pain, she suspected. It only now registered with her that the two bundles in her arms must be twins. They were about the same size, which presumably meant they were the same age. This must mean that they had come out of Lady Ealdgyth at the same time. Well, not exactly the same time, Cwen sincerely hoped. One after the other would doubtless be best.

Giving birth had always sounded like the most appalling nightmare. Doing it twice in the same day was beyond belief. Even after what must have been many months, she was surprised Lady Ealdgyth could still walk.

'What is your name?' Ealdgyth asked before Cwen could go;

not that she had the first thought about where she was going to go or what she was going to do once she got there.

'Weaver, my Lady.'

'Well, Weaver, take care of the children. You have a great responsibility.' With the removal of her burdens, Lady Ealdgyth suddenly looked a lot less flustered and panic-stricken. 'In your left arm, you hold Ulf, the younger of the boys. In your right you hold Harold.'

'Harold?' Cwen couldn't help the question coming out.

'The true-born King of all England.' Ealdgyth reached out a hand and stroked the child's head.

Young Harold turned his head away from his mother's caress and was sick on Cwen.

## Caput XIII A Surprise in the Loft

'Ah,' Wat was still squirming and looking away, even though the figure in the loft had released him to sit on a bale of some herb or other.

'Calm down,' the figure said. 'It's me.'

Wat now believed that it was a me, just not the one being referred to. He had to accept that this was a real person of flesh and blood and not some howling demon-ghost. Perhaps it was just someone who looked the same.

'Harold?' There was more than simple disbelief in his voice. This name was way beyond a surprise. Unexpected didn't cover it at all. It simply wasn't possible. It could not be. Everyone knew that. Everyone. If this was who it looked like, then it had to be a howling demon-ghost. 'King Harold?'

'That's right.' The man seemed to be having a lot less trouble with the idea.

Wat stood now, having given up the idea of throwing himself from the window in order to escape the hell-hound. He then dropped himself down onto another sack, which puffed a sweet fragrance into the room in protest. 'But, but.., you're dead.'

The man who would be Harold held his arms out as if to suggest to Wat that the reported death might be more report than death.

'What's going on up there?' The voice of the herbalist called from below. Hurried footsteps clattered the stairs and the head of the man appeared through the floor.

'It's all right, Brother Bodin.' Harold held a hand up in acknowledgement. 'No cause for concern.'

'How did you get in here?' Bodin demanded of Wat.

Wat was in no state to answer complicated questions like

that.

'Master Wat is an old friend.'

'You know the rules about old friends,' Bodin directed this at Harold as if friends were something you had to be very careful about. He turned his gaze upon Wat. 'And I don't think you should have friends like Wat the Weaver anyway.'

'He is just passing through.'

'Passing through my loft? He's with that monk, the investigator.'

'The King's Investigator,' Wat came to his senses. 'King William's Investigator. You know, the Duke of Normandy? That William.'

Bodin seemed to consider this with some caution.

'No telling how happy William will be to find you've been keeping information from his own investigator.'

'I do my duty upon the instruction of King William as well,' Bodin said.

'Excellent.' Wat smiled. 'We're all helping King William, then.' He waved Bodin away. 'All serving the king as is right and proper.'

Brother Bodin looked very suspicious indeed but didn't have anything more to say. Instead, he just pointed a finger at them both. 'I'm just down here. I shall be listening.'

'Well done,' Wat said, as if listening to things was going to be a bit of a challenge for Brother Bodin.

Once Bodin's head had shrunk back into his workshop, Wat turned to Harold with a hissed whisper. 'Everyone knows you're dead.' His reason was not letting his eyes get away with this nonsense. 'The whole world knows you're dead.'

At last, his mind came up with a reasonable explanation for the huge mistake he was making. He stood from the sack of herbs and took a step until he was less than a foot away from the man in the loft of the herbalist's workshop.

He looked at the clothes, which were regal in no way whatsoever. A simple monk's habit was not something Wat had ever seen the king in before. That alone was enough of a disguise.

He peered at the face and stared as hard as he could stare. There would be something here to give the game away. Once he'd done the face, he walked around the man, who stood patiently for the perusal. Wat examined height, estimated weight, considered clothing and closely reviewed the hair colour. The frown on his face did not lift. He puzzled even further about why Brother Bodin might be guarding an imposter.

He returned to his sack of herbs. 'Say something,' he instructed.

'Say something?' the man asked. 'Ah, you think I am not who I appear to be. Why Brother Bodin would be keeping watch on an imposter is an interesting question, but very well. What could I say to Wat the Weaver that would convince him? Ah, I have it. I don't suppose you have the makings here for a fine bath house tapestry? The last one, Nuns Surprised, was a wonderful piece. I was thinking something along the lines of A Knight Undone?'

'Good God.' Wat sagged into his herbs. 'What? I mean how? I mean, erm. You're dead.'

'You said that.'

'You were killed at Hastings. An arrow in the eye.'

'Arrow in the eye eh? Someone mentioned that a while ago. Pure nonsense. But, if it's in a tapestry it'll end up being what people believe, regardless of the truth. Nasty, though. William's man, Le Pedvin, got shot in the eye and look how he turned out.'[6]

'It's what everyone says. It's going in Earl Odo's great tapestry. Hic Harold Interfectus Est.'

'I never had you for a man of Latin, master Wat.'

'Brother Hermitage told me. "Here, Harold is killed." And there's going to be a picture of a warrior with an arrow in his eye. We heard all about it.'[7]

'Brother Hermitage? Odd name for a monk. I recall a Brother Hermitage from that ghastly De'Ath's Dingle place.[8] One of my last nights of rest before Hastings.'

Wat's reason surrendered before this blow, and it left him alone to carry on.

'So, you're not dead.'

'Well done.'

'William knows you're here and Bodin is your guard?'

'It was William who sent me.'

Wat's mouth opened to let some words out, but they didn't want to go.

'I was not killed at Hastings, although I was shot.' Harold's hand inadvertently dropped to the area of his wound. Wat noticed this and looked away, politely. 'I escaped the field and, after long trials that I will not retell now, William sent me here.'[9]

'To the loft of a herbalist's workshop?' Wat knew the loft would come back sooner or later.

'Not specifically, no. I have come to this abbey as an anchorite.'

---

6 *The Domesday Book (No, Not That One)* and other tomes include a lot about Hastings and Le Pedvin -and it's all true, honest

7 And you can read all about it in *The Bayeux Embroidery*

8 *The Heretics of De'Ath* takes place in the ghastly De'Ath's Dingle place.

9 Long trials that you can re-live - *The Domesday Books, I and II*

'A who what?'

'Your Brother Hermitage would explain. It is usually someone who retires from the world for religious reasons; preferably into a small cell where no one ever bothers them again. And Saint Werburgh's was chosen as a nice quiet place, to begin with. I am retired from the world, but the reasons are far from religious.'

Wat was still having trouble taking it all in. 'I don't believe this.' After a few more moments, some of his senses came back and he moved from his sack of herbs to kneel on the floor. 'Your Majesty.' He bowed his head.

'Majesty no more.' Harold took Wat's shoulders and half pushed him back to his seat. Harold now sat beside him and lowered his head so that they could converse in confidence.

'But,' Wat began. Then he stopped. Then he started again. 'You, you were the king. Then you got killed and William was king. Now you're not killed, aren't you king again? Isn't that how it works?'

'Not in this case. If an old king decides he wants to be king again he has to get rid of the new one.'

'Ah.' Wat recognised a scheme when he saw one hatching.

Harold held his hands up. 'But I tried that, and it didn't work either.'

'Oh.'

'William's grip is strong. He has moved quickly and those who would have supported me lie dead on the field of Hastings. The earls are Normans now, and it is hard to raise rebellion from the loft of a herbalist's workshop.'

'Especially when the herbalist is keeping an eye on you,' Wat whispered even more quietly.

'More than just the herbalist, I suspect.'

'Does the abbot know it's you? He told us you were called

Brother Odwin.'

'Odwin, Godwin, Godwinson,' Harold explained. 'He knows someone is here, but not who. He is a fellow of deep belief and pious honesty. It would be wrong to embroil him in something like this.'

'And if he's that honest, he might tell someone.' Wat saw that this was a sensible approach.

'There is that.'

'He might tell some Norman who may think you should be dead for real.'

'There are some of them, I fear.'

'How many of the brothers here are real monks, and how many are here to make sure you don't get out as much as you'd like?'

Harold gave a shrug. 'That, I do not know. I am restricted to this loft at the moment, supposedly under the care of Brother Bodin. I dare say there are others whose duty is defined by William rather than Our Lord.'

Wat nodded as his thoughts formed themselves into some sort of pattern. 'Brother Abel,' he said, very quietly.

'The dead one? I heard something had happened.'

'Something murder-like came over a brother called Abel. When I went to see the body, I recognised him.'

Harold gave Wat a sideways glance.

Wat took a breath and explained. 'After the murder of Abel, the abbot sent for Hermitage as he's the King's Investigator.'

'Ah, yes, now I recall, I appointed him. You were there at the time.'

'And I've been with him ever since. William appointed him as well, although I don't think he knew what he was doing. You wouldn't believe the things we've had to do since then.

But never mind that. The abbot called us, obviously not knowing the death of Abel could have anything to do with you.'

'And you think it does?'

'This Abel. I'm sure I know from more settled times.'

'A Saxon then?'

'Almost certainly. Could be a merchant, could be connected to one of the old nobles. I never did trade with him directly, but I know the face. And he turned up here claiming to be a priest.'

'Could be coincidence,' Harold suggested. 'I'm sure there are many who seek sanctuary from the Normans. Abel may well have turned to the church.'

'Could be. But then, before we could even get here, Brother Pendle is murdered as well. Abel was killed with a chasuble and Pendle with an amice.'

'How very peculiar.'

'Handy weapons in an abbey, I suppose,' Wat said.

'Not as good as a candlestick, or even a sharp stick.'

'But still connected. Two murders with clothing? You have to admit it's a bit odd. Two monks dying in an abbey is one thing. Two monks murdered is odd. Two monks murdered in a very similar manner, in an abbey that happens to be home to the old king? If there isn't some connection, I'm an honest man.'

Harold smiled at that suggestion.

'Did you know Pendle?'

'No,' Wat shook his head. 'Doesn't mean he wasn't Saxon. I never met them all. You haven't seen anyone you know?'

'I've not met any other brothers at all. Bodin keeps me to himself. He calls himself my "protector". I've witnessed nothing at all. I got the news about Abel and Pendle from conversations I managed to overhear. And I gather that they'd been here for some time. If they were Saxons, they didn't seem to know I was here.'

'There must be a connection,' Wat insisted.

'Not necessarily,' Harold shook his head gently. 'It is quite possible that Abel and Pendle were as in the dark as I am. If the abbot of this place only thinks that he's got a sick monk in his herbalist's loft, the rest of the abbey may well think the same. Abel and Pendle could be genuine brothers, Saxons or not, who have simply fallen to some evil.'

Wat looked at Harold and gave this careful consideration. He came to his conclusion. 'I don't believe a word of it.'

'Then why were they here for so long without any trouble?'

Wat thought about this. 'Could be that they were here as ordinary monks, or Saxons seeking sanctuary. But then they found out you were here and decided to do something about it.' He lowered his head and his voice and leaned in close to Harold. 'And when Bodin found out, he did for them.'

Harold looked at the floor, on the other side of which, Bodin was doubtless trying to listen.

'They found out that the king was here and were going to rally men to your cause. Bodin couldn't have that so he killed them. He is William's man, after all. And he was suspiciously close to the bodies.'

'Really?' Harold raised an eyebrow.

'He found Abel in the chapel as he was distributing herbs. Then he was in the corpse house when Pendle was found.'

'Corpse house?'

'There's a brother called Merle who looks after the dead.'

'Merle?'

'I know, another odd name for a monk. And he's an odd monk, believe me. He looks after them so well he gives them lodgings.'

Harold was starting to look rather confused.

'I imagine he must bury them eventually.' Wat wasn't too sure about this, even as he said it. 'We looked at the bodies, just to make sure they were properly dead and had been murdered. And we discover Bodin popping up on each occasion.'

Harold puffed his cheeks and blew out as he considered this more seriously. 'And where is Brother Hermitage now? The King's Investigator. My Investigator, I suppose.'

'He's gone to look at Saint John.'

'The saint?' Harold sounded surprised.

'Not the real one. There's another religious house here, called Saint John.'

Harold just shrugged at this. 'As you say, I haven't got out much. And Brother Bodin tells me very little.'

'That doesn't surprise me. Anyway, this Saint John place thinks of itself as the prime house of Chester and wants nothing to do with Saint Werburgh's. We thought they might have something to do with the deaths; trying to show Werburgh's up as a place of sin and have it closed down.'

'Sounds a bit extreme for a religious house,' Harold observed.

Wat shrugged that that wasn't his problem. 'So, Hermitage went to find out what he could, being a monk.'

'And he hasn't come back yet?'

'Only just gone.' Wat suddenly sat up straight and stared at Harold.

'Something occurs to you?'

'Cwen!'

'Another monk?'

'No, no. Cwen's a weaver.'

'Of course, she is.' Harold humoured Wat.

'She went off to find out if there was any connection to the deaths somewhere else.'

'Really.'

'Yes.' Wat held Harold's eye. 'Because we thought Abel might be a noble, she went to see Ealdgyth.'

'And who's Ealdgyth?' Harold asked, nonchalantly.

'Your wife.'

Harold stopped looking quite so nonchalant. 'My wife?'

'Yes. You know, the woman you married.'

'I do know what a wife is. Are you saying that Ealdgyth is here? In Chester?'

'I am. She's been here for a while. Came with her brother.'

'Edwin?'

'Brought her here after Hastings, apparently.'

'Good God.'

'I take it you didn't know.'

'I did not know.' Harold was looking very thoughtful.

'You think the murder of two monks in your monastery is still a coincidence?'

'Does William know she's here?'

'Who knows what William knows? You'd think so, wouldn't you? I mean, you nobles tend to make a bit of noise wherever you are. Someone would have mentioned it.'

'Then why would he send me here as well? Why choose Chester?'

'I can't imagine he thought you'd like to be together.'

Harold snorted at this. 'Quite the opposite, more likely. Keep everyone where he can see them. Makes it easier to kill us all quickly if he has to. Ealdgyth is still daughter to old Aelfgar, Earl of Mercia. If there was a chance of rebellion against William, she could be key. If there was some rebellion brewing, involving Abel, Pendle and Ealdgyth, it would be no surprise to find Normans wanting to put a stop to it.'

Wat looked worried. 'And we've sent Cwen into the middle of it all.'

'What did she hope to find out?' Harold asked.

'If we knew that, we wouldn't have sent her to find out,' Wat replied, with some irritation. 'All we knew was that Abel was dead, he might have been connected to some Saxon noble, and there was a nest of Saxon nobles in town.'

Harold nodded. 'I can see that would worry anyone. This Abel could have been a friend of those in Chester or an enemy. If the latter, they wouldn't let the simple fact of the Norman conquest get in the way of revenge. If this isn't some rogue Norman doing it all anyway.'

'Hm,' Wat creased his face in thought. 'Have you ever heard of a Norman called Adversane?'

'Adversane? I've never heard of anyone called Adversane. Why do you ask?'

'This Adversane told Saint Werburgh's about Hermitage, apparently.'

Harold shrugged. 'Could be anyone. There were plenty of Normans living here before William brought the rest of them over. But, as I say, some Saxon nobles are quite capable of murdering one another without help.'

'Charming,' Wat said. 'Cwen went to find out what sort of trouble there might be, and whether there could be any connection to Abel and Pendle.'

'You think my wife actually killed them?' Harold didn't sound very happy at this suggestion.

'Of course not. It's only the male noble that actually does the killing, isn't it? But then she'll probably have a few of those to hand if she needs them.'

'But she could have something to do with it?' Harold asked a genuine question.

Wat felt some annoyance at this, even if it did come from his old king. 'The ordinary people don't go round killing one another. Only nobles do that sort of thing. If you got some dead bodies and a noble nearby, it doesn't take an investigator to work out who probably did it.'

Harold stood from his bale of herbs and paced slowly around the small space of the loft, an intense look of deep thought on his face.

Wat did nothing but watch. He couldn't tell if Harold was mightily offended at the suggestion that his wife might be a monk-killer, or whether some other great thoughts were occupying the regal head. Whatever it was, he hoped something helpful might come out of the short stroll.

After a few moments, Harold returned. He sat and then bent over to let Wat know his conclusions. 'Who were Abel and Pendle?' he asked. 'We need to know more about them.'

'The abbot seemed to think they were genuine monks.'

'But then the abbot doesn't know he has a king in his loft.'

'True. So, you think they could have been your men, discovered you were here and started to foment rebellion, only to be finished off by Bodin before they could get anywhere?'

'That's possible, although you would expect them to make themselves known to me. Or, it could be they were discovered by someone in Ealdgyth's court who had a score to settle. We need to know what they were up to.'

'They're a bit beyond asking,' Wat pointed out.

'Others will know. Brothers they associated with. Perhaps the abbot has records?'

'I suppose I could see what I can find.'

'Good man. And in the meantime?'

'Yes?'

'Can I suggest you get this Cwen out of Ealdgyth's court?'

'There could still be useful information there.'

'It's not that. It's just your comment about nobles and murder...,'

'Ah, yes, sorry about that.'

'No, no. You're quite right. If some of them find out what your Cwen is up to, she might end up in the corpse house as well.'

Wat snorted at this. 'You've never met Cwen, have you?'

Harold looked nonplussed.

There was one other thing he had to check with Harold. 'When we come down from here and meet the others?'

'Yes?'

'I want you to swear something to me.' He gave Harold a very serious stare.

'If I can,' Harold agreed.

Wat even pointed his finger to emphasise the point. 'You swear to tell no one that I screamed. Especially not Cwen.'

## Caput XIV Into Saint John

'Brother?' Hermitage didn't like to be rude, but being dragged into Saint John's by his arm seemed unnecessary. All he wanted was some information.

'Follow.' Only when the door was closed behind them did the monk release Hermitage's arm. He then strode away with the simple word of instruction.

Hermitage quickly concluded that he'd really rather not follow at all. This monk raised his suspicions, which were never easily motivated. Being inside Saint John's with the door locked was not comfortable. However, if he was going to find anything out at all, including the location of any other exits, he would have to do as he was told.

The monk led away from the door and into the body of Saint John's. They were immediately in a large courtyard which, to Hermitage's eye, had something wrong with it. A frown creased his brow as he sought to identify exactly what it was.

There were several other brothers in the space, all of them working at some task or other. Some were sweeping, some appeared to be carrying out repairs to parts of the building while others were wheeling barrows, taking rubbish away or bringing supplies for the works.

The whole place was remarkably clean, well-ordered and neat. That was it. He'd never been in a clean, well-ordered and neat establishment before. Saint Werburgh's was obviously a massive improvement on his old home of De'Ath's Dingle, but that dread place set the standard against which all others were measured. Any place worse than De'Ath's Dingle probably wasn't capable of supporting life at all anymore.

Saint Werburgh's had appeared to be a very average sort of community. Yes, the brothers kept it in order, but they didn't go mad. You still needed straw scattered about, in case the need to use it came over you when you were in the middle of something. And there was really no point scrubbing the refectory after every meal; after all, you were only going to use it again.

The brothers in this courtyard almost appeared to be putting the stones of the floor in order.

'Very, erm, neat,' Hermitage offered.

His escort gave him a very odd look; more questioning how Hermitage had the temerity to speak at all, rather than surprise at the comment.

The monk now led the way around the edge of the courtyard, keeping close to the walls of the buildings. As they turned a corner, it became clear that they were heading for a place on the opposite side of the yard. Walking straight across would have been much more direct, but Hermitage could already see that walking on the courtyard would not be allowed.

With only a short time inside the walls, he had already formed a good impression of what sort of place this Saint John's was going to be. And he knew it wouldn't suit him.

He was all for devotion, commitment and adherence to the rule. After all, that took away all the worries that people outside the monastic life had to deal with. It enabled concentration on the life spiritual. He had heard about places like Saint John though: the sort of place where if you didn't do your devotion, commitment and adherence to the rule quite right, there would be consequences.

And what constituted "quite right" would be determined by the abbot and enforced.

As these worrying thoughts seeped through his mind like drizzle through his habit, they arrived at their destination.

This was a large building, made of wattle and daub, but it looked as if it had been here for some considerable time. The brother pushed open an old, weather-beaten door and beckoned that Hermitage should step inside.

He knew that he had no choice but to obey, but found himself thinking like Wat - find the way out before you go in.

The single room inside contained a desk, a candle and a monk. It was not much for a whole building, but then the theme of this place was order; having two things going on in one room would be considered messy.

The monk in the room sat behind the desk and by the light of the candle was applying a quill to parchment in a careful and deliberate manner.

'I've got another one,' Hermitage's guide announced.

There was no doubt about it. Being "another one" was not a good thing to be.

The monk behind the desk put down his quill and looked up at the arrivals. There was no smile, no frown, no sign of satisfaction or of annoyance. For some unknown reason, Hermitage had the urge to call out "cheer up". He could tell that would not be well received.

The monk with the quill acknowledged the delivery of Hermitage with a short nod, and the other monk now turned and left. It was clear that Hermitage was expected to stand at the desk, and so he did.

Putting the parchment he had been working on to one side, the brother took up a book that had been resting on his desk. This was a very large book. Quite alarmingly large. Not broad or tall, but thick. There must be dozens of pages of parchment bound into this one volume. Whatever it was, it must contain a huge amount of information. Despite himself, Hermitage was desperate to know what was in it.

The monk opened the book and turned the parchment until he was near the back pages. All Hermitage could see was tiny writing, completely illegible when read upside down.

Taking up his quill once more, he turned his empty eyes to Hermitage 'Name?' he asked.

'Name?' Hermitage only wanted to come in for a look round, he didn't want his name taken. He certainly didn't want it written down in a book where it could be referred to and used again. He didn't know why he worried about this, there was just something in him that said "don't give these monks your name, it won't end well."

'Do you have one?' The scribing monk sounded as if a monk with no name would be quite normal.

'Erm, yes.'

'Good. What is it?'

'Brother, erm,'

'Brother Urm. Good.' The scribe started writing.

Hermitage hated to see errors put down on parchment but didn't like to correct this one.

'Where from?'

'Where from?'

The writing monk did now give Hermitage a look of impatience. Resigned, weary and hugely disappointed impatience. The sort of impatience that said this person loathed their allotted task, and that the whole awful experience was being dragged out unnecessarily. They might drop dead if this took much longer, and wouldn't that be tiresome.

'Derby,' Hermitage said. It had the benefit of being true.

'Derby,' the monk repeated as he added the word to the

record. 'Brother Urm of Derby.'

Hermitage could see that the monk had come to the last column in the book so there was obviously one more question. The brother lifted his eyes from his work and held Hermitage's gaze. This was clearly going to be an important question.

'Are you now, or have you ever been a member of the community of Saint Werburgh?' The monk crossed himself.

'Saint Werburgh?'

'You are a repetitious fellow,' the monk sighed. 'Yes, Saint Werburgh.' The monk crossed himself again.

'Well, no.' This too was true. Thankfully, the monk with the book had not asked if Hermitage had ever set foot inside Saint Werburgh's. And he sincerely hoped there wasn't another page for that question.

'Good.' The monk completed his writing, blew gently on the ink to start the drying process, and then set the book to one side.

Hermitage felt as if he had been imprisoned in that book. At least it didn't have his right name.

Setting down his quill, the monk sat straight on his stool and faced Hermitage with his blank and disinterested expression.

'Saint Werburgh's,' he said as he crossed himself yet again. 'Is a house of sin and a blight on the city of Chester.' A touch of passion emerged from the monk at these words although it sounded as if he was reciting a lesson, rather than giving a considered opinion.

'Really?' Hermitage tried to sound interested.

'Yes, really. And the brothers there carry out the most unholy rites and are destined for the darkest reaches of hell.'

'All of them?' It was all Hermitage could think of.

'Yes, of course, all of them.' The brother sounded annoyed at this questioning of his lecture. 'How can you have a monastery full of sin and unholy rites if only some of the brothers are involved?'

It was an interesting question, but Hermitage felt that it wasn't being opened for debate.

'I see.' He nodded politely. In his own mind, he was letting the brother know that he had heard the words, not that he agreed with them.

'No right-thinking person has anything to do with Saint Werburgh's. It is only a matter of time before they are cast adrift from the righteous.'

'Cast adrift,' Hermitage repeated helpfully.

'So,' the brother came to his point. 'You are now a member of the community of Saint John.'

'Am I?' Hermitage now saw what all this was about.

'Of course, you are. I've put your name in the book. We make sure that all brothers who enter the town are saved from the evil that is Saint Werburgh's. You're very lucky we got to you first.'

'Thank you very much.'

'And if you are ever approached by anyone of that disreputable house, you must report it immediately. You must not talk to anyone from Saint Werburgh's, you must not even look at them.'

Hermitage was desperate to know how he was supposed to tell the difference between two monks but thought that this would only distract the brother before him.

'And if you discover anything about that place, or have the opportunity to reveal the true depths of their depravity, you must make it known.'

'Show them in a bad light, you mean.' Hermitage already

thought that this hatred for Saint Werburgh's was a bit unreasonable, but was now seeing that the brothers of Saint John really did consider it their mission to destroy the reputation of the other house. Would that go so far as murder though? He didn't like to ask if it would be all right to kill a monk of Saint Werburgh's. He thought it an outrageous question, and he wasn't confident that he would like the answer.

'Reveal their bad light for all to see.' The monk was starting to sound just a little bit mad now.

Hermitage nodded some more. 'I will see what I can do when I'm out and about.'

'When you're what?'

'Out and about. Upon my daily business.'

'Your daily business is here now,' the monk explained. 'Your name is in the book.' The monk patted the book, almost as a source of comfort.

'Ah, yes,' Hermitage gave a little smile. 'Of course.' He knew that he would be expected to attend the daily orders and be given tasks if he stayed here. Such was only reasonable exchange for his accommodation. He dearly wanted to explain that he'd only come in for a moment and wouldn't be staying at all, but it didn't seem the time, somehow. 'When I move on, then,' he tried.

The monk was looking a bit lost now. 'When you move on?'

'Yes, you know. Head back to Derby.'

The brother shook his head as if it had suddenly filled up with nonsense. 'Your name is in the book,' he repeated slowly. He looked a bit worried that Hermitage wasn't showing due respect to the book.

'Yes, and thank you for that.'

'You are a member of the community of Saint John. You're not going anywhere.'

Hermitage felt his stomach give warning. 'As I have come from Derby, so I must return.'

The monk spelt out the situation very clearly and very plainly and now added a hint of annoyance. 'Your name is in the book.'

Hermitage considered his situation very rapidly, urged on by his sense of panic. If he mentioned that the name in the book was the wrong one, he could see all sorts of trouble emerging; emerging right here and now as he was dragged away to a cell by some very large monks and locked up.

He would have to bide his time and take an opportunity to leave as soon as one arose. Either that or wait for Wat and Cwen to rescue him. If he wasn't back by nightfall they would probably come looking; he hoped.

'In the book, ah yes,' he said, wanting to assure this monk that there was no danger of him trying to climb over the walls and run away.

'I shall show you to your cell,' the monk said, rising from the desk.

'Marvellous,' Hermitage managed to get out.

Tidying the parchment and the book, the monk came round from behind the desk and beckoned Hermitage back towards the door.

As they emerged into the growing gloom of the evening, Hermitage thought he should take the opportunity to make some further enquiries; before he was buried in a cell and never saw the light of day again. 'I hear talk in the town that there have been deaths at Saint Werburgh's.'

The monk turned his head to Hermitage. 'I'd advise you to make the sign of the cross if you have to mention that name.'

Hermitage did so.

'Deaths, yes.' The monk nodded as if that sort of thing was going on all the time at Saint Werburgh's. 'It is surely a sign of their depravity and that the Lord himself is visiting death and destruction upon them.'

'Well, quite.' Hermitage said. 'Through the agents of the Lord who actually did the deed, I expect.'

'It is no sin to send a sinner to their end.'

'And it shows Saint Werburgh's for the truly awful place it is,' Hermitage offered.

The monk now nodded that this was an excellent point. 'I am sure that our abbot will be informing the authorities of events. The sooner we get the stain of Saint Werburgh's removed from the city, the better.'

Hermitage swallowed. He could easily see that these people might well have something to do with the deaths of Abel and Pendle. If they didn't actually do it themselves, they were jolly pleased about it. That was enough of a sin in its own right. It could well be that this particular monk would have no specific knowledge, but that someone higher up in Saint John's would.

Perhaps he would loiter here and see what the gossip of the place was. Despite its austere exterior, he knew what monks were like; being one himself. There would be chatter in the cells at night, there would be discussion of the abbot and other senior office holders. Any death was a topic of conversation; two murders just down the road would keep tongues wagging for weeks.

He found himself hoping that Wat and Cwen would not come to rescue him tonight, he had more to discover. It was actually quite exciting. He just had to tell himself that he was Brother Urm, and not give away his real mission.

As he pondered these developments, he saw that they had come to what must be the dormitory block.

'We will be just in time for Vespers,' the monk told him. 'I will show you your cell and then we will go to chapel.'

Hermitage quite looked forward to that. His devotions while staying with Wat were occasional, to say the least. Chapel was also a good place to pick up on the conversations taking place in any monastery.

They passed through the door into the dormitory but had to step aside to let another brother come out.

The monk of the desk bowed his head in acknowledgement and Hermitage did likewise.

As he rose, he saw the other monk considering him carefully.

'What the devil are you doing here?' Brother Longor asked, in a very inappropriate manner.

'This is Brother Urm,' the note-taker did the introduction.

'No it isn't,' Brother Longor said with some anger. 'This is Brother Hermitage, the King's Investigator.'

Oh dear, thought Hermitage.

## Caput XV Out of the Mouths of Babes; and Other Places

Little Harold, the true born King of England, was very lucky Cwen wasn't sick on him when she saw what was in his swaddling.

'Oh, my God.' She couldn't stop the exclamation bursting forth as she considered the task before her.

She had both infants on the floor in the room she'd been taken to, and it had required very little investigation indeed to determine that Harold was the source of the appalling smell. She knew where it had come from and what she was going to find when she explored further, but she still wasn't prepared when she parted the cloth.

'What have they been feeding you?' she asked the child as she backed away from the revolting sight.

All she could do was look. She had no idea what to actually do. Presumably, all the "stuff" needed cleaning up somehow, but what to use, and where to put it was a mystery. She had never had a younger sibling from whom to discover things like this.

Her childhood friends had had baby brothers or sisters and some of them cared for these little bundles while their mothers worked. Cwen had joined in, but only so far. As soon as things got messy, she went home.

"Don't you want to look after little John or tiny Brona?", her friends would ask.

"No," Cwen would reply.

But now, here she was. She'd got herself in this situation, she would just have to deal with it. Actually, Wat had got her into this situation, so it was all his fault. He'd suggested she come here, so he should be here now, clearing up this mess. And it really was a mess.

She gave tiny Ulf a warning look that if he was thinking of doing anything like this, there would be trouble.

Tiny Ulf gazed at her blankly before his eyes took on a distant look. They then descended into an expression of intense concentration, followed by what could only be described as painful straining. His little face went red and his eyes now squinted with effort of some sort.

This was followed by a revolting noise; the sort of gurgling a toad might make as it drowned in a bog. Ulf's face cleared and rested into quiet satisfaction at a job well done.

The smell in the room now doubled and Cwen had to swallow hard to avoid adding to what was becoming a disaster area.

She looked around to see if there was anything here she could use; like a window to jump out of and run away.

There was a jug of water on a stand in one corner and a substantial cupboard stood against one wall. Leaving the children to wallow in their filth, she opened the cupboard and found a supply of clean cloth. Well, that was a start. She had water for cleaning and cloth for re-swaddling. Now all she had to do was actually touch the disgusting creatures she'd taken charge of and get her hands dirty; quite literally.

In preparation for getting down on her knees, and a lot closer to the children than she wanted, she held her breath. If she was quick, she might be able to avoid breathing until the whole sordid business was done.

Before she could make any move, the door to the room opened and a large young woman entered. Cwen quickly moved to the cupboard, as if carefully selecting the best cloth for the task ahead.

'Ah, bless them,' the new arrival, said, beaming a smile at the besmirched infants on the floor.

Bless them, eh? That hadn't been one of Cwen's thoughts.

Without introduction, the new woman knelt straight at the side of the boys and cooed at them. She then proceeded to say revolting things like "have you made a mess then?" and "who's a clever boy", neither of which Cwen could understand; the mess was there for all to see, and it didn't seem to be a very clever thing to have done at all. If she'd done it herself no one would have called her clever.

'Oh, let me, let me,' the woman said, looking up at Cwen.

Only too glad to move out of the way, Cwen watched as the woman fetched the water, chose the cloth and quickly had the twins clean and dressed once more.

'These will have to go to the wash,' the woman said, holding the dirty swaddling up as if she'd won a prize. 'You'll be the new nurse, Weaver?'

'Erm, that's right.'

'I said as how we didn't need no new nurse. I said as how I would do it, but oh, no.'

'Really?' Cwen didn't like to ask who this woman was; she was so grateful that someone had rescued her from a fate worse than a very smelly death. She would be perfectly happy if this was a witch come to steal babies for the pot.

'Couldn't you just eat them all up,' the woman said, beaming at the children and rubbing their stomachs one at a time until they gurgled.

Rubbing their stomachs seemed a very bad idea to Cwen; something horrible might come out one end or the other.

'I am mistress Lyveva, Her Majesty's maid,' the woman called up from her position on the floor.

'I see.'

'My Lady Ealdgyth says as how I have enough to do looking after her, and we must have a nurse for the babies. I say as how that's nonsense. I can do both and be glad of it.'

Cwen was thinking as how she'd be glad of it as well.

Lyveva rose from the floor now, a boy in each arm, and Cwen marvelled at how she'd managed to do that without falling over.

'I must say, you're a bit of a young thing for nursing.'

Cwen decided that there might be a way out here. 'To be honest,' she confided. 'I was the only one the Ealdorman had. He wanted to send someone when he heard that the last old woman was gone.'

Lyveva nodded at this and looked as if she had her own confidence to share. 'I sent that one away.' She gave a little shiver at the bravery of her act. 'She wasn't looking after them right. I could see that and wanted rid of her. Ealdgyth wasn't having it, but I gave the old so-and-so a coin and she left like a bat up a chimney.'

Cwen just nodded and smiled at this. It felt as if there could be an escape from the awful baby situation if this woman wanted to take over their care. She was plainly mad, but then that was up to her. One thing she might prove useful for though was information. If she really was Ealdgyth's maid, she might know about Saint Werburgh's, if there was anything to know.

'If it's all right with you then,' Cwen said. 'I could get off. If the children are cared for and Lady Ealdgyth won't mind?'

'Oh, don't you worry my dear. I shall straighten out Her Majesty. Can't have a slip of a young thing like you looking after the little lovelies. Can we? Can we?' She actually addressed the question to the swaddled-up children, neither of whom had a constructive answer to offer.

'That'd be good. I was supposed to be going to Saint Werburgh's when the Ealdorman diverted me.'

Cwen didn't know whether to be pleased or disappointed at the horrified look that arrived on Lyveva's face.

'What you going there for?' she demanded. She even clutched the babies closer as if they'd had a very narrow escape from this awful woman.

'There have been deaths.' Cwen tried to sound as if she was confiding a juicy bit of gossip.

'Well, of course, there have. The devil himself lives at Saint Werburgh's.'

'The devil?'

'That's him.'

'What? The devil? The real one?'

'Absolutely.' Lyveva looked quite terrified just discussing the subject.

'How do you know?'

'How do I know? How do I know the devil lives in Chester? How can you ask such a question?'

'Well..,'

'It's the devil. This is not just some hobbledy-hoy, you know.'

'It's the devil.'

'Exactly.'

Cwen tried to act as if she was in awe of this information and hide the fact that she thought Lyveva was an idiot. 'Have you seen him?' she breathed.

Lyveva crossed herself. 'God spare me, no. I'd drop dead on the spot.'

'So, who told you?'

'People as have seen.'

'Other people have seen him?'

'That they have.'

'And they didn't drop dead on the spot?'

'Of course, not. Simple folk like you and me, well, we're meat and drink to the devil.'

'Are we?'

'Oh, yes. We'd as soon drop dead at the sight of him as we would fall down a well with a hole in the top.'

'So, who?' Cwen was finding it very hard to take this seriously. If she was going to hear anything useful, she would have to play the part of simple folk who fell down wells.

'Noble folk,' Lyveva whispered, presumably in case the devil was listening.

'Oh, noble folk.' Cwen nodded as if everything a noble told you was bound to be true. She did not miss the point that the nobles were involved already. Perhaps Abel's killer was in the house with them.

'The nobles need to take care of Her Majesty; protect her from evil. And Saint Werburgh's is full of it.'

'So, if they saw some evil there, they'd have to get rid of it.'

'Of course, they would. And Her Majesty herself told me about the place.'

'Did she?' Now that was interesting. 'And did one of her nobles tell her about it? I can't imagine she went off and saw the devil herself.'

'Oh, great heavens, no. We've only been here a while. Apparently, one of the monks of Saint John warned us about Saint Werburgh's. And they'd know about devils.'

'A monk of Saint John, eh?' No surprise there, then.

'Her Majesty gave me fair warning to stay away from the place. The devil has taken up residence in Saint Werburgh's she said.'

'Did she?'

'She did. And you stay away Lyveva. He'll gobble you up as soon as say "break fast".'

'I can see that would be a worry.'

'So, it's no wonder there's been deaths, is it?'

'Obviously not.'

Lyveva turned her head slightly sideways to look at Cwen. 'Why you going there then?'

'Well, I won't,' Cwen said decisively. 'Not now you've told me about the devil.'

Lyveva was happy again.

'The Ealdorman wanted me to go and find out about the deaths. He has to know about dead people, it's part of the job.'

Lyveva looked impressed.

'But now I can see why he wanted me to go. It's just so he won't get eaten by the devil.'

'Typical,' Lyveva huffed. 'If he wants to check on the devil, let him go himself.'

'He probably knows, doesn't he?' Cwen went on. 'I mean, if the nobles know, and the Normans know, the Ealdorman is bound to know.'

'You mean he knew about it all the time?'

'Could be.'

'That's awful, that is. And he wants to send you there. He sounds like a bad lot.'

Cwen paused a moment before the next question. 'Does Lady Ealdgyth know who's dead?'

Lyveva checked the room, probably to make sure there were no devils in the corner listening in. 'Some other devils,' she confided.

'There's a lot of them, then?'

'Oh, yes. Place is swarming with them, it is. And being devils, they like nothing better than killing one another.'

'What happened to the abbot and all the other church

people?'

'Probably possessed.'

'Of course.' Cwen let a frown develop. 'But the Ealdorman told me it was two monks that got killed. What did he say they were called? Abel and Pendle, that's it. That's who I was supposed to go and find out about.'

'Disciples.'

'What about them?'

'Your Abel and Pendle, they'll be disciples of the devil.'

'That must be it. Or they were disciples of the devil before they were murdered.'

'Exactly. That's what you get for being disciples of the devil.'

Cwen continued to look unhappy about all this. 'If the nobles know it's the devil, why aren't they up there doing something about it all right now? I mean, when there's trouble it's always the nobles who sort it out. Isn't it? Look at the Normans.'

'The Normans?' Lyveva had some trouble making this connection.

'The Normans come over here and the nobles go off to sort them out. The nobles all get killed, of course; well, ours do. But that's their job, isn't it? What's the point of being a noble if you don't go and do noble things when there's call? What are they doing sitting about when there's a devil down the road?'

'Plans,' Lyveva said with an air of mystery.

'Plans?'

'They got plans.'

'Have they?'

'The nobles. Her Majesty's nobles.'

'They've got plans for the devil? And all his little disciples?'

'That's it. I heard Her Majesty talking about it.'

Cwen contained a smile. 'And this was just before the disciples got murdered?'

'I expect the devil's in a panic now. Killed his own disciples, he did.'

From what Cwen had seen of Ealdgyth's nobles, she concluded that they wouldn't induce panic in an easily startled rabbit. Still, perhaps there were some better ones at the back of the house. Sneaking into a monastery and killing two harmless monks might well be in their line. But why?

This business of the devil had obviously been made up for some reason. An excuse for killing monks? Or was it possible that Ealdgyth's nobles were so stupid they really did believe the devil was in Saint Werburgh's? She thought about this and concluded that yes, it was quite possible.

But who would put them up to it? And why frighten them into keeping away from Saint Werburgh's if there were devils to be killed?

The monks of Saint John who had mentioned the devil in the first place sounded suspicious, but then they were starting to sound suspicious most of the time. And Ealdgyth herself? The nobles she'd seen appeared to be idiots, but surely the so-called queen wouldn't be taken in by tales of devils. What was she up to?

This was all proving very informative and she would have a lot to discuss with Wat and Hermitage when she got back. The trip had been worth it after all. Only down to her success in wheedling the information out of Lyveva though. She couldn't imagine Wat getting anywhere at all.

'I shall make sure I go nowhere near the place,' Cwen said, trying to look as horrified as she could. She gave Lyveva a smile and moved towards the door.

'You do that, my dear.' Lyveva turned her attention back to her charges and hugged them close, looking confident that she could keep even a devil at bay.

Before Cwen could pull the door back, it was opened from the other side and the noblewoman who had found her in the first place came in. 'Ah,' she cried out, pointing at Cwen.

'It's all right,' Cwen said. 'Mistress Lyveva has said she'll care for the children.'

'Saint Werburgh's,' the woman wailed out now, for no apparently good reason.

'I just been warning her about the place,' Lyveva said. 'Telling her as how she shouldn't go anywhere near it, even if the Ealdorman has told her to.'

'Go anywhere near it?' the noblewoman positively screeched. 'She doesn't need to go anywhere near it. Saint Werburgh's is where she's come from.'

Lyveva took one look at Cwen before she joined in the screeching and ran from the room. Her tiny bundles were clutched tightly as if she was pulling them from the very jaws of that devil she'd been going on about.

The noblewoman soon had a gathering of noblemen at her back as they crowded the entrance to the room.

'We've got you now, devil,' she said.

Cwen just looked at them, blocking the only way out. There was only one conclusion to draw; this was all Wat's fault.

## Caput XVI Creeping to the Crypt

Wat got nothing useful at all from the abbot. He had no more to tell about Abel and Pendle than he had already imparted. As far as he knew they were genuine brothers who had joined the community in the normal manner, and had then died, in quite an unusual manner, he had to admit.

With no hope of getting anything more, Wat headed back to the herbalist's workshop.

From his assessment of Abbot Fulmer, he concluded that if Abel and Pendle had been the king's men, the last person to find out would be the abbot. He would probably be the last person to find out if three of his monks were actually nuns, the Archbishop of Canterbury lived in his wine cellar and Saint Peter himself looked after the keys at night. He reminded Wat of Hermitage, in so many ways.

'Where are you going?' Bodin the herbalist asked Wat as he entered the workshop.

'Upstairs,' Wat nodded towards the loft.

'There's nothing for you there.'

'Apart from King Harold,' Wat snorted.

Bodin's face took on a quizzical look. He appeared to be thinking about this carefully. Eventually, he shook his head slowly. 'No. No kings in my loft. Harold's dead anyway. Everyone knows that.'

'Oh, come on,' Wat chided, half-jokingly. 'I was just up there talking to him, you know that. You saw us.'

Bodin's head shook some more. 'Must have been another loft.'

Wat's demeanour hardened in the face of this nonsense. 'I'm going up there,' he said firmly. He could see Bodin was a young and fit man, but herbalists probably didn't get in many fights. If he was a herbalist at all, of course. That could all be a ruse. Was this man really some sort of soldier pretending to be a herbalist. Or vice versa? Wat was about to find out.

'Please yourself.' Bodin stepped aside.

Wat kept his eyes on the herbalist as he went to the ladder and climbed a few steps to put his head into the loft. He was not surprised to find it empty of kings.

He stepped down again and considered Bodin. 'Where is he?'

'You know,' Bodin said, turning his back and going over to his workbench. 'I think you may have been sleeping with the moonlight getting to your head. Not sure if it's frenzy, mania, melancholy or fatuity at the moment, but I could give you some herbs.'

Wat just shook his head in a disappointed manner. 'You can try this if you like, but it's not going to work. No one sees kings in the loft without there actually being one there. And I saw Harold. I've met him before, I know him very well and we had a nice chat; including about you.

'We know you're a Norman of some sort, guarding the old king, making sure he doesn't stray, and that's fair enough. But don't try to pretend he's not here. Unless it's you who needs the herbs, having kings in the attic and not knowing?'

Bodin just shrugged as if there was nothing he could do and no help he had to offer.

'I shall just find him,' Wat said calmly. 'Saint Werburgh's isn't a big place. Not many spaces to hide a king, particularly as you don't want anyone to know he's here.'

Bodin simply turned to his workbench and began grinding something or other with a pestle and mortar.

'Just have a final check up here before I go,' Wat said, and he darted towards the stairs to the loft before Bodin could move.

Once fully in the space above, there was nothing of any help to be seen. The sacks and drying herbs were just as Wat had last seen them, and he could make out no message left by Harold to say where he had been taken; not that he'd have known of course.

'No one there, eh?' Bodin called from below.

'No, there isn't,' Wat replied. 'And I don't know what the King's Investigator will make of that. Looking into murders and one of the most significant clues is taken away. Can't think William will like to see that in the report.'

'Ah, well,' Bodin sounded nonchalant. 'William gets all sorts of reports, I imagine. From all sorts of people.'

Wat scowled at Bodin's back as he came down from the loft and made for the door.

'Good luck,' the herbalist called after him, not sounding very sincere at all.

. . .

'Now,' Wat said to himself once he was back in the courtyard. 'If you had to hide a king in an abbey, where would you put him?' He turned full circle and considered the buildings around him. 'Not where there are any other monks, that's for sure.' He cast his eyes towards Merle's dread realm. 'Dead or alive.' He screwed up his face in thought as if that might help.

'Dead, eh? What did Hermitage say about burying important monks? Sometimes they get put in the walls? And old Abbot Abbo's brother got his own crypt.' [10]He looked at the floor as if the entrance to a crypt would just present itself. 'The abbot would know,' he said, 'but it might be a bit suspicious asking him if I can look at his dead monks. Merle's

[10] *The Case of the Cantankerous Carcass* - sounds intriguing, doesn't it?

the man, then.' He didn't feel at all happy about this but headed off for the house of the dead anyway.

Merle was obviously surprised at getting more than one knock on the door in a single day. He was even more surprised to see that it was someone who'd come back for a second visit.

'No, no, I won't come in,' Wat said, despite the gracious invitation. He coughed slightly as the odour of the place rose around Merle like a host of guardian angels; guardian angels who had died some time ago and had been left out on a warm night. 'I was just wondering where the dead go after you've erm, dealt with them.'

'Into the presence of our Lord,' Merle replied. 'If they've behaved themselves.'

'Sorry, I mean where do the bodies go? Where do you put them?'

Merle raised his eyebrows at Wat. He was clearly a man in a unique position who had to deal with all sorts of things the average monk wouldn't know about. He had also clearly never been asked this particular question before. 'Why do you want to know?' he asked, very suspiciously.

'Is there a crypt? I suppose that's the question, really.'

'Is it?'

'Yes. Do your monks go in a crypt somewhere? Some of them, anyway?'

'They might.' Merle was obviously worried that if he gave this information away, Wat would go and do something uncalled-for in the crypt.

'Could you take me?'

'Could I take you?' Merle half shut the door now and was starting to look quite nervous.

'That's it, could you take me to the crypt?'

'At this time of night?'

'It's not really night yet, and it is quite urgent.'

'How can going to the crypt be quite urgent?'

'I think there might be someone down there.'

'There's plenty of people down there,' Merle confirmed. 'But they're not receiving visitors anymore.'

'You don't understand.'

'And I'm not sure I want to.' Merle looked back over his shoulder. He leaned out of the door a bit and looked up and down outside before addressing Wat quietly. 'I've still got Abel and Pendle in here if you want to come in?'

'Good God, no,' Wat was shocked at the suggestion.

'There's no need to be so upset about it. You're the one who just asked to go down the crypt in the dark.'

'I think there's someone alive down there.' Wat realised he hadn't explained this bit and could understand why Merle might be a bit concerned.

'Oh, yes?' Merle sounded as if this was a common complaint. 'Heard the dead calling, have you? It happens now and again.'

'It's nothing like that. I think a living person has been put in the crypt.'

Merle was mightily offended at the implied slur on his professionalism. 'I can assure you I have never put anyone in the crypt still alive.'

'You didn't put him there.'

'What?'

'Someone else put him there.'

Now Merle looked quite angry. 'Someone else has been putting people in my crypt? Without them being dead?'

'Erm, possibly.'

'Are you a loon?' Merle asked, peering hard at Wat.

'Absolutely not,' Wat said clearly and firmly. He didn't like to add that he thought the person in the crypt was King Harold.

'And you think there's someone down in the crypt? Have you heard them?'

'No, but someone is missing, and I can't think where else he would be.'

'There's lots of places people would be that aren't the crypt.'

'Not if they need to be hidden.'

Merle was looking increasingly as if he wanted to not only close the door but bar it from the inside. Abel and Pendle were much safer company.

'It is on the king's business,' Wat said. 'For his investigator.'

'Not sure that makes it any better.' Merle frowned. He did look as if he was considering the request a bit more seriously now though. 'You just want to look?'

'That's right.'

'You don't want to, erm, do anything.'

'What would I do?'

'Well, I don't know, do I? You're the one who wants to get into the crypt. How am I to know what your sort gets up to in crypts.'

'My sort?' Now Wat was taking offence. 'What's my sort?'

'The sort who want to go down crypts of an evening.'

Wat thought this was a bit rich, coming from the man who kept dead bodies in his parlour.

'Look, can we just go down to the crypt and look inside. That's all I want to do.'

'On the king's behalf?' Merle checked.

'That's right.'

'And does the king know you like going in crypts in the

dark?'

'I don't like going in them, I need to look in this one. Can we get on with it?' Wat's irritation at least had an effect on Merle.

'Please yourself,' he said. He took one look over his shoulder, perhaps to make sure that Abel and Pendle were comfortable, and then pulled the door closed behind him as he indicated Wat to follow. 'You could have just gone,' Merle grumbled. 'We don't keep it locked, you know. Never had anyone try to escape.' He gave a disturbing little laugh at this.

'If I knew where it was, I would.'

'Never had anyone want to go in either unless they're moving in for good if you know what I mean. And then they don't get much choice.'

'Fascinating.' Wat wished they could just get this over with. He didn't really know what to do if Harold wasn't there. He could ask Merle where else there was in this place to hide someone, but he wasn't sure he could tolerate waiting for the answer.

'This someone still alive, then?' Merle asked as he led the way to the chapel.

'I hope so.'

'That's good.'

'Is it?' Wat couldn't see how any of this was good.

'Oh, yes. Live people in the crypt is nothing to do with me. It's the dead I put down there. If someone else is putting dead people in my crypt, well, I mean to say. Where would it end?'

'I really can't imagine,' said Wat, who really couldn't.

'You'd get people putting all sorts down there. Them as don't deserve it. And if I put dead people in the crypt, I don't want them coming out again.'

'Well, quite.'

'Here we are then.' They had arrived at the door of the chapel and Merle pushed it open. 'It'll be Vespers soon, so we'd better hurry.'

That suited Wat.

Merle scuttled over towards the back of the chapel, behind the altar, and here Wat could see a tiny opening, like the doorway for a child, that was set in the wall at the back. It looked very small and very dark and very unwelcoming.

'Is that it?' he asked rather nervously.

'That's it,' Merle sounded full of pride. 'Lovely isn't it?'

'Oh, yes, lovely.'

'It's a bit dark down there,' Merle said as he took a candle that was burning on the altar. 'We'll need this.'

'Are you supposed to take those?' Wat asked, thinking that Hermitage's sensibilities must be starting to get through to him.

'It's either that or stumble about down there in the dark. With all the bodies.'

'Bodies?' Wat asked.

'That is what you generally find in a crypt.' Merle tutted.

'Aren't they in boxes, or stone tombs or something?'

'Boxes?' Merle sounded confused now.

'You're the crypt expert, obviously,' Wat said, his nervousness growing. 'But I understood that bodies in crypts had their own tombs?'

'Why would anyone do that?' Merle sounded a bit lost now. 'Why have a crypt and then put boxes in it?'

'I'm sure I don't know. It's just what I heard. Protect them from animals? Keep the smell down?'

'What smell?' Merle was very puzzled.

'Had you ever organised a crypt before you came here?'

Wat asked, as nonchalantly as he could.

'Nope,' Merle said happily, as he approached the opening with his candle.

'Oh, marvellous,' Wat sighed.

There were two small steps just inside the tiny entrance that led down to a small wooden door set in the stone of the wall.

'This is what you need to keep the animals out,' Merle explained. He pushed on the door. 'Who's locked it?' he complained.

'Locked it?'

'It's locked.'

'Do you have the key?'

'There isn't a key, there's just a bolt.' He reached up to the top of the door and drew back a large bolt.

Wat's hopes rose as now he thought it more likely that Bodin had taken Harold to the crypt and then bolted the door.

Merle pushed on the little door and it swung backwards with difficulty as it didn't actually fit the hole very well.

'At last,' a voice called from the depths of the crypt where only corpses were supposed to be.

At hearing these words come from a room full of dead people that had been bolted shut, a scream of shock rang around the chapel. Wat was surprised to note that it had come from him. He looked at Merle with embarrassment.

The crypt keeper seemed not to be disturbed in the slightest that one of his bodies was up and about.

'Aha,' Wat said, trying to disguise his outburst as a coughing fit. 'There we are then, there is someone down here.'

'You said there would be.' Merle couldn't hide his

disappointment that Wat had screamed when what he expected to happen, had happened.

'Just so.'

The door was now pulled from the inside and Harold emerged, also looking very calm and collected, considering who he'd been staying with for the past hour or so.

'I thought you might come.' Harold brushed himself down and considered Wat and Merle. 'The keeper of the dead?' he asked Wat, nodding his head towards Merle.

'That's right.'

'You're supposed to put them in boxes, you know,' Harold explained.

Merle shrugged. He seemed to have very little interest in anything that wasn't dead. Which at least meant that Wat didn't have any explaining to do.

'Thank you very much, Brother Merle,' Wat said, with a bow. 'We'll be off then.'

Merle gave them both rather hard looks before returning to his door, closing it and pointedly throwing the bolt back again. He wandered off back down the chapel, tutting at what people got up to these days.

'You'd think he'd want to know who was in his crypt,' Wat said.

'He probably thinks I'm dead anyway. He might try to put me back in again.'

Wat had started to breathe more normally now. 'Bodin put you in there, then?'

'As soon as you'd gone. I think he planned to get me moved out of Chester as well, now that it was known I'm here.'

'Perhaps we could go and surprise him that you've risen from the dead, once more.'

Harold gave this some thought. 'Can we look at this Abel

fellow first?'

'The dead one?'

'That's him. If you're right, and it is someone from the days before William, we might have more that we need to ask Brother Bodin.'

Wat nodded that this was a good idea, even if it did mean another encounter with Merle.

Knowing the way only too well, Wat led back from the chapel to the door of Merle's unique residence. 'He's going to love seeing me again so soon,' he said as he knocked on the door. 'Mind you, I'm not that keen on seeing him.'

'What now?' came from inside as Merle shuffled over to the door. He opened it and considered the two men. 'If you want to get back in the crypt you only have to throw the bolt.'

'We don't want to get back in the crypt,' Wat said. 'I didn't want to go in there in the first place.'

'Brother Merle,' Harold interrupted with a smile for the monk. 'I understand that you are caring for Brothers Abel and Pendle?'

Merle gave Wat a glare but replied amicably to Harold. 'That's it. By all rights, they should be on their way now, but the abbot says not, as they were killed. And now there's this king's man holding things up.'

'Quite,' Harold got in before a full diatribe began. 'May I look?' He nodded towards the interior.

'You too?' Merle looked askance at Harold and gave Wat a sidelong glance as if this sort of thing was all his fault.

'It's just that I may know Brother Abel, from a previous life.'

Merle seemed very doubtful about people who had previous lives. 'You're certainly not going to know from this one anymore. Who are you, anyway? I've not seen you before.'

'I have been ill,' Harold explained. 'In Brother Bodin's care.'

'Oh, you're him, are you?'

'That's right.'

'Better now?' Merle sounded cautious.

'Mostly.'

'What were you doing in my crypt then?'

Wat thought that was a very good question

'Did that idiot Bodin think you were dead?' Merle asked. There was clearly no love lost with the herbalist. 'Even though you were walking around?'

Harold just shrugged a bit.

'Typical. That man can't tell a corpse from coriander.'

Wat couldn't really believe that anyone would believe a herbalist could mistake the living for the dead. But then, this was Brother Merle.

'Brother Abel?' Harold asked.

'Oh, please yourself,' Merle stepped aside and threw the door wide with some exasperation. 'I don't know why I don't just leave them outside; the number of people keep coming and going. It's not decent.'

Wat and Harold quickly entered the room, before Merle could change his mind. Wat led over to Abel's resting place and directed Harold's attention to the deceased.

Harold considered the rather sunken face, not seeming to be put off by the smell at all. After the briefest of examinations, he nodded. 'That's Lefsius, or it was. Earl Waltheof's man.'

Wat snapped his fingers. 'Of course, it is. I should have known. Waltheof had a very particular interest in, erm...,'

'Yes,' Harold got in quickly. 'We all knew what his

particular interest was, and we don't want to be reminded. He was married to William's niece, Judith. Although how she put up with him and his interest is hard to understand. It's not surprising that his men could escape William's attentions, being related.'

'What was he doing here though?'

'Just keeping out of harm's way, I expect.'

Wat considered the body. 'He didn't manage that very well, did he?'

'He was a loyal servant to his master though. If he found out I was here, he might have taken ideas into his head.'

'Ideas that Bodin might want to bring to a quick stop.'

'Just so.' Harold nodded his head gently as he thought about the implications. He glanced over to the other body that was on the next table. 'And this is Brother Pendle, is it?'

'So we're told. Don't know him at all.'

Harold took a step over and looked at Pendle. 'You don't know him because he's a Norman.'

'A Norman?' Wat couldn't quite take it in. 'What's a Norman monk doing in Chester?'

'Not a Norman monk. Obviously, he's a bit more dead than when I last saw him, but this is Walter, one of Hugh de Montfort's men.'

'Erm,' Wat said.

'And he is no more a monk than Lefsius was.'

'I don't understand,' Wat had to say, none of this fitting together at all.

'Lefsius might have taken refuge here and then found out who the sick brother in the tower was. Walter could have been sent to make sure the sick brother didn't leave. One of Bodin's companions?'

'Or even sent to watch the watcher,' Wat suggested. 'And

now they're both dead.'

'Both murdered,' Harold corrected. 'Someone is killing Saxons and Normans alike.'

## Caput XVII Hostile Hospitality

'I think the abbot better see you,' Longor said, right in Hermitage's face. It didn't sound like a very pleasant invitation at all.

Hermitage had been taken to see abbots many times in his relatively short monastic life. While they were all memorable experiences, none of them was happy. Even his dear friend, Abbot Abbo, could be brusque and short with him at times.

He had never really reasoned why abbots tended to be intimidating and aggressive characters; perhaps they needed to be in order to manage their flocks. But Abbot Fulmer seemed a gentle soul. Why couldn't more abbots be like that?

Then Hermitage wondered if it might be him. Was there something about him that brought out the brusque and short in all abbots? If he spent time with Abbot Fulmer would that fellow turn into some raging loon who threatened to do things to Hermitage that were specifically prohibited in several passages of the bible?

No, that was ridiculous. No leader would have favourites, or whatever the opposite of favourite was. They would be rational, thoughtful types, how else would they have been elevated to leadership?

The short journey to see the abbot of Saint John gave him time to consider all of this, and come to the conclusion that the imminent meeting would be one of the bad kind. What had this abbot's name been? Kenwald? Something like that. Hermitage was confident that he'd soon be able to add that name to the list of abbots to be avoided.

Longor said not a word as he led the way through the corridors and passages of Saint John's. His silence seemed to be deliberate and was having a terrible effect on Hermitage.

By the time they arrived at the door to the abbot's study, he was ready to use the first pile of straw he saw.

Longor knocked, all the while giving Hermitage a withering stare.

'Enter.' A voice from the inside commanded. Hermitage thought it noticeable for its brusqueness as well as being quite short.

Longor pushed the door open and stepped through ahead of Hermitage. He stood by the door and waved an arm to indicate the abbot would receive him now. As Hermitage stepped through, Longor spoke up in a loud voice. 'A Brother Urm arrived today,' he said sneeringly. 'But it turns out to be Brother Hermitage, The King's Investigator.'

Well, that was some sort of introduction, Hermitage concluded; it could have been worse.

He stood in surprise as Abbot Kenwald rose from behind his desk and stepped across a very well-furnished room to face him.

Then Abbot Kenwald did something which confused Hermitage no end. He bowed.

Hermitage wondered if the abbot wasn't getting ready to butt him in the stomach; that would certainly be a surprise.

'My Lord investigator,' the abbot said as he rose from his bow.

Hermitage looked around him. No, there was only the abbot and Longor in the room with him. Kenwald was smiling now, which was most disconcerting. Longor was quietly growling behind him, which was much more like it.

'Aha,' he said decisively.

Abbot Kenwald now beckoned that Hermitage should come and join him in comfortable chairs by the fire. Moving very cautiously, in case the plan was to throw him in the fire when he least expected it, Hermitage did so.

'Longor,' the abbot instructed, once they were both seated. 'Send for wine and food for the investigator.'

Longor's growl was now the sort that could scare away mad dogs.

Once Longor had gone, slamming the door behind him, Abbot Kenwald turned to Hermitage with a smile that would make a sycophant look quite rude. 'We are honoured,' he said, and even bowed his head again. 'The great King's Investigator.'

'Oh, well, I don't know about that,' Hermitage said, very nervously, still expecting something horrible to jump out at him.

'And how fares King William?' the abbot asked.

'He, erm, fares pretty well, I think.'

'When did you last see him?' The abbot sounded truly fascinated.

'A few weeks ago, I suppose,' Hermitage said. He tried not to remember his meetings with William, they tended to come back to him in the middle of the night of their own accord. He thought he better make some conversation though. This abbot seemed very keen. Some people were keen on William until they met him.

'I had to deal with an issue for the King and his brother, Odo.'

'Odo?' Kenwald seemed to be in awe now.

'That's right, in Kent. Some nuns were reported dead.'[11]

'No!'

'Just so.'

'And do you see the king often?'

Hermitage's immediate thought was "too often" but that

---

[11] *The Bayeux Embroidery* includes dead nuns.

wouldn't go down well. 'Oh, yes,' he said. 'Quite frequently. He and his fellow Le Pedvin deal with most of the investigations directly.'

Now Abbot Kenwald crossed himself. His face also became more intense and thoughtful, somehow. If Hermitage was a suspicious fellow, he'd think that the abbot had just been testing him.

'And now your work brings you to the sorry abbey of Saint Werburgh.'

Hermitage noted that, unlike his brothers, the abbot did not cross himself at the name. He nodded. 'The deaths of Abel and Pendle.'

'A blight on the town, and on the community. I am sure that Abbot Fulmer must be beside himself. Have you discovered anything?'

'My enquiries are still at an early stage.' Hermitage liked the sound of that; he might use it again.

Before there could be any response. The door opened and a monk came in bearing a tray with bread, a flagon and two fine cups.

'Ah, excellent,' Kenwald smiled broadly. 'Set them down there, by the side of the King's Investigator.'

The tray-bearing monk looked suitably impressed and left the supplies by Hermitage's side.

Abbot Kenwald leaned over and filled the cups with a fine-looking wine. He handed one to Hermitage and sat back with the other. He raised it to Hermitage and they both drank.

Hermitage wasn't used to wine at this time of day. He wasn't really used to it at any time of day, but Wat insisted on having it with every meal. What did people expect him to drink, he would ask, water?

And this was very good wine, the sort Wat only brought out when he'd sold something very expensive. It slipped down Hermitage's throat as if it knew the way. It sent a little tingle to the back of his head, just to let him know it had arrived safely.

'Of course.' Abbot Kenwald went on, considering his wine cup more than anything else. 'It is a pity for poor Saint Werburgh's,' he mused. 'Obviously, it depends upon your findings, but this could be the end of them. A great loss to our town.'

Hermitage thought that if Longor was anything to go by, the loss of Saint Werburgh's would be celebrated. Some of Wat's words drifted into Hermitage's mind. "Stop believing everything anyone tells you", being most prominent. Could it be that Abbot Kenwald was not being entirely open and honest? He took another sip of wine, which was a bigger sip than he'd intended.

'If the king's own Investigator finds that Saint Werburgh's is at fault in any way, I can imagine the consequences could be dire.' Kenwald looked deeply saddened as he said this.

Hermitage hadn't thought of that at all or anything like it. He would find out who the killer was, he hoped, and then he would let everyone know. What happened after that was hardly up to him. Other people generally stepped in at that point; Normans, usually.

He didn't like to say anything so simply sat quietly.

This seemed to worry Abbot Kenwald slightly. His eyes darted about, and he looked as if he desperately wanted to press Hermitage further, but didn't dare.

Instead, he shook his head, sadly. 'But what brings you to our humble establishment? And under an assumed name?' He was still managing to look absolutely enthralled, and there was not a hint of criticism in his question.

Hermitage swallowed. He had played the part of the king's most high representative before, and now Kenwald seemed to be treating him as one. He just wasn't sure he could carry it off. Perhaps more wine would help; it seemed to be making his worries drift away slightly. He found he had got to the bottom of the cup, so Abbot Kenwald kindly filled it up again.

'Brother Longor,' he started.

'Brother Longor?' the abbot asked, glancing towards the door.

'Brother Longor came to Saint Werburgh's with a delegation.'

'Ah,' Kenwald nodded his head in a knowing manner and scratched behind his ear. 'He can be an impetuous fellow.'

Hermitage had guessed that.

'And the delegation included a number of others.' Hermitage took a deep breath for his next falsehood. The breath was very deep and quite quick and seemed to make the wine in his head spin round a bit. 'All of whom we are looking into.'

The abbot went quite pale now. 'Looking into?' he asked.

Hermitage had not the first idea what looking into someone actually meant so he didn't have an answer. He just nodded slowly. He thought that nodding quickly might make him feel quite peculiar.

This seemed to have an even worse effect on Kenwald, who started fiddling with his hands. 'You can't think that we had anything to do with the deaths?'

Hermitage's feelings at this moment were truly bizarre. Yes, his head was swimming rather, with the effect of wine on an empty stomach, but he'd never experienced anything like this in all his encounters with kings, nobles, abbots, monks or even other people. He couldn't immediately put his finger on it but suspected that this was what it felt like to be in charge.

He had an almost overwhelming urge to lean forward, look Abbot Kenwald in the eye and ask him to explain himself. Nay, to demand that he explain himself. That was too much though, it would be unspeakably presumptuous. Even the wine wouldn't let him go that far.

'Who can say?' Hermitage eventually came up with; he certainly couldn't.

That didn't appear to help the abbot at all.

'Why would we?' Kenwald almost whimpered now.

Hermitage couldn't see any harm in telling him. Perhaps it would elicit some useful information, and perhaps his newfound power was going to his head.

'Well, when we met Brother Longor he made it quite clear that he would be glad to be rid of Saint Werburgh's.'

'Brother Longor.' Abbot Kenwald said this in a very unhappy manner.

Hermitage could tell that Longor's next meeting with his abbot would not be a happy one. He was deeply ashamed of the quiet satisfaction he took from that. He also wondered about the tales of Abbot Kenwald being a very difficult man. He tried hard to remind himself that people sometimes lied, particularly when murder was involved. With yet another revelation, he concluded that he'd rather trust Abbot Fulmer than Kenwald.

He felt a little frisson of excitement as he wondered if he might not try a little ruse, just to see how far Kenwald would go.

'Do you not think that Saint Werburgh's is a problem house? You said they would be a loss to the town, but would it be better if Saint John's were made pre-eminent?'

Abbot Kenwald held his hands out. 'That is not for me to decide, of course. But it may be that your investigations will throw some light on the situation of Saint Werburgh's. Some light that could illuminate the king in any decision he sees fit to make.'

'So,' Hermitage plunged on, washed along by the wine. 'It would be to Saint John's advantage to see Saint Werburgh's fail.'

Abbot Kenwald looked around the room now, and seemed to be weighing up his options and carefully considering what he should say next. He leant over towards Hermitage and dropped his voice.

'It is true that I have worried about Saint Werburgh's for some time. I don't believe that they are following the rule in the true spirit. They are a lax and sometimes lazy house.' Abbot Kenwald was starting to get a bit excited. He calmed himself with some effort. 'But that does not mean I wish them ill. And I would certainly not do anything to bring them harm.'

'Not you personally,' Hermitage said. He was slightly surprised to hear that come out as "pershonally".

Kenwald dropped his voice. 'You mean someone here may have taken things into their own hands?'

'Hands? Feet? Who knows?' Hermitage thought that was very funny and smiled to himself.

'By murder?' Kenwald sounded appalled.

Hermitage just shrugged at that.

The abbot shook his head sorrowfully. 'How, erm, how will you find out?'

Hermitage waved a finger in front of his face. 'That,' he said, 'is a very good question. It's all in the investigation, you see.' He nodded at this profound truth.

'I do see,' Abbot Kenwald said, although he obviously didn't.

'Who could have done it? Why would they want to do it, and how was it done? We know the last one; clothing.'

'Clothing?'

'They were both murdered with clothing. Vestments to be preshoo, prespri, precip, accurate.' Hermitage got out. He looked at his wine cup and realised that he was drunk. This was awful. How could he? He only drank wine with Wat and Cwen when they were there to look after him. He should have known better. He told his mind to sort itself out, but his mind stuck its tongue out.

He put his cup down on the table, which was quite an achievement in its own right. 'I had better get back.'

'Really?' Kenwald's disappointment was clear.

Hermitage scratched his ear and started wondering if the abbot hadn't given him too much wine on purpose. Why on earth would he do that?

'Oh, yes,' he went on. 'I said I would be back at Saint Werburgh's by sunset.'

'Nearly too late already,' Kenwald pointed out. 'You are welcome to stay in our guest lodgings.'

'No,' Hermitage said, more quickly than he expected.

'Have you got all you came for, then?'

'I think so. I have your assurance that you would not do harm to Saint Werburgh's.'

'But you still think someone might?'

'Someone did kill Abel and Pendle. They didn't do it themselves.'

'Perhaps there were other reasons?'

Hermitage nodded as sagely as he could manage. 'All will

be investigated.'

'If I may ask?' Kenwald sounded more interested than annoyed. 'Why come here as an ordinary brother. Why not simply ask me as King's Investigator?'

'Aha,' Hermitage nodded at this question, and quickly tried to think of an answer. 'Those alerted to the presence of the King's own Investigator may be cautious, for fear of King William, you understand.'

Kenwald nodded that he understood this bit very well. 'Catch them unaware, eh?'

Hermitage thought that sounded like a good idea and nodded.

'Well,' Kenwald moved in his chair. 'I must not detain the king's man any longer. Allow me to allocate a brother to see you safe back.'

Hermitage took the offer gratefully. He thought he could probably work out the way, but his head was feeling very peculiar and he thought that he might find a comfortable spot for a little sleep.

The abbot rang a small bell and a moment later the door was opened and a young brother put his head around the door.

'Ah, Brother, would you see the King's Investigator safe back to Saint Werburgh's please.'

The brother, who Hermitage was pleased to see was not Brother Longor, looked very surprised at this request.

'We wouldn't want to keep King William's own representative from his duties,' the abbot explained.

The young monk looked even more alarmed at this but bowed his acknowledgement.

'And if you have any more you need to know, please don't hesitate to call again,' Kenwald bade Hermitage goodbye.

As his escort led him away from the study and towards the door of Saint John's, Hermitage could have sworn he heard Abbot Kenwald bark out an instruction. 'Bring me Brother Longor,' he said. 'Now.'

## Caput XVIII The Queen was in her Parlour

'What's going on here?' A male voice demanded from behind the press of nobles, who looked like they wanted to get at Cwen and do something uncalled for.

The woman who seemed to be leader of the pack spoke over her shoulder. 'We've caught this devil from Saint Werburgh's.'

'Indeed?' The man at the back sounded calm and only slightly interested. 'And you're going to do what, exactly? Without informing Her Majesty?'

There was hesitation among the nobles now, along with some shuffling of feet.

'Sorry, I didn't quite catch that?'

'Nothing.' The woman sounded like a petulant child who's been asked what they're going to do with that frog.

'Excellent. I thought that would be the case.'

'We were going to bring her to Her Majesty,' one of the young men of the group spoke up brightly.

'Of course, you were. And now you can.'

The crowd broke up slightly, and Cwen could see the stiff-looking attendant who had opened the door at the top of the stairs. He still held his staff, and even it managed to look at the rough gathering of Saxon nobility with some disdain.

'Here she is.' A young man reached out and took Cwen's arm pulling her towards the door. 'Ow,' he added, as Cwen stamped on his foot.

A flicker of a smile bothered the man with the staff. 'I will take her to Lady Ealdgyth.' He even gave Cwen a small nod of acknowledgement, then addressed the nobles. 'Why don't you all go outside and, erm, do, something?' This man had a clear understanding that whatever it was these people did, it would be completely pointless.

There was muttering of the nobles, and they milled about for a bit, before finding their way to the door. A few unhappy glances were cast back over shoulders, but they did as they were told.

'So?' The man cast his weary gaze on Cwen as if she was just the latest in a long list of life's trials. 'The nurse has come from Saint Werburgh's, eh?'

Cwen gave no reply.

'We had better discuss this with Lady Ealdgyth.' He beckoned that Cwen could lead the way back up the stairs.

She momentarily considered turning for the door and making a run for it, but thought that the dismissed nobles were probably out there sulking, and would only bring her back.

At the top of the stairs, the functionary nodded that Cwen could open the door. She did so and saw Ealdgyth sitting by the window that looked over the street. Another woman sat by her side doing some embroidery on a small wooden frame she held in her lap.

At the far end, to Cwen's right, Lyveva had the twins on her lap; the burbling baby noises being the loudest sound in the room. When she saw Cwen, Lyveva stopped making burbling baby noises and clutched the boys protectively.

'Ah,' Lady Ealdgyth said. 'The nurse who is not a nurse.'

'And from Saint Werburgh's,' Lyveva wailed.

'Just so,' Ealdgyth agreed. 'You may leave us now, Lyveva. 'And you mistress.' She nodded at the woman doing the embroidery who packed up her things and stood with a bow.

Lyveva was only too happy to get out of the room with the devil in it and scurried away as quickly as she could. She even walked around the edge of the room to keep as far away from

Cwen as possible.

Cwen was awfully tempted to say "boo" to her as she left, but thought she might drop the babies, and that would not go down well.

Once they were alone, the attendant with the staff opened the door once more, checked that there was no one outside and closed it again.

He nodded to Ealdgyth, who beckoned Cwen to draw near.

Telling herself that this was not the Queen of England, that it was only some Saxon who probably owned nothing anymore, didn't help much. She stood before the seated woman, but at least refused to bow.

'So, Weaver, if that is your name?' Ealdgyth was quite fierce.

'It is,' Cwen said. She was a weaver and it was common for people to be known by their trades. Why shouldn't she be Cwen Weaver?

'Here from Saint Werburgh's then.' This wasn't really a question.

'Could be,' Cwen shrugged.

'And what were you doing in that place?' Ealdgyth's manner was serious and quite intimidating. Unfortunately, she'd never met Cwen before and didn't know that this was entirely the wrong approach. Mistress Weaver didn't usually give as good as she got; she went way beyond that.

'The king sent us.' She said, her glare never wavering for a moment.

'The king?' Ealdgyth gave a light and entirely false laugh.

'William. Know him?'

'What is the king doing sending the likes of you to Chester?'

'I'm with his investigator. It's from the Latin, vestigare, to track. We track killers. We're looking into the murders of Brothers Abel and Pendle.'

Ealdgyth looked as if she was trying very hard not to be put off by this and wasn't quite managing it. 'And you track them to my house?'

'Of course,' Cwen held tightly on to the upper hand. 'One of our party recognised Abel. A Saxon from days gone by. Possibly with a noble connection of some sort. And what do we find in the middle of Chester? Why, a whole house full of nobles. And who better to murder a noble than another noble?' She turned her gaze on the attendant and his staff, both of whom looked rather offended at the examination.

Ealdgyth tried to wave this away. 'You're just a slip of a girl.'

'That's probably why King William finds me useful. And Le Pedvin, of course. Do you know him as well?'

The pale flush that ran down Ealdgyth's face said that she knew Le Pedvin; and the sorts of things he did.

'Why would the king be interested in the death of some monks?' Ealdgyth was still trying to dismiss this as nonsense but wasn't doing very well.

'May not be monks, you see. If Abel was a noble, or someone's old retainer, it could be that revenge is in the air. The king can't have people running around the country killing one another. That's his job.' Cwen was delighted to see quick looks of shock fly between Ealdgyth and her man.

'And,' Cwen went on, after just the right length of pause to add to the worry in the room. 'Lyveva tells me that Saint Werburgh's is full of devils. Or so the nobles here have told her.'

'Superstitious rumour,' Ealdgyth said.

'Superstitious rumour that Lyveva says you've got plans for. She heard you.' Cwen folded her arms now. 'Plans for dealing with the devils of Saint Werburgh's, two of whom are now dead.'

Ealdgyth and her man were now exchanging looks heavy with suggestion. Cwen took the opportunity to look around for a seat. She saw one by the wall, went to bring it over to Ealdgyth and then sat comfortably.

'The king's what, did you say?' Ealdgyth asked, with more genuine interest now.

'Investigator. The investigator himself is a monk, Brother Hermitage.'

Ealdgyth opened her mouth.

'Odd name for a monk, I know,' Cwen got in first. 'Nonetheless, he has been appointed by William to look into murders and the like. Well, mainly murders. Actually, only murders so far. He investigates and finds out who did what. He then reports to the king who takes the next step.'

'Next step?'

'Depends on the circumstances. Could be exile, could be something worse.'

'And where is this Brother Hermitage now? Why isn't he here?'

'Two reasons; one, he's not very good with babies and wouldn't pass for a nurse. Second, he's, what does he call it? Interrogating? That's it, he's interrogating the monks of Saint John.'

'Interrogating them?' Ealdgyth obviously didn't know the word, but she didn't like the sound of it.

'From the Latin, again,' Cwen gave a little smile.

'The monks of Saint John are a powerful force,' Ealdgyth's man spoke up.

'So is the King's Investigator,' Cwen said, the image popping into her head of Hermitage being trampled to death by the monks of Saint John.

There was a very long silence in the room now, although it seemed that the man and his queen were talking to one another without words.

'I think we'd better tell her,' Ealdgyth suggested.

He just shrugged in return that it was her decision. It was a shrug of mild encouragement, though.

'Tell me what?' Cwen leant forward.

Ealdgyth looked around the room, clearly thinking very carefully about whether to say more or not. Eventually, she took a breath and spoke. 'We have had our suspicions about Saint Werburgh's.'

'Like Saint John's have their suspicions?'

'No,' Ealdgyth dismissed that. 'Saint John's hates Saint Werburgh's as religious houses just naturally hate one another. There's nothing unusual there. No, we think there's more to Saint Werburgh's than meets the eye.'

'We?'

'Mathias and I.' She nodded towards the man with the stick, who was obviously Mathias.

'You think it is full of devils?'

'Of course not. We just spread that rumour to stop our idle nobles from putting their feet in dangerous waters. You are right that a noble with nothing to do can be dangerous. There's nothing like the promise of a devil to keep the superstitious at bay.'

'Like Lyveva.'

'Exactly. She wouldn't dare go anywhere near the place now.'

'So, what do you suspect? And more interestingly, what

have you done about it?'

'Done? Nothing. We have done nothing.' Ealdgyth was insistent on this point. 'We have been here for many months now, brought by my brother, Edwin, after the defeat at Hastings. We only escaped by the flick of a rabbit's tail. If it hadn't been for Edwin's quick thinking and some help from friends on both sides, we would have been lost.'

'Friends on both sides?'

'There are Normans who have lived in England for many years. There are even some in Chester.'

'Adversane?' Cwen asked.

Ealdgyth nodded. 'Yes, Adversane was a help.'

'I think we need to meet this Adversane, he keeps popping up.'

Ealdgyth had no comment on that. 'Anyway, all was quiet here, but then we started to notice things about Saint Werburgh's.'

'Things?'

'People.'

'People. Ah, well that is unusual, people in an abbey.' Cwen gave a heavy sigh that she wasn't being told anything interesting here.

'People arrived. New monks and priests. And they slipped quietly into Saint Werburgh's never to appear again.'

'You think they vanished?'

'No, they simply stayed there. Never came out and never participated in any of the town's ceremonies.'

'And what's odd about that?'

'Monks who hide themselves away give me concern.' Ealdgyth took another deep breath and seemed to pause before she went on. 'You can imagine that William would have been very happy with our capture at Hastings. Harold dead and his wife imprisoned.'

'Of course,' Cwen nodded, and tried to look as if she thought this was quite a good idea as well.

'And there were Saxons at Hastings who would have complied with his wishes.'

'Handed you over.'

'Just so. And they may not be satisfied with seeing us escape, they may be following. We cannot be too careful.'

'I think I begin to see.' Cwen was thoughtful. 'Fresh brothers arriving at Saint Werburgh's who may not be brothers at all.'

Ealdgyth acknowledged this with a tip of the head. 'Saint John's is so anxious to make sure travellers join them that they have boys at the gates, paid to direct monks into their care.'

'Really?' Cwen thought that would at least be a help to Hermitage in not actually getting lost between the gate and Saint John's.

'So, why would anyone go to Saint Werburgh's? Unless it was a deliberate destination.'

'Which it could be. Monks are funny people, believe me, I know.'

'And then they lock themselves up? And you have said yourself that this Abel may not be a monk at all.'

It was Cwen's turn to nod agreement. She put the story together for all their benefit. 'You think these Saxons, who would happily give you away to William, have come to Chester, presumably knowing that you're here.'

'That is what we believe. But we've managed to get no information out of Saint Werburgh's at all.'

'Are they here to capture you, kill you or just keep an eye on you?'

'Again, that we do not know. We are here in numbers so it would be hard for just one or two of them to do us harm.'

'And you've told your court that the place is full of devils so they'll keep away, and shout to the hills if they see anyone from Saint Werburgh's even coming close.'

'Which works admirably. The ones who escaped Hastings with us tended to be the ones more concerned with their own skin than the good of the land.'

'Lovely.'

'So, you see, there is no need for the king to be concerned about us, rather the other way round.'

Cwen gave all this careful thought. Or, rather, she tried to look as if she was giving it careful thought.

'Of course, there is an alternative,' she said.

'Really?'

'Yes. You escape to Chester after Hastings and start to make yourself comfortable. After all, William is miles away and it could be months, if not years before he gets this far north. Then, what do you find? Some Saxons who have gone over to William's way of thinking turn up.

'They settle themselves in Saint Werburgh's and get up to goodness knows what inside the walls. Perhaps they really are people who have had enough of war and battle and want to spend the remainder of their days in peace. You don't know, because you haven't spoken to them. They won't come out.

'That must be a bit of a worry. People in Saint Werburgh's watching you, plotting against you, or worse.' Cwen held up a finger as if she'd just thought of something. 'Here's an idea. Why not tell your rather stupid followers that Saint Werburgh's is full of devils. Not so that they keep away, but so that they deal with the devils in a more permanent manner. You could even offer a reward to the first one to kill a devil for you.'

'That's ridiculous,' Ealdgyth complained.

'Not at all. It's very sensible. It's what I'd do if I were in your shoes.'

Ealdgyth looked at her feet for a moment, obviously thinking that there was no way she was giving her shoes to this woman.

'And bring William down on us in a moment?' Mathias said.

Cwen turned to face him.

He explained. 'If these men are here to watch us, or do us harm, or even just report on us, what would be gained from getting rid of them? Once word got out, a force of Normans would be here in days. It would be just the excuse William needed: we killed his friends, so he gets to kill us.'

Cwen had to admit that did sound perfectly reasonable.

'In which case, who did kill Abel and Pendle?'

Mathias raised a single eyebrow. 'I believe you said you were with the investigator.' He gave a knowing smile. 'We look forward to finding out.'

## Caput XIX Lost and Found

Hermitage supposed that he should feel some relief that he had escaped Saint John's at all. He suspected that if Brother Longer had his way, the King's Investigator would be languishing in a cell somewhere; the sort of cell that didn't encourage languishing.

Outside of the main gate, he looked up and down the street as the activities of the evening took over from those of the day. He imagined that the town gate would be closed by now, and so he would have to hurry back to Saint Werburgh's if he was to be allowed admittance.

Far from being any actual help in getting him to Saint Werburgh's, the brother assigned as his guide simply pointed down the road and grunted, 'It's that way,' before he went back in again. Despite Abbot Kenwald's assurances, Hermitage was finding the Brothers of Saint John to be a positively difficult bunch.

As evening darkened further, he realised that he might have to seek out Cwen; she'd be good with the gatekeeper of Saint Werburgh's who didn't want to open his gate.

Still, Chester was not a huge place like London. He had his directions for the road to take and he knew that Saint Werburgh's was downhill from Saint John's. The road led downhill, so that must be the way.

Somehow, his surfeit of wine gave him a confidence that didn't feel natural. Still, he assured himself, things would get back to normal soon enough; his head would start aching, his stomach would churn,, and things would start going wrong once more.

After reaching the town wall, after which the only choice was to walk back uphill, Hermitage realised he was lost. Still, he reasoned, Chester was enclosed, and he could simply walk around the walls until he came to the main gate. From there he was sure he'd be able to find his way. Or perhaps find someone else who knew what his way should be. A further thought bothered him, Chester might have more than one gate.

This part of the town he was in was remarkably quiet. Nobody was about at all. The houses here seemed shut up and there were no taverns or other places for people to gather once the work of the day was done. He couldn't even see a church, for goodness' sake. Had this area been abandoned for some reason?

Could this be a plague quarter? Was that why it was empty? Hermitage looked about nervously. He didn't know what the signs of plague were that one should look for, he hardly expected to see dead bodies lying in the streets. He decided to move on a bit quicker.

Following a narrow lane that hugged the town wall as it made its circle, he came to darker and darker corners, where the buildings looked as if they were starting to plan an attack on the walls. The one nearest would lean against the wall, while the ones behind climbed up its back and escaped.

"Be sensible, Hermitage", he told himself. Telling himself things seldom worked, and it didn't now. He just couldn't work out whether the buildings were going to fall on him before the robbers jumped out, or afterwards.

'Eek,' he squeaked as a figure appeared out of the shadows in front of him. The robbers first, then.

'You look lost, Brother.' The figure stepped forward and was revealed as a very ordinary-looking fellow.

There was no sign of disease, no ragged clothes of the robber or the beggar, in fact, he looked quite out of place in this part of town. He clearly wasn't a noble, his clothes were not that fine, but he was no pauper either. Nor a man of the church. Just a perfectly normal inhabitant of Chester who just happened to be loitering in a dark alley and who had decided to jump out on a passing monk. And he looked a bit old for that sort of thing, being well over forty, by Hermitage's estimate.

'Oh, erm.' Hermitage thought about saying no, that he was perfectly fine and that he would be on his way now. The man appeared to be no threat though, and he had to admit he was completely lost. 'I was making my way from Saint John's to Saint Werburgh's.'

'Really?' The man sounded very surprised at this. 'And you ended up here? How did you manage that?'

'Well, I just sort of walked downhill from Saint John's and, erm, here I am.'

'Took the wrong road, to begin with, then,' the man explained.

Hermitage thought that statement accounted for quite a lot of his troubles in life as a whole.

'Not to worry, soon have you back on the path.' The man smiled and beckoned that Hermitage should carry on along the road the way he was going.

As Hermitage drew close, the fellow turned and joined him.

'I am Adversane, by the way.'

'Adversane? Good heavens.'

Adversane raised his eyebrows.

'I am Brother Hermitage, the King's Investigator.' He beamed a smile.

'No!' Adversane looked genuinely surprised by this.

'Yes.'

'As you say, good heavens. And what a coincidence.'

'I understand it was you who told the monks of Saint Werburgh's about me.'

'That's right. I have some contact with King William's court, and your position seemed perfectly appropriate in our circumstances. I have heard wonderful tales of the King's Investigator.'

Hermitage sincerely hoped there weren't actually any tales of the King's Investigator. How embarrassing would that be? And what would there be to tell? There was no way any of his experiences could be dragged out into a tale more than a page long.[12]

'King William?' he asked, feeling a tinge of worry.

'I am Norman by birth,' Adversane explained. 'But I have lived here for more years than I can remember. Since William's arrival, of course, things have changed. He wants to know who all the Normans are, and where they live.'

Hermitage could see that this made sense.

'Not that I've had many dealings with William himself.' Adversane started to look a bit apologetic for some reason. 'I am sorry to say that I am a distant relative of a rather awkward fellow called Le Pedvin. Have you heard the name?'

Hermitage felt the shiver run down his back and he looked quickly around, even though Le Pedvin was probably hundreds of miles away. He wouldn't put it past that ghastly man to be hiding in the shadows as well; all shadows, especially the ones in his room at night.

'I have come across him,' he managed to say.

'Terrible man,' Adversane said. 'He was all right when he was miles away, but now he's in the country, more's the pity.'

'And he's, erm, contacting all the local Normans?'

---

[12] Not that this stopped your author

'Quite. So, when I heard of the deaths at Saint Werburgh's I had a word with the abbot and suggested he might send for help.'

Hermitage managed to say, 'That was very thoughtful of you.' His real response was a bit less charitable.

'And have you made progress?'

'My enquiries are still at an early stage.' That phrase was coming in useful.

'How fascinating. But you have been to Saint John's.'

Hermitage wasn't sure how much he could tell this Adversane. The man was a Norman, after all, even if he had lived in England for a long time.

'I have. I need to gather as much information as possible, from as many people as I can.'

'Those of Saint John are of a difficult disposition,' Adversane said. 'Their hatred of Saint Werburgh's is clear for all to see. And most unchristian, if I may say.' He nodded an apology to Hermitage.

'That's fine,' Hermitage said. 'We encountered Brother Longor at an early stage.'

'Ah.' Adversane nodded heavily. 'That brother. A troubled fellow, if ever I saw one.' His look said that there was a lot more to tell, but it was not for him to do so.

They walked on together for a few more moments in silence.

'And now you return to Saint Werburgh's.'

'I do.'

Adversane shook his head sadly. 'Who would kill two brothers like that? Who would kill two brothers at all?'

'You know of erm?'

'Brother Pendle, yes. I must confess that I am a very minor benefactor to Saint Werburgh's, hence my contact with the abbot. I heard all the awful details.'

'It's usually a case of finding out who would gain from a death.'

'Usually?' Adversane sounded intrigued in a slightly macabre manner.

'In my other investigations.'

'Ah, of course.'

'We know how they were killed. We just need to find the person who had the opportunity and the motive.'

'A motive for killing two brothers in an abbey. I'm sure I can't think of one.'

Hermitage didn't like to say that he couldn't either. There was still the question around Wat knowing who Abel was, or rather not knowing who he was but knowing that he was someone. Despite Adversane's apparent knowledge of events, and his involvement in the investigation already, Hermitage was reluctant to tell him too much. If Adversane thought that Abel was a monk, then it was probably best to leave it like that.

There might be other knowledge to be gleaned though. If Adversane was a benefactor of Saint Werburgh's he could have all sorts of useful information.

'Is there anyone else who has problems with Saint Werburgh's?' he asked. 'Anyone who might wish them harm?'

'Good heavens, no,' Adversane seemed disappointed by the question. 'Saint Werburgh's is a quiet house of contemplation and service. I suspect Abbot Fulmer would rather the doors were kept closed at all times; stop anyone from the outside world getting in.'

Hermitage could sympathise with that. If he had doors that could keep King William and Le Pedvin out of his life, he'd nail them shut.

'They take no part in town life?'

'Oh, they do their part. Their saint's day in February is a great event.'

Hermitage nodded to himself, mainly nodding that this was of no use to him at all.

'We are told that many of the houses in town are owned by the churches and by Saint John's and Saint Werburgh's.'

'That's true. But it's been the case since their establishment.'

'No disputes at all then?'

'None that I am aware of.'

'I see.' Hermitage knew that it was perfectly normal for people to cause trouble over houses and property. He didn't really understand why, but then that was perfectly normal as well.

'Perhaps these individual brothers had upset someone?' Adversane suggested.

'Abbot Fulmer said that they had been here for several months. Strange that this should occur now. Particularly as Saint Werburgh's keeps itself to itself.'

'True.' Adversane was looking as lost for explanations as the official investigator.

'You have had an arrival of Saxon nobility recently.' Hermitage tried to make this sound as nonchalant as possible as if it had nothing to do with anything.

'Noble no more,' Adversane said with a sorry shake of the head. 'All of them deposed by William and resting in Chester because it's a long way away, I suspect.'

'And they show no interest in Saint Werburgh's?'

Adversane appeared surprised by the suggestion. 'They show no interest in anything but themselves. I was able to assist them with lodgings when they first arrived, but I think they largely attend Saint John's, anyway.'

'Really?'

'Of course. Abbot Kenwald would have made sure he was the first to greet them. And to get his denigrations of Saint Werburgh's in, I imagine.'

'So, these Saxons could have concerns about Saint Werburgh's as well. Put there by Abbot Kenwald.'

'I hardly think Saxons fleeing from King William are going to bother killing a couple of quiet monks. What would they gain from it?'

Hermitage had nothing to offer to that.

Adversane frowned and rubbed the back of his head. 'Unless they weren't monks, of course?'

'Not monks?'

'We know these Saxons fled to Chester, they make no secret of the fact. I am sure there will be others who want to simply disappear in the face of William's advance. People who may have made firm enemies in the conflict. What better place than an abbey, or monastery? Become a monk and vanish.'

Hermitage was a monk, but he hadn't managed to vanish.

'Are you saying that Abel and Pendle weren't brothers at all?'

'I really don't know, I only ever saw them in chapel. It's only an idea.' Adversane shrugged. 'Still, I expect you'd already thought of that, being the King's Investigator and all.'

'Oh, quite,' Hermitage tried to sound confident. 'Although, I really don't know what you've heard.'

'The story of the murder of Umair?'[13]

'Oh, yes,' Hermitage didn't like to bring back to mind all

[13] *The Case of the Curious Corpse* - in which Umair gets murdered.

the horrible things he'd already dealt with. The one in front of his face was more than enough.

'I must say, I never knew a king would need an investigator.'

'Me neither,' Hermitage sighed.

'From the Latin, vestigare?'

'It is.' Hermitage brightened a little. He was always happy to talk about where words came from. What they did when they got here was more of a problem.

'Remarkable. Well, here we are.'

Hermitage looked out from his reverie and saw that they had arrived back in the bustling centre of Chester. And there was Saint Werburgh's. He'd never thought he'd be grateful to see an abbey with dead monks in it. He did notice that the door was firmly shut now, which could be a problem.

'I cannot thank you enough, Master Adversane.' Hermitage bowed his acknowledgement. 'I could have wandered the streets of Chester for hours without your help.'

'It's nothing,' Adversane waved the thanks away. 'It has been a pleasure to meet the King's Investigator, having heard so much about you. I can only apologise for bringing you into this sorry business in the first place. But then, I suppose this is the sort of thing that intrigues you and is your daily bread.'

'Oh, yes,' Hermitage said, thinking that there was no reason for Adversane to make him feel any worse than he did already.

'Will you get in though?' Adversane nodded towards the closed gates of the abbey. 'It is past sunset, and I know the rule is quite strict on these matters. Even I have no influence over that.'

Hermitage prepared for a new set of worries, but then saw his salvation coming down the road.

'Oh, it'll be fine, I'm sure. Here comes Cwen.'

'Cwen?'

'Yes, she, erm, works with me. On the investigations.' Hermitage didn't really know what else to say. For a moment it occurred to him that maybe he shouldn't have mentioned Cwen. Too late now.

Adversane and Hermitage moved to the door of Saint Werburgh's and waited for Cwen to join them.

'Ah, Cwen,' Hermitage said brightly. 'This is Master Adversane, he helped me find my way back here when I got rather misplaced in the streets of Chester.'

'Oh, yes?' Cwen said. She gave Adversane her customary appraisal; blatant, bordering on the rude. 'The same Adversane who brought us here in the first place?'

'I have apologised for that.' Adversane smiled.

'And the same Adversane who welcomed the Saxons to Chester, I hear?'

'I organised a roof for their heads. It seemed the least I could do. I am fortunate to own one or two houses in the town.'

'Hm.' Cwen sounded as if putting roofs over the heads of Saxons was very suspicious.

'But I shall leave you now.' Adversane bowed. 'And wish you a pleasant evening. If you are denied admittance at this late hour just come and find me. Perhaps I can find another roof. Ask for Adversane, everyone knows me.'

Cwen said nothing, but Hermitage nodded his head gratefully. It was nice to be wished a pleasant evening, even if he was pretty certain he wasn't going to get one.

'Right,' Cwen said, once Adversane had gone. 'Let's get back in and find Wat. I've got quite a lot to report. You?'

'Oh, erm, yes.' Hermitage realised that he probably had

found out quite a bit, particularly about Brother Longor.

'And we'll find out who the sickly one in the tower is as well.'

'Ah, yes. Of course, it could be simply a genuinely ill monk who is being properly cared for and is of no help at all.'

'More than likely.' Cwen agreed. 'Here, lend me that.' She nodded at the staff that Hermitage had been carrying all this time.

Hermitage frowned but handed it over.

Cwen held the thing up and banged the bottom of it three times on the door of Saint Werburgh's. There was no response and so she started banging again, this time without any indication that she would stop until she was answered.

When there was still no response, she simply gave Hermitage a smile, indicating that she was prepared to keep this up all night.

Eventually, a small window opened in the door and the face of the gatekeeper appeared.

'We're back,' Cwen said.

'Then I shall open the door for you,' the door monk even gave a little smile.

'Thank you.' Cwen looked pleasantly surprised.

'In the morning,' the door monk added as he slammed the little door.

Cwen simply shrugged and started banging on the door again. After what felt like an embarrassingly long time, when there was no response, she moved over to the small side door and continued her hammering on that. As she did so, she noticed something and stepped back to consider the door.

Hermitage was pleased that she'd stopped hammering but was worried about what she was going to do next.

She bent to peer at the door quite closely and then looked

to its left and right. Apparently coming to some conclusion or other, she took a pace back. She then stepped quickly forward once more, lifting her right leg as she did so to give the door a firm kick.

Her foot landed right by the handle, which immediately surrendered to her blow and flew off completely. The door swung back on its hinges with a mighty crash into the wall behind.

Cwen stepped back now and bowed to indicate that Hermitage could go first.

He wanted to do no such thing, so Cwen stepped inside and then waved him to follow.

He did so reluctantly, deeply ashamed to be involved in any of this.

He felt even worse as he considered the crumpled heap of the monk who had been standing behind the door when it opened.

## Caput XX Meetings to Die For

'Now to find Wat,' Cwen announced. 'I suppose the herbalist's would be the best start. He must have got into the tower by now, but you never know.' She stepped off smartly into the body of the abbey.

'I think we should make sure the fellow behind the door is still alive, perhaps?' Hermitage suggested, with a hint of a reprimand.

'Who?' Cwen turned to look. 'Oh, him? What an idiot.'

'Cwen, you kicked the door open right into his face.'

'He shouldn't have been standing behind it.'

'That was his job. Might you have called out a warning?'

'If I'd called out a warning, he might have put a bar across the door or something. Then we'd never have got in.'

Hermitage just tutted and went over to the door monk, who was just starting to stir. At least there wasn't another death to be investigated. Hermitage didn't know what he'd do if he had to report that Cwen had killed a monk with a door.

'There you are.' Cwen waved a hand. 'He's fine.'

Hermitage gave her an open stare. 'He is not fine. You and I are fine, we're standing up talking. He is lying on the ground moaning with the imprint of a door on his head.'

'He's probably used to it.'

'Used to it?'

'Being a door monk. This sort of thing probably happens all the time.'

Hermitage picked up the broken pieces of door handle that were laying there. 'I don't think it's ever happened before.'

'He's an awkward so-and-so who wouldn't let us in,' Cwen complained. 'What else were we supposed to do?'

'Wait?'

'While there are monks being murdered?'

'No monks are being murdered. They've already been murdered, it's quite a different thing.'

'Please yourself. You stay and look after the monk, I'll go and find Wat and we can get on with finding the killer.'

Hermitage found this attitude quite irritating. He knew Cwen was fierce and fearless and determined, but knocking an innocent monk to the ground and then leaving him was just heartless.

'He was only following his instruction; quite reasonable instruction to keep the gate shut after sundown. We didn't even explain why we needed to get in.'

'He should have been more cooperative.' Cwen did sound as if she might be starting to see the edge of the shadow of a reason to conclude she might have been wrong. She wasn't going to take any notice of it, though.

'I shall give the poor fellow here your apologies,' he said. He also thought he'd better store this event away for a later discussion with Cwen.

'If you like,' Cwen said, and then she was gone.

Hermitage turned his attention to the monk who was now recovering more of his senses.

'Here, let me help you.' Hermitage pulled the man into a sitting position. He then squatted down and looked at him with sympathy. He did wonder if he ought to get some clean water or fetch the herbalist, or something. Looking sympathetic seemed best, just at the moment.

The door monk lifted a hand to his damaged head and groaned. 'Oh, my Lord,' he said in a low voice.

'Are you all right?' Hermitage asked, immediately seeing that it was a bit of a stupid question.

The monk moved slowly and painfully. He mumbled something that Hermitage couldn't quite make out. He bent in close to hear.

'Where is she?' the monk asked.

'She? The woman who wanted the door open? Cwen?'

The monk nodded.

'She has gone off into the monastery to continue our hunt for the killer of Abel and Pendle. I am sorry that you got injured in this manner.'

The monk managed a nod to acknowledge Hermitage. 'Could you fetch the woman?'

'Fetch her. I suppose I could see if I could get her to come back.' That was the best Hermitage could offer as he knew perfectly well that Cwen wouldn't come back. 'Do you want to see her?'

The monk shook his head in a painful manner. He beckoned Hermitage to draw close again and he whispered his words. 'I want to kill her.'

Hermitage stepped back as the monk wound himself around to get back to his feet. 'Oh, really. You're as bad as one another.'

Having lost all sympathy for the injured monk, Hermitage turned to find Cwen and Wat.

'Is everything all right here?' a voice from the door asked.

Hermitage looked over and saw Adversane standing there.

'I heard a mighty crash and thought there had been some other calamity.'

'Oh, er, no, no,' Hermitage said. 'It's all fine. The door got a bit stuck, that's all.'

Adversane looked at the door monk who was standing now but was still rubbing his head and had a vicious look on his face. He stepped forward to assist the man.

'I must, erm, get off.' Hermitage waved towards the interior of the monastery.

'Oh, quite, quite,' Adversane agreed. 'I'll make sure this fellow is cared for.'

Grateful that the worry was taken from his hands, Hermitage set off once more. He was quickly back in the main courtyard of the abbey and saw no sign of anyone. As Cwen had suggested the herbalist's workshop, he thought he would go there first, but then he saw that the door to Merle's less inviting residence was hanging open.

He knew that few of the inhabitants of that place were likely to get up and leave, but it did seem odd.

He wandered slowly in that direction, hoping that Merle would emerge any moment and he could go back to looking at herbs instead of bodies. When he was only a step or two from the door, he heard voices from inside.

He quickly told himself that no, Abel and Pendle had not got better and the whole business had not turned out to be a simple mistake. Voices meant people; living ones. The voice that was speaking rang a very vague bell in the back of his head, but he couldn't put a name to it.

The next voice was perfectly recognisable: Cwen. And she sounded quite excited. That was seldom a good thing and so he hurried his paces into the room.

There were four people in there, sitting on stools around the still empty fireplace. Wat and Cwen, Merle the man of the dead and one other. Hermitage recognised him and breathed a sigh of relief. Ah, that was all right then. It was only King Harold. Everything would be fine now.

Then he thought that King Harold was looking remarkably well for a man who'd been killed quite some time ago. He followed this with the recollection that he was in a room that already contained a number of dead bodies. Next, he felt his head go round and thought a bit of a lie down would be nice.

Soon after that, he thought that Cwen didn't need to slap him quite so hard just to wake him up. His head was now throbbing nicely from the wine of Saint John's, and Cwen hitting it was not helping at all.

He opened his eyes and saw the four faces looking down on him. Brother Merle's expression was abject disappointment that he wasn't going to have some more preparation to do.

There was Wat and Cwen, and there was Harold again. He knew it was Harold and he could see that the king was alive and well and not in the least bit dead. Nonetheless, his certain knowledge that the king had been killed at Hastings refused to be put away. Instead, it just made him whimper a bit.

'I am not dead, Brother.' Harold said with a smile.

Hermitage was forced to agree; it seemed sensible in the circumstances.

Wat leaned down now and took Hermitage under the arms, heaving to get him back on his feet.

'The king escaped Hastings with some help and has now been settled here as an anchor.'

'An anchor?' Confusing Hermitage, even more, was not kind.

'Anchorite,' Harold corrected.

'Ah.' At least Hermitage understood that. He still gave Harold a slightly sideways look, half expecting the trick to be revealed at any moment.

They all returned to the hearth and sat in a close huddle.

'It's really him,' Wat confirmed Harold's identity for

Hermitage. 'He knows all about the tapestries he bought from me.'

That wouldn't be Hermitage's chosen means of identification, but he supposed it would suffice.

'Then?' Hermitage had so many questions that they all rolled themselves into one and became complete nonsense.

'Quite.' Wat seemed to understand anyway. 'What are monks doing getting themselves murdered in the monastery that houses the old king?'

Hermitage just nodded.

'And it's even more odd when we discover that Brother Abel was, in fact, a Saxon Noble's man called Lefsius.'

Hermitage moved his head round in a bit of a circle; a nod that he had heard the words, a shake that he didn't understand them.

'And Pendle was called Walter, a Norman Noble's retainer.'

'A Norman?' Hermitage was really puzzled about that. 'Who would kill a Norman?'

'Anyone who could?' Cwen suggested.

'Unless they didn't know he was a Norman,' Hermitage suggested. 'The killer may have thought he really was an ordinary monk.'

'And that's better, is it? Killing ordinary monks instead of Normans?'

Cwen should know the answer to that question. 'And Abel was a Saxon?' Hermitage checked.

'That's right.' Harold confirmed.

'Ah.' Hermitage had managed to ignore the fact that the dead king was in the room with him. 'Erm, Your Majesty,' he added.

'No need for that now,' Harold said. 'It is as Master Wat

said, I have retired to this place, albeit at the behest of Duke William. He obviously hid the fact of my escape from Hastings. After all, as a new king, he wanted it believed that the old one was dead.

'I then travelled over the sea with the help of the Danes before eventually returning here. One more attempt to unseat William failed and so I agreed to come here.'

'You mean William told you to come here or die?' Wat suggested.

'That was about it, yes.'

Hermitage had now managed to incorporate all this new knowledge. He thought he'd achieved it quite quickly; it normally took weeks of careful study.

'If Abel was really a Saxon, did he know you were here?' He asked the erstwhile king.

'That's just what we've been discussing, and we think not. Not to begin with, at least. Brother Bodin is my guard, and not even the abbot knows who he has in his tower.'

'If someone did find out who Abel was, I can understand a death. But killing a Norman as well?' Hermitage couldn't really understand any death at all. Even if Abel had been a Saxon of some import, he was an older and broken man. The poor fellow didn't look as if he'd be a threat to anyone. Mind you, he had been dead for a while now, so that probably didn't help his looks.

'Saxons,' Cwen said, nodding knowledgeably.

'What about them?' Hermitage couldn't see that the word was much help.

'Saxons would kill a Norman. And I've just been with the Saxons of Lady Ealdgyth, I was just about to tell the others.'

Harold nodded that she should continue.

'As far as I could tell, Ealdgyth and her man, Mathias, are a sensible pair.'

'I know Mathias well,' Harold said. 'Always a cautious and careful fellow. I can't see him doing anything like this.'

'Quite,' Cwen agreed. 'They both saw that killing monks would only be trouble. William might use it as an excuse to bring death to everyone.'

The room nodded sombrely at this; only Merle seemed to perk up at the suggestion of widespread death.

'The others with her though? Not so sure.'

'Do you know who they were?' Harold asked.

'I got no names, but they all seemed to be idiots. There must be at least six or eight of them. A woman and two men had been sent off to find a nurse.'

'A nurse?' Harold raised his eyes.

'Ah, yes,' Cwen looked as if she shouldn't have opened her mouth; a rare occurrence for her. 'There are, erm, children. Well, babies, really.'

'Babies?'

Cwen swallowed and took the plunge. 'Ulf and erm, Harold. Twins.'

Harold sat back with a sigh and look that was hard to fathom. It could be fear that there were now two more innocents who could fall to William's sword, or was it triumph that he had at least inflicted some sort of defeat on William? 'My sons,' he said.

'Some more sons,' Wat mumbled quietly, reminding Harold that he already had three sons who had dealt with the Norman invasion spectacularly; by running away.

No one else had anything constructive to say and left Harold to his contemplation.

'Does Ealdgyth know that Harold is here?' Hermitage asked when the silence had gone on a bit too long for comfort.

'I didn't know he was here myself until I got back,' Cwen replied. 'There was certainly no mention of it when I was there. Everyone was worried that the Normans would be coming for them. That's why Ealdgyth and Mathias wanted St Werburgh's left alone.'

'You said there were others?' Wat asked. 'Six or eight altogether?'

'That's right. The ones I came across think Saint Werburgh's is full of devils. One of them could well be stupid enough to think that killing devils would put them in good stead with Ealdgyth.'

'They might not even know that this particular devil was a Norman,' Wat said.

'Probably wouldn't. And they might kill Abel, not knowing he was Saxon either. And using religious clothing to kill devils is probably the way you're supposed to do it.'

Hermitage just gave this nonsense a little snort.

More silent thought didn't really take them any further forward.

'And what did you find out at Saint John's?' Wat asked.

'Oh, yes,' Hermitage remembered where he'd been now. 'Well, the abbot there seemed genuinely concerned about the King's Investigator being here and how he might be shown in a bad light to the king. I mean, the new, er that is, William.' He gave Harold an apologetic glance.

'There was one other though, Brother Longor.'

'The one we met coming into town?'

'That's him. He seems a very aggressive fellow, and perhaps a bit out of control. The abbot didn't seem at all happy with him.'

'So, even if the abbot didn't have anything to do with it,

Longor might have taken things into his own hands, and killed Abel and Pendle, not knowing who they were.'

'It is possible.' Hermitage had to nod. 'I also met Adversane while I was coming back here.'

'Ah,' Wat said. 'The famous Adversane. We're all here and it's his fault.'

Hermitage ignored that. 'He said that he thought Longor was a troubled fellow.'

'He'd have to be pretty troubled to start murdering monks.' Wat rubbed his hands together. 'I think we need another word with friend Bodin first. It's certain that he knows more than he's telling. If he's the Norman guarding Harold, he could well have removed Abel as a threat.'

'And Pendle, another Norman?' Hermitage asked.

'That is a bit more unlikely,' Wat admitted. 'It's a shame they went in the order they did. If Abel had killed Pendle, having found out he was a Norman, Bodin might have killed Abel in revenge.'

'Lovely,' Cwen said. 'I think Abel was a bit too dead for that though.'

'Right,' Wat stood. 'Off to the Herbalist.' He gestured everyone to leave the room and they bade Brother Merle farewell. It was alarming that he looked at them all as if he hoped to see them again very soon; in a much more official capacity.

Back at the workshop, Wat hammered on the door and got no response.

'Could be out tending a brother?' Hermitage suggested.

'He does seem to know his herbs,' Harold added. 'Even if he is a Norman guard as well.'

'We'll go in and wait.' Wat lifted the latch and the door swung open easily. 'I don't suppose he needs to lock it now that he doesn't have a king in the loft anymore.'

They filed in and saw straight away why Bodin didn't need to lock the door anymore.

'Oh, no,' said Brother Hermitage. 'Not another one?'

## Caput XXI The Herbalist's Cure

'This is getting ridiculous.' Cwen seemed to hold the dead body of Bodin responsible for the whole situation. 'First a Saxon, then a Norman, now the guard who was supposed to be looking after everything.'

The four of them drew close to the prostrate figure of Brother Bodin. There was no doubt that the herbalist was dead; no doubt at all. No herbalist in Hermitage's experience had ever done anything quite so personal with a sprig of hawthorn. More than a sprig, really, more like a whole branch. And knowing how sharp the thorns on hawthorn were, it was going to be a bit messy getting it out again.

'Erm,' was all he had to say on the topic before them.

'Good Lord,' Harold said, as he was the first to go over and kneel at Bodin's side. 'Who would do such a thing?'

'And how,' Wat added.

'With a hammer?' Cwen suggested, helpfully miming the hammering of a hawthorn branch into a herbalist. She added a charming impression of the gurgling noise such a herbalist might make at the time.

'Cwen, really,' Hermitage chided.

'Well, he wasn't very nice, was he?'

'That's as may be, but killing people because they aren't very nice is still appalling.'

Cwen shrugged that they weren't going to agree on that.

'He's only very recently dead,' Harold reported. 'Still warm.'

Hermitage held a hand to his mouth, instructing his stomach to stay where it was.

'But who?' Wat asked. 'It's not that long ago that we left him alive. Someone's been pretty quick to get in here, do that and then get away.'

'Follows the pattern as well, doesn't it,' Cwen said.

'Follows the pattern?' Hermitage asked, not understanding.

'Yes. Like you follow a pattern to make a tapestry, these murders are following a pattern. Two monks killed with holy clothing and now a herbalist done to death with a herb; quite a big one on the end of a stick, but still a herb.'

'Holy clothing?' Hermitage was aghast at that.

'You know what I mean.'

'Brother Bodin was also a monk,' Hermitage pointed out. 'He too could have been killed with,' he swallowed, 'holy clothing.' He crossed himself at the atrocious description of religious regalia.

'Who knows who the monks are?' Wat asked. 'Abel was a Saxon from the old days and Pendle was a Norman. They could have come here for genuine reasons, but to choose the abbey with King Harold in it? And Bodin we know was a Norman guard. It's all too much of a coincidence.'

'Bodin could be a Viking for all the dangerous and stupid people Ealdgyth keeps around her knew,' Cwen offered. 'They'd have just killed another devil.'

'Or Brother Longor came over to do more damage to the reputation of Saint Werburgh's, this time by killing their herbalist.' Wat shrugged.

Harold stood now, obviously satisfied that the herbalist was dead from a surfeit of hawthorn.

They gathered around the body of Bodin, perhaps hoping that something would become clear that would help explain all this.

'What's the third thing?' Wat waved his hand around in the air as if trying to retrieve a word that was just out of reach of his tongue.

'The third thing?' Hermitage asked, looking around. 'Third thing of what?'

'You know.'

'I'll have to take your word for that.' Hermitage tried to look lost, which he did very well because he was.

'Murders.' Wat was now snapping his fingers in irritation at not being able to recall.

'The third thing of murders?'

'That's it. What is it?'

'Sorry, Wat. I don't have a clue what you're talking about.'

'Yes, you do,' Wat contradicted. 'The first one is how they were done, the second is why they were done?'

'Oh,' Hermitage had it now. 'Opportunity. We know how they were all killed. We have two main motivations at the moment; the Saxons and Brother Longor. Who had the opportunity?'

'That's it. I knew it began with opp. Who had the opportunity?'

'Could have been either group,' Hermitage said. 'We don't actually know when Abel and Pendle were killed.'

'But we know when Bodin was, near enough; very recently.'

'The killer could still be here,' Cwen said, with some unfortunate relish.

Hermitage felt like another sit down.

'And the door is locked,' Harold said. He gestured outside, where it was now fully dark. 'No one could get out as it's always locked at sunset. Bodin assured me that the gatekeeper is most dedicated to his task, another reason for me to stay where I was put.'

'Ah,' Cwen said, looking more at the floor than anyone else.

Wat gave her his disappointed look. 'What have you done

to the gate?'

'Nothing,' she protested.

'Nothing?' Hermitage almost shrieked. 'I would hardly describe that as nothing.'

'I didn't do anything to the gate that isn't normal. I just opened it, that's all,' Cwen insisted. 'The gatekeeper just objected.'

'And?' Wat pressed.

Hermitage gave the rest of the explanation. 'He objected by getting in the way of the door when Cwen kicked it open.'

'Oh, nasty.'

'He was conscious when I left, but that's about the best I could say for him.'

'So, the door isn't locked anymore,' Wat said. 'And hasn't been for some time. Our killer could have got away while the gatekeeper was having a lie-down.'

Cwen's look said that it wasn't her fault while acknowledging that it was, really.

'But who could it have been?' Harold looked very thoughtful. 'Brother Hermitage, you were at the monastery of Saint John.'

'I was.'

'And you only got back here after the gate had shut; before it was opened again.' He gave Cwen the same disappointed look Wat used.

'That's right.'

'And this Brother Longor was with you at Saint John's?'

'He was.' Hermitage confirmed.

'And Mistress Cwen,' Harold turned to her. 'You were at Lady Ealdgyth's?'

'Actually, he wasn't,' Hermitage interrupted.

'Who wasn't what?'

'Brother Longor. I mean, he was there. He took me to see Abbot Kenwald but after that, I don't know where he was. I certainly heard the abbot summon him as I left, but I never saw him again.'

'Aha,' Harold said.

'Oh, you can do it too,' Cwen said brightly.

'Do it too?' Harold looked confused.

'Yes. When Hermitage works out who did it, he says "Aha".'

'Does he?'

'He does.'

'Well, that's very interesting. But I don't know who did it.'

'Oh.' Cwen was disappointed and looked daggers at Harold for leading them on like that.

'All I meant was, "Aha", Brother Longor is not accounted for.'

'Right.'

'So he could have come here, got in before the gate closed and then escaped when it was open.'

'Or the Saxons did the same,' Cwen said. 'One of Ealdgyth's lot could have got in, did the trick with the hawthorn and the herbalist and then made their escape.'

'Or,' Wat said, quite loudly. 'There is someone else in this monastery who is killing people close to King Harold. I still think it's a bit too much of a coincidence that the old king is here and people keep dying. Never mind monasteries who want to make one another look bad or Saxons who think they're killing the devil. The king is real and here and now. And someone is killing those around him.'

Everyone looked very thoughtful for quite a while, without coming up with anything helpful.

'Should we tell Brother Merle about the herbalist?'

Hermitage suggested. 'I'm sure he'll need to know.'

'I'm sure he'll want to,' Cwen said. 'Make his day.'

'And the abbot,' Harold added. 'He must be told that there has been another death.'

'Poor fellow,' Hermitage sympathised. 'If there is one person we should not suspect it's Abbot Fulmer. He doesn't even know King Harold is here and he sent for me to investigate the murders in the first place.'

'Could be a trick,' Cwen suggested.

'A trick?'

'Yes, throw you off your vestigare.'

'My what?' Hermitage wondered why Cwen had started babbling.

'Your track,' she explained with some impatience. 'Vestigare, to track?'

'No, no no.' Hermitage shook his head. 'Vestigare is to track. A track would be semita. A path or footway, if you will.'

'What?' Cwen looked quite angry now.

'To say that you are doing some tracking is a different word than saying you are on a track.' Hermitage was happy that this was clear.

'Stupid language,' Cwen concluded. 'Anyway, the abbot could be tricking us. He knows Harold is here, he killed the monks and brought Hermitage in to find it was someone else. He goes around being all innocent just to confuse us.'

'Or because he is all innocent,' Hermitage suggested.

'And why did he kill the monks?' Wat asked. 'What's his motivation?'

'He's a secret monk killer.' Cwen wasn't giving up.

'As he's had a monastery full of them for years, he's a bit of a late starter,' Wat pointed out.

Cwen just grumbled to herself that it could have been him and that no one ever listened to her.

'I suppose,' Hermitage said with careful deliberation, 'that everyone is suspect.'

'There you are,' Cwen crowed.

'As we have no clear indication of who it might be, we must assume it could be anyone, until we can, erm, remove them.'

'Remove them?' Wat sounded rather alarmed. 'That seems a bit drastic.'

'From the investigation,' Hermitage clarified hurriedly. 'We remove them from the investigation. If we can show who could not have done it, we'll be left with the one who did.'

'Sounds like that could take a while,' Wat seemed a bit bored with the whole thing.

'But, if we can't prove who did do it, we must prove who didn't.'

'Is there another word for that then?' Cwen complained.

'For what?'

'Investigating people to prove they didn't do it. Your wonderful Latin must have a word for it. It has a word for everything else.'

Ignoring Cwen's tone, Hermitage gave it some thought. 'Perhaps eliminate.'

'Eliminate?' Cwen frowned. 'Sounds a bit, sort of, final, somehow.'

'From ex, out and limen, the threshold. Out of the threshold of the investigation.' He was quite happy with this. 'That's it, we shall go and eliminate the abbot.'

'I think someone better warn him,' Wat said quietly.

'If we're suspecting people, why not Merle?' Cwen suggested as they left the room. 'He likes dead people. Perhaps he just went out and made some more?'

Hermitage pondered this but only for a moment. 'He would be in the same position as the abbot. If he kills people, why hasn't he been doing it for years?'

'The supply of dead monks suddenly dried up?' Cwen offered. 'Pendle was found in Merle's workplace after all.'

'When Merle was not there.'

'Only because he'd killed Pendle but wanted to leave him for someone else to discover.'

Hermitage sighed. 'Oh, this is hopeless. We have some people who could have done it and quite a few who might want to for various reasons.'

'We do have more questions for the abbot though,' Wat said. 'About Bodin, mainly.' He turned to Harold. 'Was he here when you arrived?'

'He was. He seemed to be well established here.'

'But he was obviously William's man. How could William have placed him here in time to guard you?'

'Maybe he didn't. It could be that Bodin was a local herbalist, loyal to William. He could even be Norman himself. Sorry, he could have been Norman himself.'

'But William must have sent word that you were coming and what his duties were going to be.'

They all nodded at that, but no one could see that it was much help.

'We tell Merle he's got another body to play with, and then we go to Abbot Fulmer.'

'I don't think Brother Merle plays with the bodies,' Hermitage objected.

'I wouldn't be so sure about that,' Cwen said.

Hermitage tutted at her. 'And it could still be as Wat says, there is another in the monastery who is doing this. One we do not know about. We had best ask Abbot Fulmer about his other brothers.'

'There don't seem to be that many. And we already met four of them.' Cwen obviously thought that this wouldn't take long.

'It won't take long then,' Hermitage smiled. 'I just feel that we don't have enough information yet.'

'Oh, yes, let's find that everyone's a possible killer, that'll help.'

'I suppose the abbot is going to have to find a new herbalist now,' Wat observed. 'Can't be very convenient, having one of them die.'

'And not a very good thing for a herbalist to do anyway,' Cwen added. 'They're supposed to cure people, after all.'

They all gave Brother Bodin a respectful look and left him with the hawthorn that had very successfully cured him of being alive.

## Caput XXII The Compline Collation

Brother Merle took the news of Bodin's death with surprising irritation. 'How many more of them am I supposed to deal with?' he complained.

There wasn't really an answer to that.

'Can't you bury the first one to make room?' Cwen suggested.

'Abbot doesn't want them taken away,' Merle grumbled. 'Says as how we've got to know who did it before we can give them Christian burial. That's all very well for him to say, isn't it? He's not the one who's got to find space for them all.'

'There's only three,' Wat pointed out.

'That's three more than I had this time last week. One at a time, that's the decent way. Take 'em in, prepare them, take them out, then do the next one. I've only got one pair of hands you know.'

Wat nodded that this was indeed the case.

'Leave him where he is then,' Cwen said, clearly thinking that this was not their problem.

'I can't leave a dead herbalist in the herbalist's workshop. He'd make everything go off.'

'Go off?'

'The herbs and such. Can't be good for them having the humours of the dead seeping out all over the place.'

Hermitage didn't want to think about that. 'Well, we're off to see the abbot now, so we can let him know you've got a problem.'

'Tell him to stop people dying,' Merle instructed as they left him to his overcrowding.

Making their way back through the convolutions of the abbey to the abbot's study, Hermitage thought that he was perfectly entitled to be irritated by all the dead people if even the man whose job it was to deal with them was finding them annoying. He assumed that Brother Merle had chosen his area of specialism. Kings had dropped Hermitage's right on his head. And now one of those kings was here with him. He still didn't feel this was the moment to start complaining about his lot in life.

And anyway, Harold wasn't king anymore, he could hardly relieve Hermitage of his burden if he didn't have the authority. Still, perhaps if he got one king to say he was no longer the investigator, that would only leave one to go. Of course, William was another matter altogether; a much more intransigent and difficult one, but Hermitage's moment might come.

He even found himself walking alongside Harold, there could be no better moment.

'It sounds as if you have had a troubling time, Your Majesty,' Hermitage said, by way of conversation. It wasn't very good, but then he wasn't very good at conversation.

'Majesty no more,' Harold replied. 'Even kings have to realise that their time has passed. Most of them are not lucky enough to still be alive when it happens. Ends of reigns tend to be bloody affairs, most of the time.'

'King Edward died peacefully.'

'That he did. But he left the country in a complete mess by not declaring his heir with any clarity. That led to more bloodshed than one simple dead king.'

Hermitage nodded. 'And so to William.' He gave a sigh of disappointment. 'We have had to deal with him on more than one occasion.' He was quite proud of getting to his point so quickly. Whenever he saw a point he generally circled it for a considerable time before getting anywhere close. By that time it had usually ceased to be a point at all.

'Still King's Investigator then, but with a different king. I congratulate you, Brother Hermitage.'

'How so?'

'Most people who held office for King Harold had the ability to hold anything taken away from them most abruptly.'

'Ah, of course. But then,' Hermitage swallowed and told himself to say the words. What harm could words do? 'I never really wanted to be King's Investigator at all. The events at De'Ath's Dingle were pure coincidence. I happened to be there at the time and managed to be of some service.'

'In sorting out a gaggle of miscreants, many of them in supposedly high office.'

Hermitage nodded that this was the case.

'Well, just go and tell William you'd rather not do it anymore. People can resign from royal office if they want to retire to their estates in old age, or take to a monastery, that sort of thing.' He considered Hermitage for a moment. 'But then you're not very old and you're already in a monastery, so that won't work.'

'And I don't think William would see any benefit from me not being his investigator anymore.'

'You've investigated for him directly?'

'Once or twice,' Hermitage said, thinking that it was more like four or five times; a lifetime, anyway.

'I don't think you have any choice then, I'm afraid. I certainly don't need an investigator anymore, and I'm not even a king. But there's still one on the throne and if he wants you, that's that.'

Hermitage thought that was as good as he was going to get. Harold had effectively unappointed him. He was no longer the investigator for multiple kings, only the one. Mind you, before today he'd thought that Harold was dead, so he wasn't actually sure how far this had got him.

He still told himself that this was good news; before he told himself that he was in exactly the same position as when he got up this morning.

'And your reputation must be a good one, or you wouldn't be here doing this now,' Harold added unhelpfully.

Hermitage gave a little shrug that he didn't want a reputation either.

By this time, they were approaching Abbot Fulmer's study, and Hermitage was troubled by the question of how to break the news. Simply barging in and announcing another dead monk, might give the poor abbot a fit of some sort.

Starting a conversation about the weather and eventually leading up to the suggestion that Brother Bodin wouldn't be worried about it now that he was dead, seemed a little long-winded.

He could always rely on Wat to deliver in these situations; deliver in the most inappropriate manner, usually.

So it was that Wat knocked once on the door and then pushed it open before walking in uninvited. Cwen followed behind and then Harold and finally Hermitage.

Fortunately, the abbot was not there.

'He must be in chapel,' Hermitage concluded. 'It is the hour for Compline. We should really be there ourselves.'

A small snort emerged from Cwen at this idea. 'Do all the monks go then?'

'Only those who are sick or infirm would be excused.'

'Or dead?' Cwen asked, most impertinently.

'Yes,' Hermitage managed to load his tone with criticism. 'Obviously the dead don't attend services.'

'Unless it's for them, I suppose,' Cwen continued her disrespectful commentary. 'At least the abbot will notice that Bodin isn't around anymore.'

'If the herbalist was attending a patient, he might be excused from the orders of the day.'

'We'd better find the abbot then,' Wat said.

'We cannot interrupt with news such as this,' Hermitage protested.

'That another of his monks has been murdered? I rather think he'd like to know.'

'How long are they going to be?' Cwen asked, sounding as if the monks attending their holy duties was a great inconvenience.

'Compline itself will take about half an hour. If Saint Werburgh's is anything like my own establishments, it will start with Collation.'

'Collation sounds good,' Cwen said.

'Collation is the reading from scripture.' Hermitage would really need to take Cwen on one side when they got home; her knowledge was lamentable and her behaviour not much better.

'The abbot may hear any petitions for exemption from the rule.'

'He'll what the what?'

'If anyone has good reason not to attend, they seek permission from the abbot.'

'Like being dead?'

'Cwen, will you behave,' Hermitage almost snapped.

Cwen adopted an expression that tried to say she didn't understand what she'd done when she understood perfectly well.

'So,' Wat spoke up with a cautionary look for Cwen.

'Brother Bodin would have to go and ask to be excused?'

'That would be normal. After all that, the abbot will join the Collation and then it's into chapel for Compline itself. I must say, I haven't actually heard the Compline bell ring out, but then we have been rather preoccupied.'

'If he's still doing these permissions we could go and find him. Before he starts collating.'

'Collation. Yes, I suppose we could go and look.'

'Come on then.' Wat sounded impatient as if they should have gone to the chapel, to begin with.

At least it was only a short step from the study to the chapel, where they found Brother Paul just going in.

'Ah, Brother,' Hermitage called.

Paul turned and saw them, and his face fell. 'Oh dear,' he said. 'I'd rather forgotten you were here. Have you resolved our issues?'

'Issues?' Cwen coughed. 'Oh, you mean the dead monks. Have we found out who murdered them? No, we haven't yet. We're just looking for the abbot.'

Paul regarded Cwen with a mixture of shock and surprise. 'Are you the one who injured our gatekeeper?'

News of that had obviously spread.

'Just a misunderstanding,' Cwen dismissed the question. 'The abbot?'

'He is in his parlour, hearing petitions.' Paul said, with a very wary look at Cwen. He nodded towards a small door just to their right, then turned and hurried into chapel, before someone could hit him with a door.

Once more, Wat knocked and opened this door without any preliminaries. This time the abbot was in. He was on his own though, there obviously being few petitioners this evening.

His parlour was a very simple chamber with just one wooden chair and a lectern carrying a book; probably the record of those excused from the orders. Abbot Fulmer was sitting on the stool, his eyes closed probably in quiet prayer.

'Ah,' he called out at the sudden disturbance. He quickly recognised Wat, Cwen and Hermitage. He frowned at Harold. 'Are you not the sickly brother in the care of Brother Bodin? Should you be up?'

'It's about Brother Bodin we have come to speak,' Hermitage said. He thought that he'd better get in first before Wat or Cwen said something completely heartless.

'Oh, yes?'

'Yes.' Hermitage dropped his head. 'We fear that Brother Bodin has followed Abel and Pendle into the arms of the Lord.'

'I think we know that he has,' Cwen said, but at least she was quiet about it.

'Bodin?' The abbot asked, his voice trembling. 'Dead?'

Hermitage just nodded as sombrely as he could manage.

'Oh, good Lord above.' The abbot sank his head into his hands. After a few moments, he emerged and considered them again. 'Another killing?'

Hermitage nodded once more.

'What curse is upon us?' Abbot Fulmer wailed, looking to the ceiling for some solace. He dropped his eyes to Hermitage again. 'Have you any idea who is doing this to us?'

Saying that his enquiries were still at an early stage seemed a bit pathetic somehow. He didn't know how long an early stage lasted, but it must surely be over by the time the third dead body arrived.

He also felt somewhat guilty that murders were still happening in the middle of his investigation. Surely it was the job of the investigator to find out who had killed someone, and stop them. If the killers simply carried on as if no one was there, what was the point?

'We have some thoughts,' he said. 'But what would really help us is knowing more about the brothers of Saint Werburgh's.'

'You're not suggesting anyone here had anything to do with it?' The abbot had found his authority once more.

'We have to consider all possibilities.'

The abbot turned his disappointed eyes to Harold once more. 'I saw you briefly when you arrived here, as you were taken into the care of Brother Bodin. But there is something else about you that is familiar, Brother Odwin.'

Hermitage, Wat, Cwen and Harold all exchanged looks, carrying out a silent debate as to whether they should tell the abbot anything or not. The conclusion seemed to be that it was unavoidable.

Hermitage looked to the others to see who was going to break the news. The replies were quite clear; it was him.

'Brother Odwin,' he began.

'Yes?' the abbot asked.

'Brother Odwin is, as you know, an anchorite at Saint Werburgh's.'

'Yes,' Fulmer confirmed with a little impatience. 'I was aware of that, being the abbot of Saint Werburgh's.'

'Quite.' Hermitage took a breath. 'And he became an anchorite at the suggestion of, erm, King William.'

The abbot frowned now. 'Did he?'

'Yes.' Hermitage wondered how much further he could beat around the bush; he wasn't sure he could actually see the bush at all from here. 'He met the king at Hastings.'

'The battle?'

'That's the one. He was, erm, on the other side. From the king, the current king. William, that is.'

Abbot Fulmer sighed. 'Perhaps you could just tell me who he really is?'

Hermitage took a deep breath. 'Harold.'

'Brother Harold?' The abbot looked very puzzled about why a monk would need two names.

'Well, yes, but before he was a brother, he was more a sort of, erm, king. King Harold. Of England.'

Now the abbot gazed at Harold with an open mouth. 'King Harold?' he asked in a stunned whisper.

'King no more,' Harold said. 'An anchorite on retreat from the world.'

'We've got King Harold in our abbey?' The abbot seemed to think this was akin to a plague of rats. It sounded as if he thought it was almost as bad as having Wat the Weaver; almost, but not quite.

Harold nodded.

The abbot looked at him hard, then at Hermitage, Wat and Cwen in turn. 'Well,' he said. 'It's no wonder people are getting killed, is it?'

'That's what I said,' Wat agreed. 'I said it was too much of a coincidence, didn't I?'

Cwen looked rather annoyed that he might be right.

Abbot Fulmer's face seemed to be having trouble making its mind up whether it should be doing anger or despair. Both flitted about, neither taking complete control.

'How many other people know this?' he demanded. 'Obviously, it was not the sort of information that could be passed on to a mere abbot.'

'As far as we know, only Brother Bodin,' Hermitage said.

'The dead Brother Bodin,' the abbot specified. 'And Abel

and Pendle? I suppose we now find out they were something to do with all this?'

Hermitage looked at the others once more, but no one else seemed ready to take up the tale. 'Possibly, but not necessarily,' Hermitage said. 'It does seem that Brother Abel had previously been a Saxon Noble's man called Lefsius.'

'And Pendle? I suppose he was a Norman.' The abbot sounded as if he was trying to say the most outrageous thing he could think of.

'Erm, yes, he was. Called Walter.'

'Wonderful,' the abbot said, the despair now taking control of pretty much everything.

'But it is quite possible that, like Harold, they had simply come here to follow a religious calling. After all, they had been here for some time before Harold arrived.'

'We wanted to know about the other brothers.' Wat got back to the topic. 'Obviously, Bodin and Abel and Pendle are accounted for. Paul, Hengard, Brede and Girunde are the ones who came and got us. Who else do you have?'

'So that we can line them up to be murdered as well?' The abbot was quite cross now.

'No,' Wat said, equally firmly. 'So that we can see if anyone else has a dark past they're hiding. After all, we've already found your abbey is full of Normans and Saxons and one ex-king. Who else do you have hiding themselves away?'

'Wat!' Hermitage spoke up. 'Poor Abbot Fulmer has just discovered that another of his brothers is dead and that he has King Harold hiding in his tower. This is hardly the time to be badgering him.'

'Just the time, I would have said, before someone else needs the attention of Brother Merle.'

'There is no one else,' the abbot snapped at Wat. 'No one.

We are all that is left. And now we are three fewer than we were.'

Hermitage couldn't quite take that in. He added up quickly in his head; the four who had summoned him, the abbot, Merle and the Gatekeeper. 'There are only seven of you in the whole of Saint Werburgh's? Not counting the king, here.'

'There are now. Just a few days ago there were ten. And now I find out that three of them weren't even proper brothers.'

'Good heavens. Why so few?'

'Saint John's.' The abbot sounded very resigned now. 'Every new arrival is snatched away to be taken into that place. We've had no genuine new brothers for months and months. Hengard was our last. My hopes started to rise when Abel and Pendle arrived, but now I see those hopes were forlorn.'

Wat looked at Hermitage with a very significant gaze. 'Three down and seven to go. Then there won't be a Saint Werburgh's at all.'

'Why do you say that?' the abbot asked.

Wat indicated with a nod that Hermitage was better at speaking to Abbot Fulmer, just at the moment.

'I visited Saint John's,' he said.

'You did?' The abbot sounded impressed by Hermitage's bravery.

'One of the possibilities was that Saint John's had taken their rivalry with you too far and that someone there may be responsible for the deaths.' He shrugged that this was obviously ridiculous and didn't bear thinking about.

'I wouldn't be surprised,' the abbot said, which shocked Hermitage.

'Really?'

'Oh, yes. I told you that the abbot, Kenwald, is a very nasty piece of work, but then there's Brother Longor. If you want to consider the background of a monk and find something very unpleasant, take a look at Longor.'

'Perhaps you might have mentioned this when we arrived?' Wat suggested with clear annoyance.

'I am not an investigator,' the abbot replied.

'Oh, dear,' Hermitage fretted, ignoring the disagreement. 'Everyone we come across turns out to be someone else. How is anyone supposed to keep track of all this? I shall have to write it all down at this rate; and who'd want to read that?'

'Who is Longor, then?' Cwen asked the abbot directly. 'If you say he should be looked into, you obviously know why.'

Abbot Fulmer looked away and mumbled something.

'Pardon?' Cwen almost shouted.

'I've heard they call him Skull. A quite inappropriate name for one so young.'

'Yes,' Cwen laughed. 'Brede called him that. Mind you, he does look like one.'

'A most inappropriate name for a monk, but one that obviously indicates a dark past.'

Hermitage wasn't sure a name alone was sufficient for that conclusion; particularly when the individual called skull looked like a skull.

Harold stepped quickly up to the abbot. 'Exactly how old is this Longor? The one who looks like a skull?'

'A young man still, barely seventeen or eighteen, I would say.'

'And the name.' Harold was demanding. 'Was it Skull, or Skuli?'

'Does it matter?'

'It certainly could.'

'Why?' Hermitage asked. 'Do you know someone called Skuli?'

'I do,' Harold was quite pensive now. He soon realised that everyone was waiting for an explanation. 'Skuli Tostisson is my nephew; the son of my brother, Tostig.'

'Ah.' Hermitage understood what a nephew was.

'The Tostig I killed at the Battle of Stamford Bridge.'

Everyone but Hermitage looked as if this made an awful lot of sense all of a sudden.

Harold filled in the gap. 'And if anyone is going to want me dead, it's my nephew.'

'I see,' said Brother Hermitage with a tut. 'Family, eh?'

## Caput XXIII It Was Him, Then

'That's that then,' Wat said with a happy smile. 'All sorted out nicely.'

They had left the abbot to hurry to his Compline devotions, "before things got any worse" was his precise comment. Wat and Cwen only just managed to persuade Hermitage that they needed him with them.

They stayed in the parlour, but Hermitage kept looking wistfully towards the chapel.

'Skuli Longor finds out that Harold is here,' Cwen took up the tale. 'Quite naturally, he wants to kill him. But he can't do that because of Bodin.'

'So why kill Abel and Pendle?' Hermitage asked.

'Also in the way. Abel's a Saxon who would protect Harold, and Pendle is a Norman who's here to guard him. With them out of the way, Harold is next.'

'Or it could be that he wanted to kill Abel just to damage Saint Werburgh's,' Wat suggested. 'While he's doing that, he finds Harold is here.'

Harold said nothing but just nodded quietly that this was all perfectly reasonable.

'And all under the pretext of destroying Werburgh's,' Wat added. 'I imagine Abbot Kenwald has given him pretty free rein to do what he likes in that regard.'

'But what if he doesn't know Harold is here at all?' Hermitage said. 'Very few people seem to.'

'He obviously makes Saint Werburgh's his business. He's probably been in here poking about, seeing what he can find. He waits until the useless gatekeeper falls asleep, or has a sudden attack of Stinking Leak.' Cwen seemed very confident that Longor was their man. 'It would be easy to find out there was a sick monk in the tower. He climbs up as Wat did, sees Harold and thinks, "hello, that's my Uncle. What a stroke of luck, I can kill him now".'

'Would he?' Hermitage was quite appalled by the suggestion.

'Absolutely,' Harold didn't seem appalled at all. 'I killed his father, after all.'

'I can see how that would be annoying,' Wat said helpfully.

Hermitage still wasn't satisfied. There was something else buzzing around in his head that he couldn't pin down. Mind you, pinning down buzzing things was never easy at the best of times.

'And Bodin? Bodin's only just been killed.'

'While we left the door open.' Wat gave Cwen a hard stare at this. 'Longor sneaked in, did the deed and sneaked out again.'

'But I left him at Saint John's, about to be reprimanded by his abbot, as far as I could tell.'

'But you didn't actually see him. And being reprimanded would really annoy him. Just get him in the mood for a bit of murder. Unless the abbot was lying to you, of course.' Wat suggested.

This was all getting too much for Hermitage. 'What about Lady Ealdgyth?' he said. He knew this was part of the problem, just didn't know which part yet.

'What about her?' Cwen asked.

'Skuli, I mean Brother Longor would surely know that the Lady Ealdgyth was in Chester. It's no secret, after all.'

'True.'

'So why wouldn't he do something to her? She was Harold's wife.'

'We only married at the beginning of the fateful year,'

Harold explained, obviously not wanting to say the words 'ten sixty-six'. 'And, to be honest, it was more a marriage of convenience than anything else. Skuli's father and I had already fallen out long before that. I had him exiled some time previously.'

'Marriage of convenience?' Hermitage couldn't quite understand that. 'You had two children.'

'That was the marriage bit,' Harold said. 'The convenience was that she's the daughter of the Earl of Mercia.'

Hermitage was aghast that no one showed any sign of shame or disapproval of this arrangement.

'So.' Cwen seemed keen for some action. 'What do we do about Longor or Skuli or whatever we're calling him? March up to Saint John's and deal with him?'

'Deal with him?' Hermitage was quite shocked at this. As usual, he thought that resolving the question at the heart of the investigation was the main thing. Actually doing something about whatever was discovered was normally someone else's problem.

'What can we do?' Wat said. 'There seem to be a lot of brothers up at Saint John's. There's only four of us, and seven more if you include the whole population of Saint Werburgh's. I can see Hengard and Brede being some help but not the rest of them.'

'Merle would just wait by the side for his next customer.' Cwen shrugged.

'And the gatekeeper would probably do you first.' Wat gave Cwen a smile.

'And I am supposed to be an anchorite in retreat from the world,' Harold said. 'I can only imagine what William will do if he finds Harold is marching around Chester dealing with monks.'

'We do nothing?' Hermitage asked. His natural inclination was that most of the time doing nothing was entirely satisfactory. Doing nothing was the sort of task he could tackle with a will. Even he thought that doing nothing in this situation was just plain wrong.

'This brother may have killed three people. Three monks, no less.'

'Who weren't monks,' Cwen pointed out.

'Who were still in the care of a religious house and had been for some time. We cannot simply walk away and say, "ah, yes, it was Brother Longor" and leave him to it. If you're right, we know that he'll be coming for Harold next. And then what's to stop him from finishing off the rest of Saint Werburgh's?'

'He'll probably be satisfied with me,' Harold said, without any obvious worry. 'He's only killed those who were close to me. He didn't murder that Brother Hengard, or Brede. Probably won't either; they're of no interest to him.'

'But he must be held to account for the sins he has already committed.' Hermitage was very clear on this. He was also very clear that he wasn't the best person to be holding killer monks to account.

The parlour fell into silence as they all contemplated the situation. There seemed to be an unspoken agreement that the killer needed dealing with, but no obvious method by which to do it.

'The Ealdorman?' Cwen suggested. 'Surely it's his job to deal with people who kill one another.'

'In normal circumstances, yes,' Wat agreed. 'But Saint John's is probably a powerful force in town. And he obviously didn't deal with Abel or Pendle. Hermitage had to be sent for. I'm not sure we can rely on the Ealdorman; he might simply hand us over to Saint John's.'

This brought about even more gloomy introspection.

Eventually, Wat spoke again. 'I'm not sure William will be happy with this situation.'

'Us dealing with Longor?' Cwen asked.

'No, Longor killing people. After all, Bodin was William's man, and Pendle as well. Longor's killed two of the king's guards and that's not very wise.'

Harold was nodding agreement with this.

'If the King's Investigator reported back to William, that would bring some action.' Wat gave a horrible smile.

'Like a force of Normans falling on Longor, swords at the ready.' Cwen even rubbed her hands.

'And I assume,' Wat said to Harold, 'that William doesn't actually want you dead?'

'No. He said that having me dead would only rally people. He'd rather know where I was so that he could use me if needed.'

'Excellent. If William knew that Longor was trying to kill you, he'd get here even quicker.'

'And,' Cwen added, 'if we leave Longor to get on with it and kill Harold, we know what William's response will be.'

Hermitage looked at her questioningly.

'Come to Chester, slaughter everyone and burn the place to the ground. It's what he usually does.'

Harold nodded that this sounded like a very reasonable tactic.

'This is all well and good,' Hermitage said, thinking that none of it was either well or good. 'But how would we get word to William?' He had never, even for a moment, thought that he would willingly send word to King William, asking him to come quick.

'Hm.' Wat didn't have an answer to this. 'With the dead three out of the way, Longor will be thinking he can get Harold pretty soon.'

'He would,' Cwen said. 'Before he discovered the King's Investigator was crawling all over the place.'

'I haven't been crawling,' Hermitage protested.

'You're right,' Wat smiled at Cwen, ignoring the crawling allegation. 'He'll have to be cautious now. He can't know that Hermitage doesn't have ready contact with the king. After all, you put the fear of God up Abbot Kenwald.'

'Hardly that.' Hermitage had never put the fear of anything up anyone. 'And he wasn't showing much sign of caution when he came in and killed Bodin under our noses.'

'True. But I think Kenwald will have to be more careful now. He thinks that the king will look on him with disfavour.' Wat clicked his fingers. 'Does Kenwald even know who Longor really is?'

The others looked at him.

'Chester seems to have a bit of a problem with monks who aren't monks. It could well be that Longor came here as a monk to escape his own troubles. Then he discovers Harold is here, and suddenly he has a new mission in life: death.'

There was more quiet thought as they all tried to think what their options were; or if there were any options at all.

'If I was Skuli,' Harold said, 'I'd be keeping an eye on Saint Werburgh's and the King's Investigator. The last thing he will want is any report getting out. Better to kill the investigator himself.'

Hermitage knew that didn't sound better than anything.

'We can't stay here forever,' he said, trying to control the tremor in his voice. 'And Longor is a young man; we can't wait for him to die.'

'Kill him?' Harold suggested, quite equitably.

'What?' Hermitage shouted.

'I could sneak out and kill him, I'm pretty sure.'

'Kill your own nephew?'

'He wants to kill me.'

'That is not the point. There has been enough death already. We don't solve a murder by murdering the murderer.'

The look on Harold's face said that he thought that was actually a rather sensible way to go about things. 'William will probably do it anyway.'

'I don't think William wants you getting back to old ways,' Wat said quietly.

Harold shrugged that this was probably right.

'Perhaps Wat or Cwen could get away?' Hermitage suggested. 'Get word to the king?'

'That could take days,' Cwen said, although she wasn't averse to the idea. 'Unless you've got a horse up your sleeve. Days for Longor to get on with what he does best.'

Of course, Hermitage didn't have a horse up his sleeve. A name popped into his head. He might know someone who did. 'Adversane,' he said.

'Adversane? What about him?'

'He could get word to the king. He does it all the time. He heard about me, after all. He also seems to be a wealthy man, owning houses and all. I expect he's got a horse. And he's Norman.'

'The horse?' Cwen asked.

'No, of course not the horse. For goodness sake.'

'How would we even get word to him?' Wat asked.

'The abbot knows him.' Hermitage was quite excited by this plan. 'One of the brothers could take a message.'

'What message?' Wat asked.

'That Longor is killing people?' Hermitage couldn't think what other message would be of any interest just at the moment.

'Do we tell this Adversane that Harold is here?' Wat specified the problem.

'Ah, yes, I see. Probably not. All we say is that the King's Investigator needs to get urgent word to the king about the murders at Saint Werburgh's. William knows Harold is here, he'll know what to do.'

'Can we trust this Adversane?' Wat asked.

'He advised the abbot to bring me here to look into things in the first place. He would hardly do that if he was in league with Longor.'

'That's true.' Wat turned to Harold. 'And you don't know him?'

Harold shook his head. 'Never come across him before. He was probably some minor landowner who took advantage of the conquest to become a major landowner. He could even be another pair of William's ears in the town. After all, he has me and my wife here; he'll want to know what's going on.'

'He may already suspect something then,' Hermitage suggested. 'If two of his men, Bodin and Pendle are dead, word may already have reached him.'

'It's possible, but I'm not sure we can rely on it.'

Hermitage's mind was made up. 'Adversane it is then. Compline must be nearly over now, we can ask the abbot to send word.'

As if knowing that he was wanted, the bell rang to indicate the end of Compline and the door to the chapel could be heard opening. The door to the parlour rattled and Abbot Fulmer came back in. He looked pale and worried and virtually ignored everyone as he went back to his stool.

Cwen had been sitting on this so she quickly moved out of the way.

'We have said prayers for our brothers,' the abbot said, a weary weight to his words. 'And we will meet again in the morning to discuss our future.'

'Your future?' Hermitage asked with concern.

'We are so few now, and obviously under threat, we have to ask ourselves if we should even carry on. Should we take ourselves to another establishment and offer our services there?'

'Saint John's?' Wat asked.

'Good God, no,' the abbot came to life.

'The matter may not be ended, Father,' Hermitage said. 'Can you get word to Master Adversane?'

'Adversane? Yes, I suppose I could. But to what end?'

'To get a message to the king.'

'The king?'

'William.'

'I know who the king is, Brother.' The abbot seemed to be getting quite cross. 'What message?'

Hermitage took breath. 'The message that the king's own men, put here to watch Harold, have been murdered by Brother Longor.'

'Good God,' the abbot repeated. This time it was a bit more enthusiastic. 'Are you sure?'

'As sure as we can be. If Longor is who we think he is, then he has been killing brothers so that he can get at Harold. We had the right person, just the wrong motive.'

Abbot Fulmer was quite wide-eyed now.

'And King William wants Harold alive, never mind any anger he may feel at the murder of his own men.'

The abbot nodded. 'We send word via Adversane, and William comes here to deal with Longor.'

'Maybe not in person,' Hermitage said. 'But he has a lot of people who are good at dealing with other people if you know what I mean.'

'I do,' Abbot Fulmer said.

Hermitage noticed a rather odd gleam in the abbot's eye, and a smile started to sneak its way onto his face.

'I imagine the king will not be best pleased with Brother Longor, or the house that accommodates him.'

'Erm, possibly not.' Hermitage couldn't see where this was leading.

'He may have very strong words for Saint John's.'

'I suppose so.'

'Strong words and actions, no doubt. Him being a man of action.'

'Action?'

'Of course. The king might be well advised to dissolve Saint John's completely. After all, it is a harbour to murderers.'

'Dissolve it?' Hermitage couldn't see where that had come from. 'It's only one murderer, who may not even be a genuine brother at all.' Even as he said it, he thought that one murderer was one more than was decent.

'Nonetheless,' the abbot seemed set on a path now. 'There is only one person who can be held ultimately responsible for this situation.'

'Of course,' Hermitage agreed. 'Brother Longor.'

'No, Abbot Kenwald.'

'Kenwald?'

'It is his house, and it is not in order. It is as far from order as it could be.'

'Well..,' Hermitage wasn't quite ready to debate with the abbot, who was starting to look a bit wild.

Abbot Fulmer stood from his chair. 'The king will come to us and wipe the evil of Saint John's from the face of the town,' he declared. 'I will send word to Adversane and then discuss our future with the brothers in the morning. A future without Saint John's in it.'

The others could only look on as the abbot strode from the room with a strength of purpose they'd not seen in him before.

'Oh, dear,' Hermitage said. 'I worry that this is going to end badly.'

'Really?' Cwen enquired. 'And it's been going so well up to now.'

## Caput XXIV It Could Be Us Next

With nothing to do but wait for the return of the abbot with Adversane, the four of them cautiously retired to the herbalist's workshop.

The first task was to check that the herbalist wasn't there anymore. Merle must have found room for Brother Bodin somewhere, as the fragrant room was completely free of dead bodies.

'What I don't understand, is this.' Cwen said.

'There's only one thing?' Hermitage bleated. As the official King's Investigator, he somehow felt that he had done the least work of anyone in getting anywhere with these murders.

'I think so.' Cwen furrowed her brow. 'If Longor or Skuli found Harold was here, why didn't he just kill him straight away? He was up in the loft on his own. I can't imagine Abel and Pendle were in there with you?'

'No,' Harold replied. 'I didn't even know they were here until they were dead.'

'And Bodin the herbalist must have left you alone at some point. When he went to chapel?'

'He never went. Always excused because he was looking after me.'

'And did he take you to the privy?'

'Hardly.'

'There you are then. Bodin goes to the privy, Longor climbs the wall, one dead Harold.'

Hermitage had to admit that it did sound like a reasonable plan; as far as completely unreasonable plans to murder people went.

'There could be more to it,' Wat said.

'Such as?' Cwen folded her arms.

'Who knows?' Could be Longor only wants to take Harold. You know, get all his guards out of the way, and then he can spirit him out of this place.'

'To what purpose?' Hermitage asked. He could see that getting the ex-king out into the country again might be of interest to some parties.

Wat shrugged. 'Kill him slowly?'

Harold nodded that this could be a possibility.

'Harold did kill his father, after all. He could have something really long-winded and gruesome in mind.'

Hermitage swallowed at the thought.

'Or ransom for King William,' Cwen suggested. 'Or present him to William to get into the king's good books.'

'William already has Harold,' Hermitage pointed out. 'He's hardly going to get in any good books by stealing him and then giving him back.'

'Doesn't matter, really. There could be lots of reasons why Longor wanted everyone dealt with before he came for Harold.'

'Could even be to foment rebellion,' Harold suggested. 'If young Skuli is anything like his father, he'll have ambitions way beyond his ability. He's probably got some idea that the kingdom should be his. Get me out of the way, or use me as figurehead, attack and defeat William and it's King Skuli the first.'

'Attack and defeat William?' Even Hermitage could see that was very ambitious indeed.

'Quite,' Harold agreed. 'I couldn't manage it and I'm twice the man my brother was.'

Hermitage was getting confused with all these possibilities. 'Either way, Skuli Longor wants to come for Harold. Taking him away or leaving him dead is neither here nor there.'

'Oh,' Wat said, with a horrible sounding interest. 'There's a thought.'

'What is?' Hermitage looked and sounded worried at what was about to come.

'We bait a trap.' Wat even rubbed his hands. 'We can send word to the king through Adversane as planned, but that's going to take a while. In the meantime, we let it be known that the sickly monk is now alone and unguarded since Bodin's untimely death. We then wait in the shadows of the loft for Longor to appear and we grab him.'

'Grab him?' Hermitage didn't like the sound of grabbing anyone.

'Harold, Cwen and I grab him,' Wat clarified.

'Ah, right.'

'Then we'll have him. Caught in the act.'

'What do we do with him then?' Hermitage asked. He couldn't think Longor would just sit quietly and wait for the king to arrive.

'We tie him up and gag him,' Cwen said with some relish.

Hermitage suddenly had a new worry; there was usually one to hand. 'What if he has friends? It may not be just him who comes. What if he is in league with a whole group of people. We might be overpowered.'

Cwen dismissed this. 'Saint Werburgh's hasn't been invaded for the other murders. No, he'll come alone. Why wouldn't he?'

'Because the King's Investigator is here?' Hermitage suggested. 'He's already annoyed that I went to Saint John's with questions.'

'Here's an idea,' Wat interrupted the flow. 'Let's just do it and see what happens, eh?'

Hermitage wasn't keen on that at all. Just doing things and

seeing what happened inevitably led to seeing something unexpected and frequently nasty.

'Longor is paying attention, he'll know what's going on anyway. Having killed Bodin, the last man in his way, he's going to come for Harold whatever we do. I don't think he'll let us being here get in his way.' Wat didn't seem to think being in the way was anything to worry about.

'Unless,' Hermitage went pale at his thought.

'Unless what?'

'He now has to kill us as well?'

'He can try.'

'He's killed three before us. What's three more?'

'This time we know he's coming.'

That didn't make Hermitage feel any better at all.

'What else then, Hermitage?' Cwen demanded with some irritation. 'We go and leave Harold? We take him with us? Lock ourselves in until we're rescued by the king? I think that if we do nothing, Longor will come anyway. There you are.'

Hermitage didn't have anything more to offer. All the options were awful, apart from the alternatives, which were worse.

The noise as the door opened was such a shock to Hermitage that he nearly jumped into the loft straight through the ceiling.

Fortunately, it was only Abbot Fulmer and not Longor with a handful of sharp weapons.

The abbot came in and was followed by another. The smiling face of Adversane considered the room with interest. 'My, my. The abbot explained the death of Brother Bodin and said that you had need of me, but I had no idea there would be a reception.'

He passed his smile around them all, giving no indication

that he recognised Harold.

Hermitage thought that would be for the good. Adversane didn't need to know the old king was here, just that Longor was going around killing monks. 'This is Brother Odwin, he's been ill.' Hermitage introduced the king.

Adversane acknowledged Harold and then looked quizzical, inviting someone to tell him what this was all about.

Hermitage knew that as King's Investigator, that was probably his job, but he also worried that he might get something wrong. He gave Wat an encouraging look.

'We need someone to get word to the king,' Cwen spoke up.

'I see,' Adversane gave her his attention.

'We've determined that Brother Longor, from Saint John's, is the one who killed the monks here.'

'All of them?' Adversane seemed to think this was quite a feat.

'That's right.'

'Why?'

'To show Saint Werburgh's as a place of sin. So that it would be closed.'

'Seems a bit drastic,' Adversane observed.

'Killing people generally is,' Cwen said, moving on. 'Obviously, we could approach Longor directly and deal with him as best we could, but we suspect that Saint John's may have friends in authority within the town.'

'The Ealdorman, you mean?'

'That's right.'

'And you'd be correct. He's as thick as thieves with them.'

'And there are a lot of brothers at Saint John's. If we went in and attempted to take Brother Longor, it might not go well for us.'

Adversane just nodded that he agreed with this assessment.

'You seem to have contact with the king. After all, you knew about Hermitage and got him here to deal with the murders. If you can get word back that the King's Investigator has found the Brothers of Saint Werburgh's are being murdered, we're sure he'd send help.'

'Really?' Adversane didn't seem so convinced about this.

'Brother Hermitage is the King's Investigator. He has William's ear.'

Yes, and Brother Hermitage would very much like to give it back.

'Of course,' Adversane said. 'If that is what you want me to do then I will happily send word. I don't know how much influence I have, but I will do what I can.'

'Quickly,' Cwen added. 'It's quite possible that Longor knows we have discovered him, and he will attempt to take action.'

'More killings?'

'Possibly.'

'Good Lord.' Adversane shook his head sadly. 'What times we live in where a monk will kill his brother.' He gave the monks in the room looks of the greatest sympathy.

'Do you have a horse?' Cwen asked.

'A horse?' Adversane seemed confused by the question. 'Erm, yes, I have a horse.'

'Can you use it to take the message?'

'It'll need a rider.' Adversane still seemed a bit lost.

'Obviously,' Cwen snapped at him. 'I wasn't expecting a horse to take the message on its own.'

'Oh, I see. Yes, I can organise a rider.'

'Is it known where the king is now?' Harold asked this.

Adversane looked at him as if wondering what this new monk had to do with any of this.

'I was under the care of Brother Bodin when he was killed,' Harold explained. 'I am as anxious as the others that this Longor should be brought to account.'

'Of course. Last I heard, the king was travelling north from Derby. If I send a rider out east, he should pick up word soon enough.'

'And the rider could leave tonight?' Cwen asked.

'Tonight?' Adversane sounded surprised at this suggestion. 'Is that wise?'

'We need word out as soon as possible.'

'Just so, but I wonder if going now would be best.' He held up a hand to stop Cwen's objections. 'Leaving town after the doors have been shut is an unusual event. Of course, it happens and is quite possible, but it draws attention.

'If Brother Longor is indeed killing monks, I imagine that he would not want any word getting out.'

'Not unless he's an idiot as well,' Wat said.

'So, we need our messenger to leave without Longor being aware?' Adversane asked.

'What could he do to a man on a horse?' Cwen asked.

'If you're right, he's already killed three monks. Preparations for opening the gates would not go unnoticed. If Longor is out and about, he could well discover this and try to stop the rider?

'If we wait until first light, there would be nothing unusual to note; just another rider leaving with a message.'

'Hm,' Cwen wasn't entirely happy, but could obviously see the point.

'And I do have my rider to think about. Sending a man out

across the land alone after dark is risky. He could easily fall prey to robbers, or worse, and then the message would never get through.'

Cwen gave this some silent thought and looked to the others. Wat shrugged and Hermitage had nothing helpful to say on the topic.

'First light?' Cwen sought confirmation.

'Not a moment later. And it will give me time to prepare a horse and get the message sorted out with the man I have in mind. A man who probably needs to be told to rest for the night, and not spend it in the tavern, as normal.'

Cwen gave a short nod that she accepted the plan.

'Excellent,' Adversane rubbed his hands. 'Now, the message. Is it to be trusted to word or will there be something written?'

Cwen and Wat looked at Hermitage. This was something he could do.

'Yes,' he said. 'I can write a short message. But I see no reason why the rider should not be told what he carries.'

'Then we are agreed,' Adversane said. 'If there's nothing else, I had best return home to make arrangements.'

The others all exchanged looks to confirm everything had been covered.

'That's all,' Cwen said.

'And thank you,' Brother Hermitage added sincerely.

'It is the least I can do. After all, I brought you into this in the first place, I had best see it through.'

Adversane turned back to the door and pulled it open. He stepped quickly back two or three paces and the others all stared at the shape that blocked the exit.

Hermitage imagined that this would be one of the brothers looking for their abbot. Some routine matter of abbey business, no doubt.

It was a brother who entered the room now, but not the one they expected or wanted.

The brother had others with him as well; three more figures crowded into the room, each of them wearing the very opposite of monastic garb.

'Well, well,' Brother Longor said as he appraised the room. 'All gathered together then; that is useful.' He glared at them all in turn but saved an especially intense sneer for Harold. 'Here as well then, uncle? I couldn't have asked for more.'

He nodded to his companions, who spread themselves around the room. These were clearly town guards, being well dressed and even better armed. Each of them carried swords, which they held out, making it clear that asking to leave the room would be a waste of time.

'Brother Longor!' Abbot Fulmer stepped forward. 'What is the meaning of this?'

'Brother Longor,' Longor spoke the name with some contempt. 'They have probably told you that my name is Skuli Tostisson.' He pointed at Harold. 'And that man killed my father.'

Harold showed not a blink of emotion at the accusation.

The others had nothing to say, having known this already, but Adversane was looking quickly from Longor to Harold, a frown on his face.

'But now I've got you all where I want you,' Longor said. 'The King's Investigator as well,' he gave a short laugh at this. Hermitage couldn't tell what that was about.

'Time to bring an end to it all,' Longor said. He gestured two of the guards to step forward.

'Now, just a moment,' Hermitage spoke up.

'Sit down,' Longor instructed. 'Managed to work out why

you're here yet, have you?'

Hermitage looked at him with disappointment that the habit of a monk was being abused in this manner. He considered Longor's words and shook his head slowly. Here was the killer, right in front of him, and what could he do about it? Nothing. What was the point of being King's Investigator if the killers simply got away with whatever they wanted?

And it would be even worse if what they got away with on this occasion was killing the investigator as well.

He thought that his invitation to Chester had just been the start of an inevitable road that led to this point. He felt as if the arrival of the four brothers at Wat's workshop had pushed him off a cliff, and now he was about to land.

He looked at the faces around him, a collection of individuals almost sucked into events against their will. He had heard of people being pulled into the sea by strong waves, and perhaps this was a similar feeling. Of course, he'd never so much as put a toe in the sea so wouldn't know.

He, Wat and Cwen knew why they were here, he just felt sorry for the abbot and for Adversane. This really was nothing to do with them.

Then another thought meandered into his head and made him feel as if it had been there all the time, but he had been studiously ignoring it.

He looked at Wat and Cwen and gave them a very quizzical look. They looked confused, so he added some more quizzical.

'What is it, Hermitage?' Cwen asked, still sounding annoyed at being held at sword point.

He held up a finger, alerting the whole room to the fact that he had just thought of something. 'Aha,' he said.

'What?' Longor bit at him.

'Hermitage just said "Aha",' Cwen explained.

'Is there no end to his talents?' Longor dismissed this nonsense.

'He knows the truth,' Cwen explained.

'I think we all know the truth.'

'Not if Hermitage has said Aha, we don't.'

## Caput XXV Where Did All the Honest Killers Go?

The guards were waving their swords about, mainly towards Harold, but didn't seem to know whether they should do anything with him or not. Longor had told them to get on with it, but now this monk was holding his finger up. A monk holding his finger up could not be good.

'What truth is it you know then, monk?' Longor asked with a pronounced sneer.

Hermitage considered him for a moment. 'You are a very rude fellow,' he said.

Longor looked around the room as if wanting to confirm that the others had heard the same words. 'Is that it? I'm a very rude fellow?' He gave a half-hearted clap of applause; more quarter-hearted, really. 'Well investigated. I can see that the king must be very happy with your performance.'

'Well, no,' Hermitage said honestly. 'And that's my point.'

'If you've got a point, I suggest you arrive at it quickly, before I get these gentlemen to do something pretty final with theirs.'

'You do yourself no favours, you know,' Hermitage explained. 'With the rudeness. People don't respond well to rudeness.'

Longor sighed. 'Is he always like this?' he asked Cwen.

'Like what?'

Longor didn't seem to have the words, he simply looked very frustrated. 'Like this,' he repeated, gesturing at Hermitage.

'Oh, yes,' Cwen confirmed.

'Frequently worse,' Wat added. 'We have to hear him out though, otherwise nothing will make sense.'

'I'm a busy man, monk. Ex-kings to deal with, that sort of

thing. If you could get on with it?'

'Ah, right, yes.' Hermitage told his thoughts to get themselves in order so that the others would understand them when he let them out. They seldom did what they were told so he just had to hope for the best. 'You are a very rude fellow,' he repeated.

'Yes, we got that.'

'Which makes people think the worst of you. If you were just a bit kinder now and again, the abbots and other monks and the townspeople wouldn't think such bad things of you.'

'Who thinks bad things of me?' Longor sounded a bit hurt by this.

'Well, everyone, really. It's hardly surprising, is it?' He gave Longor a disappointed look. He'd received so many from his father that he knew how to do them quite well.

'Perhaps they think bad things of him because he's bad?' Cwen suggested.

'Oh, I don't think that for a moment,' Hermitage said.

'He did kill a couple of false monks and a herbalist,' Wat pointed out. 'So he's got his bad points.'

Hermitage shook his head. 'No, he didn't.'

Longor now looked outraged. 'No, I didn't,' he complained in almost a squeak. 'Who said I killed people? Who said that?' He opened his arms to his guards, looking for some support. 'Abbot Kenwald kept going on about that. It's outrageous.'

'It's because you're so rude,' Hermitage explained, thinking that the young man would have got it by now. 'You're rude so people think the worst. Some other people are dead, they think you did it. It's quite reasonable.'

'No, it isn't. I haven't killed anyone.'

'I know that now,' Hermitage said. 'But it's a good job I'm

here, isn't it? Otherwise, goodness knows what would have happened.'

'Erm,' Cwen said. 'Well, if he didn't kill them, who did?'

'That's the aha bit,' Hermitage said.

'I think the explanation would be good now,' Wat said. 'If we've finished with the commentary on Longor's personality?'

'Ah, yes, right. Well, it was why I was brought here.'

'To solve the murders.'

'Sort of.'

'Sort of?' Cwen asked. 'The place is full of dead monks and you're the King's Investigator. Why else would you be brought here?'

'Exactly,' Hermitage was glad that Cwen had got it and gave her a smile.

She gave him one of her very pointed frowns. Ah, she hadn't got it then.

'The abbot sent messengers to fetch me because Brother Abel was dead, yes?'

'Yes,' Cwen said wearily as if she was a grandmother who had just been given written instructions on the sucking of eggs.

'He was advised to do so.'

'By Adversane, yes.'

Adversane nodded his acknowledgement of the small part he had played.

'Who had himself been told about me by the Normans.'

'That's right.' Cwen was now nodding as if Hermitage needed an early night.

'But,' Hermitage said, 'he said that he had been told of me by one Norman in particular.'

'Really?'

'Yes, really. Le Pedvin.'

'Le Pedvin,' Wat repeated with a shrug, indicating that one Norman was as good as another.

'The same Le Pedvin who thinks I'm an idiot.'

'He probably thinks we're all idiots,' Cwen could confirm Le Pedvin's opinion.

'So, why would Le Pedvin recommend me for a murder investigation, when he thinks that I am completely incompetent?'

There was a moment's pause while they thought about this.

'You're the only investigator there is?' Cwen said.

'There are local sheriffs and courts who deal with this sort of thing every day. Several times it's been suggested that the Ealdorman could have handled this. In a town like Chester, there must be disagreements and fights and even deaths all the time. Why get me in for this one?'

'You are the King's Investigator,' Wat said. 'Probably several steps up the ladder from a plain old Ealdorman. Especially one who's in league with Saint John's.'

'Is he?'

'Is he what?'

'In league with Saint John's?'

'Well, yes.' Wat was looking a bit lost.

'And who told us that?'

'Erm,' Wat thought for a moment. 'Adversane, I think.'

'Quite.'

Again, Adversane acknowledged that his humble efforts had been of some minor assistance.

Nobody seemed to reach any helpful conclusions as a result of this discussion, so Hermitage pushed them on a bit.

'Can you imagine Le Pedvin recommending me for anything? He hates me.'

'Well,' Cwen screwed up her face as she tried to think. 'Whenever King William calls for me, Le Pedvin thinks he's wasting his time. He doesn't know why I'm used because, as I said, I'm an idiot.'

Wat was looking thoughtful now. 'So, if someone went to Le Pedvin and asked for an investigator to solve a murder, your name wouldn't be top of his list.'

'Exactly. In fact, it needn't even be a direct request. It could just be overheard in conversation. Le Pedvin saying what a useless idiot the King's Investigator is and how he probably couldn't find an apple in an orchard.'

'Then?' Cwen asked, but she obviously didn't know what the rest of the question was.

'If you wanted the wrong man identified as your killer, who better to bring in than a useless investigator?'

Wat and Cwen's eyes now turned to Adversane, who wasn't looking quite so humble anymore.

'And it gets better. In the very town where the murders are being committed, there is a very rude young monk who has made it quite clear that he hates the very establishment in which the murders have taken place. If you were embarked upon a scheme such as this, you might even suggest to the investigator that the rude young monk was a likely suspect.'

'As Adversane did,' Cwen said.

Adversane made the very slightest adjustment to his feet, but it was in the direction of the door. Longor nodded to his guards, who made sure that no one was going to leave without at least one more sword wound than they had when they came in.

'But, why?' Cwen asked, with a glare at Adversane. 'It's all pretty complicated, isn't it? Commit some murders and then get a supposedly not-very-good investigator in to accuse the wrong man. Why not just do the murders better in the first place? In fact, why send for any help at all?'

'Because the whole thing must look like a simple falling out between religious houses,' Hermitage explained. 'A dead monk here and there, another one accused of the crime and dealt with. No one would think twice.'

'This sort of thing happens often then, does it?' Wat asked.

'It has been known,' Hermitage confessed. 'In older times, of course.'

Wat shook his head that monks were turning out to be as bad as everyone else in the world.

'That just leaves another why,' Cwen said. 'Why does it need to look like fighting abbeys?'

'It's as Wat said.' Hermitage nodded to the weaver.

'I did? I mean, I did, yes that's right.'

Cwen folded her arms and gave Wat one more from her stock of looks.

'Harold,' Hermitage said. 'King Harold, to be precise. It really is too much of a coincidence that it is the people around King Harold who are being murdered.'

'It's no good, Hermitage,' Cwen said. 'You're going to have to spell it out.

'Consider Adversane,' Hermitage said. He did hope that people would draw the same conclusion without him actually having to tell them what it was. He could still be wrong, and it would be nice to have some others agree with him of their own accord.

'Is it really credible that Adversane, as a benefactor of Saint Werburgh's would not have the opportunity to discover who the sickly monk in the tower was?'

They all shrugged that this might be possible.

'And,' Hermitage went on. 'Is it credible that a landowning

Norman in Chester, would not know King Harold when he saw him?'

Eyes turned to Adversane now; including Harold's.

Hermitage sighed that he really was going to have to spell this out.

'Adversane told the abbot to get me for the murders, on the clear expectation that I was a useless investigator, and that I would accuse the wrong man, Longor. He helped this along the way by pointing at Longor himself.

'And young Longor did himself no favours by being rude and aggressive and threatening the monks of Saint Werburgh's. Even his own abbot, Kenwald, was ready to believe that Longor could be a killer.'

He looked Longor in the eye and shook his head. 'You really need to make a better impression on people, young man. It nearly got you in serious trouble.' Hermitage gave a little tut. 'The fact that Longor turned out to be Harold's nephew, who could be out for revenge, was a further bonus.'

'He's what?' Adversane shouted into the room.

Hermitage managed to produce a knowing smile and gave it to Adversane.

'Oh, bloody marvellous,' Adversane complained.

'So,' Hermitage started to count out the steps on his fingers. 'One; the guards around Harold are killed and the blame is put on Saint John's and Brother Longor.'

'And once that's done, Harold is next,' Cwen filled in.

'Oh, no,' Hermitage said.

'No?'

'Not at all. Two;' he carried on with his counting as once he'd started, he couldn't leave it hanging in the air. 'In the flurry of murders, Harold disappears. With all his guards gone, no one knows he was here at all. King William won't even know he's gone, because there's no one left to report. And when he finds out, months could have gone by. After all, even the abbot here didn't know King Harold was in his loft.'

'I have never heard the like,' Abbot Fulmer said, sadly shaking his head in complete confusion. 'I knew man was sinful, but I had no idea he was so organised about it.'

'When William did find out, he might even have instructed you to come and investigate,' Wat said brightly. 'Good job you got here first.'

Hermitage shrugged. 'It was only a falling out between Saint John's and Saint Werburgh's. He probably wouldn't bother. He'd simply send some people out to find Harold, who he would assume had simply escaped. And Harold would be long gone.'

'With Adversane,' Cwen said.

'Exactly. Adversane, the Norman landowner who was quite happy here before William arrived. The man who owns many houses in Chester and who helped out Ealdgyth and the Saxons when they arrived.'

The guards with swords were now looking at Adversane, along with everyone else.

'Adversane could spirit Harold away and they would have plenty of time to rally support for a rebellion before William even knew they were gone. And a successful rebellion would see King Harold restored and Adversane as what? Earl of Northumbria, perhaps?'

The look from Adversane told Hermitage that he'd got that just right.

'He might have asked Harold about it first,' Harold complained.

'Ah,' Hermitage said. 'I did wonder if you were in on this all along.'

'Certainly not,' Harold objected. 'I've been stuck in a herbalist's loft.' He shook his head sadly. 'I didn't know my wife was here, let alone that she'd had my children. I didn't know people were plotting all around me and I didn't know I was supposed to be the centre of a rebellion.'

'I see.' Hermitage nodded. He had to acknowledge that Harold had been some help in the investigation, identifying Abel and Pendle and so forth. He would be unlikely to do that if he was behind their deaths.

'Honestly,' Harold was looking very crestfallen. 'I used to run this country, you know. Now look at me.'

'So, Adversane is the killer?' Cwen confirmed.

'He had ready access to Saint Werburgh's, being a minor benefactor, as he told me himself. And they were all killed with what was to hand, to make it look as if Saint John's may have done it. If Adversane had simply stabbed them, then we'd look outside the abbey.'

'But what about Bodin?'

Hermitage hung his head. "That is my fault.'

'Your fault?' Cwen sounded staggered by that. 'How can it be your fault. You didn't stick a hawthorn tree through him.'

'No, but I left the gate to the abbey open with Adversane tending the gatekeeper. It gave him the perfect opportunity to get in and kill Bodin. I suspect his next problem would have been us.'

'Us?' Cwen looked mightily offended that someone was thinking of killing her.

'We now know that it is Harold here. We would have to go.'

'Well, really,' Cwen snorted at Adversane. 'It's no wonder he didn't want to send a messenger straight away. He wanted to spend the night murdering us.'

'But, what about Longor?' Wat asked. 'He's just burst in here with sword-wielding guards. You can't tell me he's not up to something.'

'I suspect his abbot sent him here to apologise.'

'Apologise?' Cwen shrieked a bit. 'You don't normally take weapons to an apology.'

Hermitage nodded towards Longor that he would be the best one to explain.

Longor hung his head very slightly as he spoke. 'After the investigator had spoken to Abbot Kenwald I was summoned to his study.'

'And told off, I imagine,' Hermitage said.

'The abbot said I was suspected of the most awful and ridiculous things, and that I should go and seek forgiveness from Abbot Fulmer immediately.

'So, I came down here and found the gate open and the gatekeeper in a bad way. When I entered the precincts, I found Bodin dead. I then looked further and saw you all in discussion. I nearly screamed when I saw Harold.'

'The killer of your father.'

'Just so. I thought it best to go and get help, so I brought these fellows from the Ealdorman.'

'To our rescue,' Hermitage said with a smile. 'I think you have made your apology most effectively, Brother Longor.'

'But he was going to kill Harold,' Cwen pointed out.

'I don't think so. I think Brother Longor really has taken to the religious life, young though he is. He is still a little wild, but that will pass. When he saw Harold, it raised his anger over the death of his father.'

'I was going to take him and then tell the Normans that he was hiding here.' Longor explained.

'Which they already know,' Hermitage said. 'William

having put him here in the first place.'

'I see that now,' Longor said, although he didn't sound at all happy about the arrangement.

'I have no real evidence,' Hermitage admitted. 'But it is reasonable to assume that Adversane committed the murders of Abel and Pendle,' he said. 'I did wonder if it might have been Harold, in the brief moments he was free from Bodin. He wouldn't have helped our investigation if that had been the case. Adversane must have killed Bodin, as we were with Harold at the time.'

'Well,' Adversane said brightly. 'This has all been absolutely fascinating, but I really have to be off now.'

'Off?' Hermitage asked, not understanding.

'Yes, you know, leave? Even the useless Brother Hermitage must be able to work that one out.'

'I rather think we have you,' Wat said grimly.

Adversane smiled. 'Oh, I disagree.' He beckoned to the guards who now lowered their swords. 'You didn't think the Ealdorman would be out of this, did you? And the presence of Lady Ealdgyth and her court was just another coincidence? Surely not.' He looked and sounded astounded that this could have passed them by.

'They're in on it as well,' Hermitage sagged.

'Of course, they are. Saxon nobles? Run away from William and holed up in Chester? Bringing all their trade and money to the town? What did you think they were going to do, just live here until William caught up? My God, Le Pedvin was right; you really are an idiot. How you worked all this out is beyond me.'

'But he did work it out,' Cwen said fiercely. 'And now we all know what you've done. The abbot knows and Abbot Kenwald at Saint John's will know soon enough. You can't kill everyone. No matter how much you may want to.'

'True,' Adversane shrugged. 'And I didn't kill Abel, just for the record. He really was planning to release Harold, and so Bodin killed him.'

The abbot groaned at this news.

'God above,' Harold said. 'Does no one tell me anything anymore?'

'It was Abel's death that gave me the idea to do the rest.' Adversane seemed happy to explain. 'And it was a good plan as well. Still, live to fight another day and all that. Come.' He beckoned to the guards that they would leave now.

Longor looked very disappointed that the rescue party he'd assembled had turned out to be made up of all the wrong people.

As Adversane and the guards got to the door, Harold stood to join them.

'Where do you think you're going?' Adversane asked.

'I might as well come with you now,' Harold replied. He did give the others a slightly apologetic look.

Adversane sucked air in through his teeth. 'Oh, I don't think so. You're not much use now that everyone knows you're here. William would be on our tails by the morning. Back in the tower for you, I'm afraid.'

'What?' Harold looked very regal in his outrage.

'I'll tell Ealdgyth you said hello.' And with that, they were gone.

Harold looked around the room at the comprehensive collection of glaring faces and gave a very weak smile.

## Caput XXVI Leave by the Front Door

The speed with which an entire Saxon court could be dismantled and moved out of town astonished Hermitage. By first light, the caravan of Lady Ealdgyth was queueing at the town gate to be the first out.

'Where are they going?' He asked Wat and Cwen as they stood watching.

'I somehow don't think they'll be passing that information on,' Wat said.

They had left Harold once more in capable hands. Brother Longor had returned to Saint John's and explained all to Abbot Kenwald. In a spirit of reconciliation and recompense, that holy man had sent some of his brothers to Saint Werburgh's; some very large brothers who seemed to hold a bit of a grudge against the old Saxon regime.

They relieved Abbot Fulmer of his burden, saying that they had a much nicer and taller tower made of stone with strong locks on the door.

With some very rude comments about Adversane, and more particularly his own wife, Harold tramped away, instructed to prepare for a very long stay.

'Another killer escapes,' Hermitage complained as the doors to the town were opened and the horses and carts began to move.

'If you hadn't caught him, he could have got away with it,' Cwen said. 'Think how many more would have died if Adversane and Harold really had started a rebellion.'

'I suppose so,' Hermitage sighed.

'Look on the bright side,' Wat encouraged. 'At least he didn't kill us as well.'

'And if you tell Le Pedvin all about it, he may not think

you're an idiot anymore.' Cwen smiled.

Hermitage shivered 'I don't want Le Pedvin thinking well of me. It's bad enough being King's Investigator at the moment. Imagine what it would be like if they thought I was any good.'

Just at that moment, a horseman rode by a bit too close for comfort.

They looked up and saw the smiling face of Adversane, beaming down at them.

'You mind you don't get murdered on the road,' Cwen called up. 'There's all sorts of horrible people out there.'

'Oh, I know where the horrible people are,' Adversane replied, looking far too confident for comfort. He pointed a gloved finger. 'And I shall remember you, Brother Hermitage. King's Investigator, pah!' He kicked his horse on and trotted out of the gate.

'There you are, Hermitage,' Wat said. 'You're in the real world of the nobility now. I do believe you've made an enemy.'

'Oh wonderful,' said Brother Hermitage. 'Another one.'

**Finis**

Brother Hermitage will wander back in;
***The Hermes Parchment***

The first chapter of this is below, so if you don't want to go any further, I quite understand...

# The Hermes Parchment

by

Howard of Warwick

(Umpteen and thrice a Chronicle of Brother Hermitage)

## Caput I A Pleasant Invitation; For Once

Brother Hermitage, King William's own personal investigator, was at his happiest; he was in church, on his own, and no one was dead.

Of course, he couldn't guarantee things would stay this way. Being the King's Investigator seemed to attract death like the bottom of a cliff on a foggy night. And not the normal sort of death. Old people, nearing their time didn't simply drop at the sight of him, oh no. The perfectly healthy would find themselves suddenly murdered without a by-your-leave.

And then he would have to investigate it; frequently with King William or his awful man Le Pedvin, breathing down his neck. Why the two of them had to keep breathing when everyone else who came close stopped doing so, was not something he felt it proper to dwell upon.

But this was the Lord's day. Wat and Cwen, the weavers, were back in the workshop, having only stayed long enough in the church to be counted. Hermitage was planning to stay all day.

The priest of Derby was happy to accommodate Hermitage's devotions, although he was such a busy man he never had time to stay and debate the wide range of interesting questions that constituted Hermitage's head; mind you, it was a very wide range and the Lord's day only had the normal number of hours in it.

Once the rituals and ceremonies of the devotion were completed, Hermitage would sit in quiet contemplation until the next one began. He had even offered to assist the priest in any way that he could, but apparently, this would be unfair to all the other people of the town who might want to help; it wouldn't do to give Hermitage preferential treatment, just because of his habit.

Hermitage could see that, although he couldn't see anyone else actually helping at all. Like Wat and Cwen, most of the townsfolk made for the door as soon as they were able.

On this particular day, the rain was falling hard on the roof of the church, drumming the place into a noisy cave. Apparently, this meant that the townsfolk had to leave even earlier and more quickly than normal.

The priest was about his business somewhere beyond the back of the church, and Hermitage had the place to himself. An urge to get up and lock the doors so that no one else could come in was resisted as atrociously selfish.

He was in the middle of a fascinating consideration of why Enoch had only lived for three hundred and sixty-five years, while his son, Methuselah, lived for nine hundred and sixty-nine when a noise disturbed him.

He looked up and saw the priest coming down the church towards him, with a smile on his face. That was unusual. Even more peculiar was the fact that he had someone with him: another monk. This was not anyone Hermitage recognised, but the pair were clearly heading for him.

He briefly thought that it would be nice to engage with another brother, always assuming that brother was a reasonable fellow, and not like his old companions from the monastery of De'Ath's Dingle, where an approach in chapel was something to be very wary of.

Then he recalled his role as the King's Investigator and his heart sank. Surely not. Not in church of all places?

The priest and the monk drew near.

'Ah, Brother Hermitage,' the priest beamed his smile. 'I find you here, eh?'

That was a bit odd, the priest always found him here.

'I bring a visitor.'

'So I see,' Hermitage stood and gave a slight bow to the new arrival.

The compliment was returned, and the new monk threw back his cowl. He was a young fellow, having not many more years than Hermitage himself, with a bright and intelligent face that looked eager for their meeting.

'Brother Hermitage,' he beamed. 'I am Brother Martin and I must say it is a great honour to meet you.'

'Oh, dear,' Hermitage thought, but he extended his smile a little. 'I see,' he managed to say.

'I have travelled here from Lincoln specifically seeking you out.'

'Oh, I am sorry,' Hermitage couldn't help himself. At least he knew Lincoln reasonably well, not that his experiences of the place were altogether pleasant.

'Sorry?' Brother Martin looked a bit puzzled. 'Why would you be sorry?'

Hermitage had to admit that this Martin did look remarkably happy for someone who was bringing news of a murder.

'Well, you know,' Hermitage began. 'The reason people seek me out.'

'Indeed.' Martin was still bright and enthusiastic. Perhaps there was something wrong with him.

'Sit, Brother, sit.' Hermitage bade Brother Martin sit at his side. The priest was very happy with this and quickly skipped away back down the church to leave them to it.

'So, you seek me out?'

'I do,' Martin nodded happily.

'Even at the workshop of Wat the Weaver?' Hermitage

knew that Wat's reputation was spread far wider than his own; it was spread far wider and it was a lot worse. He couldn't believe that a monk would come looking for some of Wat's old tapestries. The crude images were widely sought after by certain individuals; they were obviously very well made but were incredibly crude. No self-respecting individual would own up to any such interest.

'That did cause me some concern,' Martin admitted. 'But I am sure there is good reason.'

'Well, good circumstance, at least,' Hermitage said. 'And I have managed to move Wat away from his more disreputable images.'

'That is good to hear. But it is not for Master Wat that I came searching you out.'

'I can imagine.' Hermitage released a great sigh. He supposed that he'd better get on with it.

'So,' he turned slightly to face Brother Martin, solemn and serious. 'Who has died?'

Martin's happiness dropped from his face. It was such a shame to bring matters down to this level.

'Died?' Martin sounded lost.

'Yes. You've come to look for me, so who is dead?'

'Erm.' Martin looked as if he were being tested somehow, but that no one had warned him the test was coming. 'I don't know?' he made it sound like a question.

'Ah, I see.' Hermitage nodded to himself. He'd had a similar experience in Normandy when it wasn't clear who the victim actually was[14] 'That'll be part of the problem then.'

'Will it?'

'It obviously makes things a little more difficult, but I'm sure that all will be revealed in the course of the

---

[14] *Hermitage, Wat and Some Murder or Other*; it becomes clear

investigation.'

'In the course of the what?' Martin now shuffled a few inches away from Hermitage.

'Investigation. From the Latin, vestigo, vestigare, to track.'

'To track,' Martin was now sounding very confused. 'Ah, I see,' he got it. 'Investigation. A fine word.'

'It is,' Hermitage nodded reluctantly. 'Appropriate, at least.'

'But, erm,' Martin was hesitant. 'Who is dead?'

'That's the question.'

'Yes, isn't it. Did you have anyone in mind?'

'Did I have anyone in mind?' Now Hermitage was getting confused.

'Has someone died?' Martin asked gently.

'I should think so,' Hermitage said. 'Otherwise what is there to do?'

'I wouldn't know.' Both monks were now frowning at one another.

It wasn't like Hermitage to want to get to the point, but they did seem to be dancing around one another. He could understand that Brother Martin might not want to talk about the gruesome details, but it had to be done.

'It is my curse,' he said. 'But also my duty. I sometimes wonder how it came to pass, but investigation of murder has become my lot.'

'Murder?' Martin almost jumped off the seat.

'Naturally.'

'It doesn't sound very natural.'

'As the King's Investigator, I have dealt with more than I care to think of. I am sure that I can help in your case.'

'My case? What case? Why do I have a case? And what does the king have to do with it?' Martin looked rather worried now.

Hermitage couldn't understand why the man was getting so excited about this. After all, he was the one who had come looking, it was no good getting all upset about it now.

'You have come to seek me out. Someone must have been murdered.'

'Why, for heaven's sake?'

'Why else would you want me?'

'Not a murder, that's for sure.'

Perhaps Martin was trying to block the idea from his mind.

'Come, Brother.' Hermitage tried to be soothing. 'You can tell me. I know it must be difficult.'

'No one has been murdered,' Martin insisted.

'Not that you know of,' Hermitage said.

'Not that anyone knows of. There is no murder.'

'Ah, Brother, there's no point keeping it from me, no matter the delicacy of the situation.'

'I promise you that no one is dead.'

'Are you sure?' Hermitage couldn't understand.

'I think it's the sort of thing I'd notice.'

'Maybe it's just a mysterious death, then?'

'Not even an un-mysterious death.'

'Not yet, perhaps?' Hermitage suggested. 'You have done well to come to me if there is a threat. Perhaps we can resolve it before any evil is done.'

'What threat, what evil?' Martin was becoming positively agitated now.

'The sort of thing I have to deal with, I'm afraid.'

'I don't understand,' Martin's voice broke a little. 'Why do you keep going on about dead people?'

Hermitage could appreciate that ordinary folk might not

be able to manage the reality of an unnatural death, but this Martin seemed to be confused by the whole business.

'As the King's Investigator, my encounters with murder have perhaps hardened me.' Even as he said this, he thought that he wasn't hardened at all.

'Ah,' Martin breathed deeply and seemed enormously relieved about something or other. 'There is no murder, Brother. That's not why I've come for you at all.'

'No murder?' Hermitage was now the one getting lost. What was the point of getting the King's Investigator involved if no one was dead? It would be a complete waste of time.

'No. No one is dead at all.'

Hermitage thought about this for a moment. 'You don't want me then.' He was actually quite relieved about this. Brother Martin had clearly come to the wrong place.

'Oh, I do. Most definitely, Brother Hermitage; there can't be another one.'

Hermitage had to admit that was unlikely, but if there was no murder then he should stay away. He shook his head slowly. 'I can assure you that you don't. Once the King's Investigator gets involved, death follows. It's become inevitable.'

'I am sure that in this case there will be no danger of that.'

'You don't know,' Hermitage warned. 'I have dealt with more murders than I care to think of. Everywhere I go, someone is either dead before I arrive or ends up dead soon afterwards. I wouldn't want that fate to befall you. Or anyone around you.'

'No one in this place is dead,' Martin pointed out, holding his arms out to indicate Derby in general.

'They have been,' Hermitage said with grim seriousness.

'An investigation even fell upon this very town. A visitor wandered in, then there he was, dead.'[15]

'Good Lord.'

'Indeed. I have been all over this country and even to Normandy; and it's full of dead people. Just waiting for me. Or queuing up to die as soon as I get there.'

'I can see that would be a worry.'

'A worry?' Even Hermitage got agitated by this understatement. 'It's more than a worry, it's a danger. That's why I say you must not ask me to come to Lincoln. No one will be safe.'

Both monks were quietly thoughtful for a few moments.

'Surely, you don't really believe that people die because you are nearby?'

'Murdered,' Hermitage corrected.

'Quite. People can't really be murdered because you're in the neighbourhood. It must be because you are, what did you call it, investigating? Yes, investigating wrongdoing. You are going to it, not it to you.'

'Hm.' Hermitage had to admit that this was a very reasonable argument. Not that he was convinced.

'And there must be murders that happen, about which you know nothing?' Martin pressed the point. 'There could even be a murder happening somewhere right now. That one can't be your fault, surely?'

'I do tell myself that,' Hermitage said. 'Not that it's much comfort to think that people are still being killed.' He sighed heavily. 'I went to a weavers' moot once,' he said, the misery of his lot clear in his voice. 'A celebration of all things weaving. And guess what happened?'

Martin chose not to answer.

15 I'm not going to say, it might spoil the surprise

Hermitage just sat and shook his head sadly. 'And I just happened to be passing through Shrewsbury once. A charming town, the very last place you would think needed a monk investigating murder. And it didn't until I walked through the gate.

'Would you believe I've even been to Wales?'

Martin did look impressed at that.

'Just in time for the murder,' Hermitage confirmed. 'And visitors from far-off lands?'

'What about them?'

'They travel halfway across the known world, get near me, and drop dead.'

Brother Martin looked thoughtful. 'Have you done anything apart from investigate murder?' he asked.

Hermitage sagged; it certainly didn't feel like it. 'In between murders, I come back here but no sooner have I sat down than another one arrives. Everyone brings them: Normans, other monks, merchants, you name it. Is Brother Hermitage in? Oh good, only we've got a murder here that he might like to have a look at.' He found himself feeling really miserable now, and he'd done that to himself.

Martin clapped his hands together and rubbed them vigorously. 'Then it is time you had some other function to carry out. I can see that doing nothing but deal with murder would drive anyone to distraction. I have come to you for another purpose altogether. One much more suited to your inclinations, I think, rather than your duty.'

That did raise Hermitage's interest, although he still wasn't convinced there wouldn't be a dead body in this somewhere; perhaps Martin was just trying to break the news gently.

'My inclinations?' He'd forgotten he even had any of those.

'Just so. I have come from the estate of Colesvain of Lincoln.'

Hermitage had heard the name. 'A supporter of William, is he not?'

'He is. And so he has kept his estates and his possessions. He is now making donations to the church. William expects it from his supporters, being a pious fellow himself.'

'Pious apart from all the murders,' Hermitage put in.

Martin ignored the comment. 'So, Colesvain is planning to give a great library into the care of the cathedral.'

'A great library?' Suddenly, Hermitage felt a lot better.

'Exactly. And I am making a catalogue of the contents so that we know what is where. Colesvain is no great scholar and so the place is a bit of a mess.'

Sorting out a library that was a bit of a mess? Hermitage felt as if he was being asked whether he was at all interested in popping into paradise for a while.

'And your reputation for the lexicography of the post-Exodus prophets is second to none. If we could persuade you to join our efforts, we would be profoundly grateful.'

Persuade? thought Hermitage. He'd been persuaded at the word "library".

Could he really afford to believe this though? 'And you're sure that no one is dead?'

'No one.'

'No shelves of books suspiciously fallen on anyone?'

'Certainly not.' Martin sounded quite offended at the accusation that the bookshelves were inadequate.

'Nobody quite old, about to die?'

'Not that I'm aware of.'

'Anyone with enemies who want them dead?'

'In a library?'

Hermitage forced himself to breathe very slowly as he let himself actually believe that this was happening. 'Brother Martin,' he said, as calmly as he could manage, even though he was jumping up and down inside. 'I would be glad to accompany you and do what I can.'

Martin beamed a smile. 'Excellent.'

'We'd better go to the workshop to let Wat and Cwen know about this.'

'Wat and Cwen?'

'Mistress Cwen is a fine weaver herself. They usually accompany me on my investigations, but this time they will not be needed. I can only imagine they will be delighted.'

The Hermes Parchment is now available - ironically, not in parchment.

Printed in Great Britain
by Amazon

62591371R20180